PENGUIN BOOKS

TRAPEZE

TRAPEZE

LEIGH ANSELL

PENGUIN BOOKS

PENGUIN BOOKS

UK | USA | Canada | Ireland | Australia
India | New Zealand | South Africa

Penguin Books is part of the Penguin Random House group of companies
whose addresses can be found at global.penguinrandomhouse.com.

www.penguin.co.uk   www.puffin.co.uk   www.ladybird.co.uk

Cover image © Silk-stocking/Shutterstock

www.wattpad.com

Printed and bound in Great Britain by Clays Ltd, Elcograf S.p.A.

A CIP catalogue record for this book is available from the British Library

ISBN: 978-0-241-43639-4

All correspondence to:
Penguin Books
Penguin Random House Children's
80 Strand, London WC2R 0RL

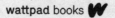

For the Wattpad readers, who have helped
take this story to new heights.

TRAPEZE

CHAPTER ONE

I once heard it said that time is a circus, always packing up and moving away.

That was true, in many ways, and I was more than qualified to comment—I'd experienced more packing up and moving away in seventeen years than most people would in their entire lives.

And yet, the saying was missing something. It failed to capture the whole story, left out the best part.

Because for there to be packing up and moving away, there first had to be pulling up and unloading. There had to be the pitching of trailers, the cranking of rusty metal, the hauling of ropes until the colors of the big top sailed among the clouds. Then came the clinking of change as coins exchanged hands, and the buzz of speculation that preceded the first show. It all came before.

And as someone who'd lived, breathed, and slept this cycle for as long as she could remember, that was always my favorite part.

At first, Sherwood, California, was just another brief stop on our never-ending road trip: another thumbtack on the giant map of the United States pinned to the wall of Aunt Shelby's trailer. The map had been there for as long as I could remember, and over its lifetime had collected such an abundance of pins that the entire American landscape had been severely butchered. I wasn't sure exactly how the ritual got started; all I knew was that each time we pulled up in a new field, the first job of the day was to stab a permanent hole in our new location, and the pin would sit there long after we'd gone.

The map proved we were no strangers to the area. The small town of Sherwood may have been new to us, but the dense collection of pins on the Northern California coastline told the stories of years past. We'd pretty much circled the area over and over. There was the whole country to choose from, but the crew could never resist the pull of the sun and the sea—and I guess I couldn't blame them.

Whenever we pitched up somewhere new, the events that followed were a strange yet predictable mix. Of course, there was the communal atmosphere: nervous energy fueling frantic conversation about openings and finales; the creaking of equipment in last-minute training sessions; long-awaited showers, now that we were finally hooked up to a water supply. On top of this, though, I had a ritual of my own.

In some sense, it was like the map on Aunt Shelby's wall. I couldn't pinpoint exactly when or how it had started, but it'd become a habit all the same. And so, hours after we'd piled into our home for the next few days, when the other guys realized I was nowhere to be found, they always knew where I'd gone.

I wasn't exactly superstitious, so I struggled to find an explanation for why the food in the first restaurant I came across always foreshadowed the fate of that evening's show. The theory wasn't strictly tried and tested, but it had yet to be proven wrong. Take for example Somerton, Idaho: after leaving the restaurant halfway through my nauseatingly undercooked meal, ticket sales for opening night hit an all-time low, and the evening was a total flop.

Good food, good show; bad food, bad show. And everything in the middle. It was just the way things worked.

Joe's was a small, fifties-themed diner that sat on a corner a few streets away from our pitch. Its blinking red sign looked close to giving out altogether, the *J* only illuminated in sporadic bursts, and the parking lot was almost empty. It neither attracted attention nor looked like it intended to. And since it was the first food outlet I'd come across—Rule Number One of my system—it would also be my first taste of Sherwood.

A bell tinkled overhead as I passed through the door, and my sneakers squeaked on polished tile. The counter was dotted with a long row of mismatched bar stools, while worn leather booths lined the opposite wall. A waitress in a long pink skirt and faded apron leaned against the counter. As I gave the diner the once over, I couldn't shake the feeling that I'd stepped through a miniature window to the fifties, where everything had been compressed and condensed into a tiny space.

Then again, that was hardly unfamiliar; I'd lived in a trailer almost my entire life.

I took a seat on one of the stools, briefly glancing at the guy next to me, who was staring down at a textbook while chomping down on a burger. He looked about my age, but that was all I gathered before I grabbed a menu and let my eyes skim over the laminated card.

The list was endless. What Joe's lacked in inspiring décor it more than made up for in culinary variety; in front of me was a choice of every burger I could imagine, plus twenty more—and that was without getting started on the sides or milk shakes. The owner had written an entire novel of options, and the sheer volume of possibilities left me stumped.

But even faced with such an overwhelming decision, I still didn't expect the stranger beside me to speak up and offer a helping hand.

"Don't even think about leaving this place without trying the curly fries."

I blinked, not sure if the voice was directed at me. It was only when I looked over that I saw the guy had looked up from his textbook. "Excuse me?"

Presented with an excuse to study his face, I was able to make a better assessment of my unexpected companion. He was fair, his milky complexion lightened by the overhead spotlights, with a head of blond hair that somehow managed to appear both neat and messy at the same time. It was ruffled, but in a way that looked calculated and entirely intentional—and as a half smile curled his lip, I noticed there was an impossible symmetry about that too. Overall, he was so polished I was sure he'd gleam in the sun.

"Sorry." He smiled sheepishly. "I'm butting in. But you looked like you were on the brink of a decision, and I couldn't let you escape without at least tasting the curly fries. They're legendary. Ask anybody."

His eyes flickered around the room, like I might do just that, instead of staring blankly back at him.

"I'll let you get back to deciding," he said when I still hadn't given him any kind of response. "It's a pretty intense choice, anyway. Just . . . bear that in mind about the curly fries, okay? You're not in Sherwood if you don't eat Joe's fries."

He went to return to his book and his plate, which I now realized was piled with a hearty serving of those very fries. But my voice made him pause. "What's so special about them?"

He grinned. "Order them and see."

So, seconds later, I slapped down the menu, caught the attention of the waitress hovering by the milk-shake machine, and placed an order for, and I quote, "Exactly what he's having."

The guy, looking incredibly pleased with himself, seemed to have forgotten about his book altogether. "You're not from around here, are you?"

I raised an eyebrow. "And what makes you say that?"

"Oh, it's easy. There's nobody in Sherwood who hasn't heard of Joe's curly fries. Like I said, they're a local legend."

"You're building up pretty high expectations here," I told him. "If they're not totally out of this world, I'm going to be severely disappointed."

But his confidence didn't waver. "They are," he said. "And I'd like to officially take responsibility for being the person who introduced you to them and therefore changed your life forever. Hi, I'm Luke."

The smile that crept onto my face was unstoppable. "Corey."

"So, Corey. What brings you to Sherwood?"

It was the question I'd been waiting for. Although conscious not to brag, I'd always secretly reveled in telling people about the way I lived. I relished the moment I transformed in their eyes, transitioning from the ordinary girl in front of them to the mysterious performer I got to be in the ring. *A trapeze artist*, I'd tell them. And there was the image, already dancing across their minds, of poise and elegance and everything that the most talented performers embodied. On the trapeze I became an enhanced version of myself, something far beyond what came across in person.

5

Trapeze was beautiful, and I was beautiful by association.

Not everybody shared such a positive view. Small towns especially didn't always give the warmest of welcomes, and I'd grown used to wary looks and judgmental whispers. But that was the beauty of life on the road—we didn't have to stick around to deal with it. As soon as trouble flared, we were already packing up and dismantling, taking to the road before it could touch us.

Life on the move was easy. It was being stuck in one place that made things complicated.

"The circus is in town," I said, "and I came along with it."

It came in perfect sequence: surprise, disbelief . . . but then, something else? I could've sworn I saw it in his expression—an impression beyond the words that had come out of my mouth. But it didn't linger, and soon enough I caught the curiosity I'd been expecting. "You're in the circus?"

"Yeah. Trapeze artist in training."

"Whoa." He exhaled. "That's pretty cool. Cooler than any of my local Sherwood knowledge I was going to try and impress you with, anyway."

I couldn't stop myself from laughing. "Sorry. I could pretend to be impressed, if that will protect your ego?"

He sighed dramatically. "No, it's fine. I'll suck it up and accept the fact that I've been majorly upstaged by a supercool trapeze artist."

"I'm sorry. I tend to have that effect on people."

I was grinning, and he was too.

By the time the waitress returned, with my order balanced precariously on her tray, we were deep in conversation about how I avoided falling to my death while hanging from the ceiling on a flimsy bit of rope. Whatever Luke had been studying was now utterly disregarded, his textbook closed and shoved aside to make room for his elbow on the counter. He was fascinated by trapeze, and I could talk for hours about it—really, it was a lethal combination. But his attention was diverted once the plate of curly fries was set in front of me.

"Seriously, prepare yourself," he said as I spun back around on the stool to face my plate. "You're about to have a life-altering experience."

"You are way too emotionally involved," I told him, rolling my eyes. "They're just fries."

He scoffed. "Yeah, okay. Let's see if you've still got that attitude in thirty seconds. Come on, eat."

Smiling at the way he was jabbing his finger at my plate, I did as he said. It was mostly down to curiosity. If the fries really were a local legend, it was my duty to try them, especially on my first day in Sherwood. And though I doubted they would be—as he so confidently put it—*legendary*, I dunked my first into a dollop of ketchup and stuck it into my mouth anyway.

In that moment, I found myself well and truly proven wrong.

Whatever I'd bitten into, it tasted suspiciously like heaven. Heaven covered in ketchup. Whether Joe's was spiking its fries with some seriously addictive substance, I wasn't sure, but they tasted *insane*.

And Luke knew it.

"Didn't I tell you?" He smirked once I'd swallowed the first mouthful and wasted no time diving for a second. "Legendary."

"Okay, okay. You were right."

"Obviously. You see, you might be a fancy circus performer jetting off to every corner of the country, but nobody knows Sherwood and its curly fries like I do."

It took hardly any time at all for me to inhale the entire serving, though I knew Silver would be pissed if she discovered I was straying from her carefully constructed diet. Nevertheless, it wasn't enough to stop Luke from persuading me to stay for a round of milk shakes, which extended my visit by another forty-five minutes. I had to get back soon, because a full dress rehearsal was mandatory before opening night, and the crew would get agitated if I wasn't back in time. And though this had been lingering in the back of my mind for the entire meal, it had been surprisingly easy to ignore when talking to Luke.

When the Elvis-themed clock on the wall hit three thirty, I knew I was really pushing it. As much as I'd have liked to stay and skip rehearsal altogether—if the fries were anything to go by, we were in for an incredible opening night—I didn't dare. The circus was my entire livelihood, and therefore never worth the risk. We may have thrived on danger, even making a living from it, but outside the circus everything had to be played safe. Taking too many chances was a potentially deadly mistake.

"I'm sorry, I really have to go," I told Luke, already gathering my stuff.

I jumped off the stool, moving to tie my jacket around my waist, when a sudden gasp from behind the counter caused me to jolt. Instinctively, my head turned to where the waitress was standing, catching sight of her just as the stack of plates slipped from her grasp and hit the floor with an earsplitting shatter.

The diner was plunged into silence, which only emphasized the sudden pounding of my adrenaline-fueled heart.

"Oh my God," the waitress said aloud to everyone who was now looking. "I am so sorry about that. Carry on, carry on."

She was already hurrying forward, reaching for the broom at the other end of the counter. Luke caught her eye as she brushed past us, fixated on cleaning up the pile of broken china. "Do you need any help?"

"Oh, God, sweetie, no," she said, shaking her head. "Don't you worry about this. Just me being clumsy, that's all."

She did seem to have it covered, and as I turned back to Luke, it occurred to me that I was standing. Before the interruption, I'd been about to make my exit.

"You're really going already?"

"Afraid so," I said, hitching my bag onto my shoulder. "We supercool trapeze artists are on a tight schedule. Especially supercool trapeze artists who are still in training. Silver won't be happy if I'm late."

"Silver?"

"She's, uh . . . my mentor, I suppose. Lead trapeze. She taught me everything I know, but she likes things done right. Absolutely no slacking."

He smiled sympathetically. "I know how that feels."

"Yeah, well. It's tough, but it has to be done. I wouldn't have got where I am today without her."

He was still smiling, but behind it was something I couldn't quite put my finger on. At first, it seemed to mimic contentment, like he would be happy to freeze the moment and live in this window of conversation forever. But there was something else lurking among the curiosity and awe and amusement—something, if I hadn't known better, that appeared almost melancholy. His eyes spoke volumes, but in a language I couldn't understand.

I shook it off quickly. "Like I said, I better be going."

"Wait," he said. "Are you just going to tell me all this stuff about you and not even invite me along to see you in action?"

The smirk crept back, materializing on my face before he'd even finished the sentence. "Are you saying you want to come along?"

"I wouldn't say no if you asked."

"Well, I'm not going to ask." I waited for the flash of disappointment across his face, barely visible, before I continued. "How about I just give you this instead?"

I fished in my bag, fumbling until my fingers enclosed a piece of glossy paper. I wasn't usually a walking advertisement for Cirque Mystique; it was a stroke of luck that Aunt Shelby had printed too many flyers, landing me with a pile before we'd left the last town. She'd told me to pin one up if I came across a good spot. As I handed it over, I realized I was probably preaching to the converted.

"We're here for the next two weeks," I told him. "The show starts tonight at seven. Maybe I'll see you there."

"Maybe you will." He folded the flyer in half and tucked it into the back pocket of his jeans. "I'm intrigued."

"As you should be. How often is it that the circus and its supercool performers rock up in this little town?" I grinned. "Bye, Luke. I'll see you around."

It was only once I'd started across the restaurant and was close enough to the door to reach for the handle, that I heard his voice. It was quiet, not bold enough to attract the attention of any other diners in the vicinity, who remained absorbed in their daily papers and cups of coffee, letting their surroundings become a blur that continued without their attention. "Good luck tonight, Corey."

It was a simple gesture of politeness, something I'd heard many times before, and was likely to hear just as many in the future. It was thrown back and forth countless times between cast members in the lead-up to every show, a safety net to make up for the lack of one in the ring. From Luke it was no different—soft and comforting, but not something I thought I'd desperately be needing.

I was wrong, but I didn't know that then, as I shot him a grateful smile over my shoulder, stepped out into the California sunshine, and set off down the street with my bag relieved of the insignificant weight of one flyer.

Good luck tonight, Corey.

Four simple words, unfamiliar by no means.

I didn't know that hours later I would be clinging to them, gripping the string of letters like they were my last hope.

CHAPTER TWO

The big top stood tall by the time I returned, secured by a myriad of ropes, its highest flag sailing among the clouds. I wasn't *technically* late, but as I ducked under the entrance flap, it became clear that I'd kept Silver waiting—and that was a crime in itself.

"Corey!"

She was pacing back and forth in the center of the ring, with the trapeze equipment in place and dangling above her. When I caught her eye, her expression relaxed and contorted all at once, leaving me wondering what exactly to brace myself for.

"You're here!" she exclaimed as I came closer. Her cheeks were flushed and her dark pixie cut was mussed, like she'd been running her hands through it all morning. It still managed to look good, though; Silver always carried off her signature style with a sense of edgy elegance that nobody else could nail. "Jesus, I was wondering if you were even going to show this afternoon."

"Sorry. I, uh . . ." I paused, choosing my words carefully. "I got caught up."

"Well. You're here now, and I guess that's what matters. We're down for first practice, and Rhona's been giving me filthy looks for the last half hour. I've wanted to scream at her. I can't make you appear out of thin air, can I? I'm a trapeze artist, not a magician."

I looked up at the stalls, following the direction of Silver's subtle nod at the mention of Rhona's name. Sure enough, she was in one of the middle rows, surrounded by her permanent entourage of her four co-performers. The aerial silk girls were the only group who tended to stick within their private gaggle, separating themselves from the rest of the crew. Rhona, the lead, was the worst of them all. Petite, blond, and three years younger than Silver, she was only capable of conversation that ended with bickering.

"Anyway, whatever. We've got fifteen minutes until their slot, and I'm not about to waste it."

Silver gestured toward the center trapeze, hanging empty above the ring. "I want you to get on center and show me the lead routine."

I froze. This wasn't what I'd been expecting—at least, not today. Our group was a trio, composed of a lead and two backups. I formed one half of the latter, alongside the third member, Kendra. There had always been three. Not just since my trapeze skills were deemed performance ready—even in my earliest memories, when I'd been nothing more than an awestruck little girl content to stand at the side of the ring for hours so I could watch the trapeze artists, there had been three performers. Over the last three years, I'd grown used to the dazzling spotlights and sweaty palms of performance, but never as the lead.

It had always been there: the unspoken agreement that I'd one day take over, stepping into Silver's shoes. But it had never been more than a distant thought, a speck on the horizon. Now that it was happening, it seemed much too soon.

"What about Kendra?" I asked, scanning the ring for the familiar bottle-blond curls of my partner. "Aren't we going to wait for her, or . . . ?"

"Kendra rehearsed earlier." Silver's dismissal was quick, emphasized by a wave of her hand. "I need to know that you can do the routine. Which you can, obviously. I just want to see how it's looking."

I took a deep breath. "Uh, okay."

It was strange that after a three-year alternating cycle of rehearsal and performance I chose *now* to be nervous. Sure, there was the common case of jitters that swept through the entire cast before an opening night, but that was easily remedied by the glare of a spotlight and a round of applause. The audience I now faced, though a fraction of the usual crowd, was still intimidating in its own right. Perhaps it was Rhona and her cronies, looking on with disdain, or merely the fact that Silver seemed to be on the brink of a decision, and the performance I was about to give would tip her one way or the other.

I tried to calm myself down as I approached the trapeze. At the very least, it was familiar, which was my main focus as I settled my buzzing nerves. How many times had my hands encircled these same pieces of wood and rope? If it was enough times to toughen their layers of skin, easing the discomfort as I gripped them with all my strength, then surely I could put my trust into them one more time.

I kicked off my shoes and tossed them aside. A hair tie around my wrist quickly slicked my dull brown hair into a ponytail, sweeping the flyaway strands from my face. The trapeze had already been lowered to the ground and was waiting for me. One deep breath, and I took a running leap at it, launching myself so my palms encircled the bar and my feet swung up to join them. Once I got started, there was no going back.

The eyes in the tent followed me as I dived headfirst into the routine, running through the musical accompaniment in my mind. I tried to channel Silver's confidence as I sat sideways on the wooden bar, my left arm twisted intricately around the rope. It was from that position that it all started, the routine I'd seen hundreds of times from behind, pieced together from fleeting glances caught when my head was the right way up.

I coiled myself around the supports, stretching out my entire body and using the trapeze as a makeshift harness. The feeling had taken some getting used to, but now I embraced it: being completely suspended in midair, supported by nothing more than a flimsy piece of equipment.

Once I got started, the movements arrived more fluidly, allowing me to transition from the first suspended trick to the second and those beyond. Silver's image remained vivid in my head as I pulled myself into an upright position, my feet curling around the rounded bar, and bent forward into a seemingly impossible version of a leg extension.

Toes pointed, chin up . . . there was barely time to remember these pointers as I leapt from one move to the next, matching the imaginary rhythm pulsing inside my head. Silver's eyes were trained on every movement, analyzing the position of my muscles, the way I held my head, the concentrated expression on my face. I pulled myself back into the seat of the trapeze, but there was no time to pause; extracting every shred of exertion from my upper body, I heaved my weight upward, forcing my legs straight into the air for one terrifying moment. Then, they fell back as quickly as they'd risen, spinning me around with impossible speed.

I could feel a breeze on my face, caressing my skin, which had already become sticky with a layer of sweat. I was exhausted, and yet the physical reality had a peculiar way of fading into the background. In moments like these, trapeze was the only thing that mattered, and I didn't want it any other way.

The big finale was fast approaching, and it was a circus requirement to go out with a bang. Swinging myself back underneath the bar, arms stretched above me, I gathered all the momentum possible. There was no room for mistakes. Squeezing the last of the energy from my muscles, I propelled myself forward, folding into a tight somersault before landing feet first on the mat.

I froze like a statue in the end position, the trapeze swinging behind me.

There was no applause. Instead, when I turned around, I was faced with the smile that had materialized across the width of Silver's face—which turned out to be a lot more satisfying.

"That," she said, "is what I wanted to see."

The raw pride on her face coaxed out my breathless grin; the misty eyes and the heartwarming smile I hadn't seen since the day she got engaged to Jack, Mystique's technical director. I didn't know what to say.

My eyes flickered toward Rhona for a moment, noticing that she was looking on with an expression of poorly concealed jealousy. Even from the center of the ring, I could see her catlike eyes were narrowed, and she clearly wasn't happy.

"Well, that makes it easy for me, doesn't it?" Silver continued, stepping closer. "You're on lead trapeze tonight. And do me a favor: please kill it like you did just then."

"Wait, are you—" Confusion cut my sentence short, and I had to find another. "I mean, are you sure? I wasn't expecting it to be so soon. I mean, I only just—"

She clapped a hand on my shoulder. "It was going to happen sometime, right? You were always in the running to take over. I'm going to be retiring soon, anyway—twenty-four's pretty much elderly, isn't it? Now that I'm pregnant, things are just going to be happening a little sooner."

"I—" There was a second's delay before her words hit me. "Wait, did you just say you're pregnant?"

Silver smiled and nodded. "Just found out last week. Guess you're going to become the star of the show sooner than you thought, huh?"

The news caught me off guard, and when combined with my ragged breathing, it was a wonder I was able to get *any* words out. "I don't know what to say. Well, first off, congratulations."

I guessed she was about to thank me, but she never got there— the moment was interrupted by an exaggerated throat clearing from across the room. "Excuse me," Rhona hollered, rising from her seat. "I think you'll find that your practice time is over. It's our turn now."

Usually, I had to brace myself for an argument any time Rhona and Silver were in the same room, but Silver just smiled. "It's all yours," she said sweetly. "After that, I'm pretty confident we don't even need the practice."

If Rhona wanted to retaliate, she wasn't given the chance. Silver had already turned back to me. "I'll see you backstage usual time, okay?" Her gaze flickered toward the stalls, in the opposite direction from Rhona. "For now, I think Dave might be after your attention."

Dave. The name sent a jolt through my chest. He was as familiar as the circus itself, his scruffy appearance and muddy-brown eyes as easily memorized as one of my trapeze routines. At nineteen, he was the only guy in the circus near my age. And for that reason alone, there was an unspoken agreement—from everyone—that we'd get together eventually. If nothing else, the pressure on all sides was sure to force us together.

While Dave seemed to have no issue with this arrangement, I differed. A childhood spent together meant he'd become like an older brother: someone I always had fun with but could never in a million years visualize myself dating.

However, this was the circus, and options were severely limited. With no permanent location, we packed up our belongings and left without a trace every couple of weeks. Outside relationships were impossible. Life on the road meant exactly that, and it wasn't to be complicated by tethers to anything—or anybody—outside the circus. Only a chosen few could hack that kind of life, and we were among them.

Despite my feelings, the decision was already made for me. With the circus came Dave, and if I wanted one, I'd have to settle for the other.

Silver had already taken off in the opposite direction, though not before shooting me a surreptitious wink. Now, alone in the ring, I was the only thing separating Rhona from her precious practice time, so there was nothing left for me to do but start toward Dave. He was slouched on one of the seats in the front row, having adopted his trademark carefree stance, the sleeves of his T-shirt straining over his muscles. A familiar smile curled his lips as his eyes followed me.

It wasn't that I didn't enjoy his company, but with each day, the wordless pressure seemed to swell, like I could feel the whole crew looking on and wondering why we weren't together yet. As kids, it used to be funny, but nowadays the knowing smirks and air of impatience had drained the sweet simplicity from our relationship.

"You looked great out there," he said when I stepped into earshot, approaching the barrier at the edge of the ring.

"Thanks," I said honestly. I reached up to run my hand through my hair, but stopped short when I remembered it was still in the tight ponytail I'd pulled it into ten minutes before. "I, uh . . . didn't know you were watching."

"Yeah, of course I was. After I finished setting out your equipment, I couldn't resist sticking around to watch you practice. You were crazy good."

"It was okay," I dismissed him lightly. "I could've pulled off the somersault a lot better, but at least I landed on my feet and didn't break anything."

He chuckled. "Well, not breaking anything's always a good result."

I peered up at him, not really knowing what to say. I couldn't count the number of times I'd found myself looking at his face. His strong jaw had been prominent even as a boy, while the rest of his features had an almost lopsided quality about them. This was particularly true for his smile, which had always been sort of goofy—but in a familiar rather than a cute way.

I wished there was some way I could force myself to feel differently about Dave, but it wasn't going to happen. And though I didn't know how this would bode for the future, I'd taken to pushing it to the back of mind, resolving to deal with it only when absolutely necessary.

Dave seemed to have leaned in slightly closer, and I wondered how this had escaped my notice. "I never get tired of watching you perform," he said. "You really are an amazing trapeze artist, Corey."

The tone of his voice made my heart pound. I dreaded these moments, when I was sure he was about to make a move. I didn't want to be thrust into a position where I'd have to turn him down, because that was sure to make things unbearably awkward for both of us.

"I'm, uh . . . not really that good," I said quickly, breaking eye contact. "I mean, I'm okay. Nothing special."

Thankfully, he appeared to sense the moment had passed, although the flicker of disappointment in his eyes didn't go unnoticed. "Well, you've got more talent than me, anyway. The circus only needs me for my muscle." He grinned and flexed, and all at once the tension shattered. My laughter was full of relief.

It was true. Dave formed part of Mystique's backstage crew, and there were at least twenty of them, all burly men with huge muscles and at least one tattoo. Dave was no exception, although his ink was limited to a single spiky design on his shoulder, which was tame by comparison. Even between the setting up and dismantling of the circus tent, they were endlessly busy, forever checking or changing equipment, or carrying heavy loads across the pitch. Dave had been born into the circus and had been recruited as soon as he was old enough to work alongside his dad. If only my own story was so simple.

"Hey, do you want to hang out tonight?" he asked. "I'm thinking late-night pizza after the show, if you're up for it."

It sounded good, the same way any other plan with Dave did—especially if it involved pizza. Tonight we'd be riding that postshow high, and I couldn't think of anything better than stuffing my mouth with pizza so greasy it would make Silver scream in horror, and laughing with Dave until our stomachs hurt.

But I still couldn't stop my thoughts from backtracking to the boy from the diner. I wasn't sure why my mind chose now to dwell on his effortlessly charming smile, his genuine interest in circus life, the way his appearance had drifted perilously close to perfection. We'd clicked, plain and simple, and I couldn't deny the easy connection that had been quickly established between us. It was worlds away from what I had with Dave.

For any other girl with a normal life, I knew what a conversation like that would mark the start of. It was the beginning of *something* with the potential to blossom. But the bottom line was I wasn't a normal girl, and the life I pursued came with its consequences.

Luke could never be more than one flirty conversation—a charming stranger, someone I'd turn my back on forever in just two weeks. So why was I thinking about him in the middle of a conversation with Dave?

That was when I realized I'd slipped into a daydream without answering Dave's original question. "I, um . . ." I pushed Luke's image into a dark corner of my mind and smiled. "Yeah, sure. Pizza sounds great."

"Cool. I'll catch up with you later, okay? I'll be in the crowd, watching you kill it on that trapeze."

"I'll do my best."

He grinned. "Well, it's not like you need it, but I'll say it anyway: good luck tonight."

There they were again—the same words, identical to those that had escaped Luke's lips not long before. In that moment, before Dave shot me a last goofy smile and turned to leave the tent, they were harmless. Luke's were too. But only in that moment.

They became ominous only when the night started to go terribly, terribly wrong.

CHAPTER THREE

"Well, well, well. If it isn't Mystique's newest trapeze star."

I didn't need to look up to match the nauseating voice to its owner, but sure enough, when I did, Rhona was heading toward me. Her pointed toes transformed her stride into a catlike prowl, and I could barely see her smirk under the thick layer of stage makeup. In fact, she was barely recognizable beneath the matte mask: falsely flawless skin, smoky black lids, dark-red pout.

We were backstage, alongside the rest of the cast, with the show already in full swing on the other side of the wall. Sound carried easily through the flimsy material, and I could hear every word of Grayson's—Mystique's resident magician's—performance. He would be onstage for another ten minutes, which meant Silver, Kendra, and I would be taking the stage in just under twenty. We'd performed the show so often our timing was accurate to the nearest second. Even my emotions ran on a schedule: fifteen minutes beforehand, the nerves would start up, but they'd disappear by the time we received our five-minute warning. The circus was nothing if not precise.

"Honestly," Rhona continued, once she'd reached my dressing table and leaned tauntingly against the wood, "I'm surprised Silver even let you have the lead spot. I was starting to think she'd never give it up. Always been a little too attached, if you ask me."

Glancing over her shoulder, she caught the eye of a redheaded girl in the cluster that stood a few feet away. They were Rhona's permanent backup: the group always ready to jump in should the situation get to be too much for their precious leader. The girl smirked, her expression mirrored by the other three, as if they were sharing a private joke that I was very pointedly excluded from.

"I wasn't asking you, actually," I shot back, meeting her gaze with a silent challenge. "Have you got anything worthwhile to say, Rhona? Because unless you have, you should probably try bothering somebody who'll actually listen to your drivel."

"Okay, okay." She leaned back, removing her hands from the tabletop to raise them in mock surrender. "There's no need to get touchy."

I took a deep breath, trying to remain calm as Rhona circled my chair. She stopped behind me, looking into the mirror so our faces were side by side. It wasn't the time to be getting riled up, but that was easier said than done with a particular blond breathing down your neck. I knew what she wanted: to slither her way inside my head moments before I stepped into the ring, screwing with my confidence and sending my entire performance off balance. I was determined not to give her the satisfaction.

"I only wanted to wish you good luck," she said sweetly. "You are on after us, of course, and that's daunting for anybody."

Had it been any other night, I could've lashed out with a comeback to wipe the smirk right off Rhona's face. She was never usually one to faze me, but not only was I closing in on the fifteen-minute mark, this was also set to be one of the biggest nights of my life.

I could practice that first moment as lead over and over, until it was carved into my brain, but it still all came down to this night. Whatever happened out there—whether I killed it, like Silver had requested, or fell flat on my face—would be remembered for a long time. It was Corey Ryder's defining moment. It'd be picked apart, assessed, analyzed to within an inch of its life. It would make or break me.

Needless to say, I was feeling the pressure.

Rhona was already looking smug that I'd failed to deflect her digging remark, her pointed features hovering above mine in the mirror. I wanted so badly to wipe the expression off her face, but the weight on my shoulders was growing by the minute. It pushed me farther down into my seat, slumping my posture, forcing down the words that would've been on my tongue on any other night. I couldn't do anything but sit there and take it.

Thankfully, by some stroke of luck, Silver descended with elegant speed at that exact moment. She was already in full costume—a long-sleeved black leotard that was identical to mine—with her eye mask dangling from her hand by its elastic.

"Well, you know what they say, Rhona," she cut in. "They save the best till last."

Rhona scoffed. "How original."

"I think it's time for you to leave," Silver said firmly. "Your minions are looking a little lost over there without you. Better get back and carry on feeding them orders."

Rhona scowled but seemed to sense that Silver was not to be messed with, particularly on a night like tonight. Still, she couldn't resist slipping one last drop of poison in my ear as she left, making sure I heard the words "Just make sure you don't screw it up for the rest of us tonight."

I watched her back as she retreated, eventually being swallowed from view by her four cronies. The loathing in Silver's expression matched my own.

"God, and every time I fool myself into thinking she can't get any more pathetic," Silver said. "You'd think she would have better things to do than go around terrorizing the other cast members."

My silence appeared to serve as its own response, because she quickly turned to me. "Corey, please don't tell me anything that just came out of her pathetic little mouth is going to bother you," she said warily. "Because I swear to God, if she does anything to get inside your head tonight, she'll be getting a slap."

"I'm fine," I assured her. "It's not Rhona. I'm just . . . I'm nervous, I guess. There's a lot riding on tonight."

I'd barely finished my sentence before Silver spun my chair around, forcing us to come face to face. Like the rest of the cast, she was also preened and powdered, ready for the spotlight, but her look was significantly more understated than Rhona's. "Don't, and don't *ever*, listen to a word that girl says. She's just trying to get into your head. I saw you in practice this afternoon, and you were incredible. We both know you're more than capable. And we *also* know that you're going to be one hundred percent outstanding tonight and upstage her completely."

I did know that, deep down. The inner confidence was there, somewhere in the back of my head, if only I could coax it out again.

"You know she's just jealous," Silver carried on, "because she saw you in practice today and knows you're going to blow her out of the water. Right?"

"I know."

"You're going to be amazing out there." Finally, I met Silver's gaze, as her tone became so level and sincere that I found myself beginning to trust it. "Not to mention, have you heard the crowd? They're loving it so far. I'm telling you, one of the best shows we've had in a while. And now it's your time to shine."

She was right. She was always right. I even managed to smile, the corners of my lips lifted by Silver's words of encouragement. "Thank you."

"No problem, kid. I'm not worried at all. I mean, I taught you everything you know, right? Of course you're going to kick ass." She grinned, her green eyes twinkling and coming to life beneath the makeup. "Now, if you'll excuse me, I really have to pee. This pregnancy thing is so not sitting well with my bladder."

I grimaced. "Too much info, Silv."

Seconds later, she'd dashed off, disappearing from view around the corner. Left alone, my attention returned to my own reflection, and the face that stared back at me. Its last traces of apprehensiveness had been wiped away by Silver's pep talk. And with Rhona and her entourage having already headed to the wings to prepare for their entrance, I finally felt like I had enough space to breathe a sigh of relief.

I studied my appearance in the mirror. I was naturally pale, but the lack of color was exaggerated by the harsh lights around the mirror, not to mention the lingering nerves. At least the makeup offered some coverage. It was pretty much identical to Silver's; the makeup artists had had so much practice with our signature looks that I was sure they had it nailed down to each stroke of the brush.

Seeing myself like this had taken some getting used to. At first, I'd found it difficult to make the connection between the two versions of myself: the first, plain old Corey, someone nobody would ever pick out in a crowd; the second, the dazzling trapeze artist who would turn any head. The makeup and costume was the best mask of all—safely hidden behind it, I was invincible.

And on a night like this, that was exactly what I needed.

"Corey!"

The voice came out of nowhere, loud enough to carry over the hustle and bustle of backstage. When I looked over my shoulder, a figure was hurrying toward me—but all I could see was a short blond bob, because the rest of Aunt Shelby's face was obscured by a giant bouquet of flowers.

"There you are!" she said, setting the bouquet down on the dressing table. They were beautiful, a pink and white collection of roses and carnations, wrapped in tissue and finished with a huge white bow. Taken aback, I couldn't quite find my words, but luckily Aunt Shelby had enough for both of us. "I've been looking for you all over. I wanted to make sure I caught you before your big night. I think you're supposed to give flowers *after* the show, but who cares? I just couldn't wait. They can be for good luck *and* congratulations."

"Oh, Aunt Shelby, you really didn't have to," I said, turning to face her. "They're gorgeous. Thank you so much."

"God, I can't believe you're on lead tonight," she said. "It still seems like yesterday you were in the playground, making me watch your 'trapeze performances' as you swung about on the monkey bars."

The smile on my face widened. "That's embarrassing. I really have come a long way, haven't I?"

"Oh, don't I know it." Her closed-lipped smile quivered, and it didn't take long for her eyes to get misty too. "Oh God, come here."

Before I could even register what was happening, she'd thrown her arms around me, pulling me in as tightly as she could. Aunt

Shelby wasn't one for doing things halfheartedly, and hugs were no exception.

"Good luck out there," she whispered, her voice breathy against my ear. "Just remember to do your best."

When she finally released me, I couldn't help but chuckle. "Do my best?" I echoed. "You couldn't sound more like a mom if you tried."

Wiping the remnants of tears from her eyes, she smiled, but didn't get the chance to say anything else as Silver bounced back into the dressing room, this time with Kendra in tow, and leaned her elbow on Aunt Shelby's shoulder.

"Hey, what's this?" she said, noticing the bouquet right away. "Flowers? Shelby, I'm offended. I've been lead for, what? Five years? And you've never got me flowers."

I had to hand it to her—although I knew full well Silver was joking, her pout was pretty damn convincing. Aunt Shelby laughed, shrugging off Silver's elbow and lightly tapping her on the cheek. "I'm not going to give you flowers for doing your job," she said. "How about after the baby's born? I'll promise you a bouquet then."

Silver touched her stomach, pretending to consider it. "Okay, deal."

"Anyway," Aunt Shelby continued, "I better leave you three to get ready. I'll see you on the other side."

She caught my eye one last time, pausing long enough for us to exchange another smile, which seemed to convey so much more than just muscle movement. Then, before I knew it, she was gone.

"So," Kendra said, pulling the elastic of her mask over her ultra-hair-sprayed bun and adjusting it over her eyes, "are you two ready to rock this?"

One last stolen glance in the mirror had my lip curling into an almost undetectable smile, and I snatched up my own mask. "I'm ready."

~

The adrenaline had begun to work, wading through enough of my body to dissipate the nerves, leaving in their place a pulsating sense of anticipation. Though tonight was different from those that had come before, the precise schedule was the same: fifteen minutes saw the nerves arriving. Five, and they were gone. Just like that.

Silver led the way as we pushed through the backstage crowd and headed for the wings. From there, we had a clear view of the ring, and we were able to catch the main sequence of the aerial silk performance. Rhona had taken her natural position in the center, with her four co-stars' scarlet ribbons arranged around her. Dressed entirely in black, the figures contrasted sharply against the silk, becoming striking silhouettes that curled themselves around the fabric. I swallowed as I watched, taking in the details of each move-ment as they twirled effortlessly in synchronization, and trying my best to maintain confidence that I was, as Silver put it, going to "blow them out of the water."

With all lights aimed at the ring, the crowd was bathed in dark-ness, which made it impossible to make any kind of assessment about its energy or size. What did stand out, however, was the faint glow of yellow high-vis vests: the mark of security guards dotted between the rows. They weren't an unusual feature, were rather a nonnegotiable safety requirement for every show. But . . . was it my imagination, or were there more of them out there tonight? It seemed like they were spaced half the usual distance apart. But why? This was our first show in a completely new town. We had no idea what the reception would be, but our usual course of action was to get through opening night and see what transpired.

There wasn't time to think about it. The music was swelling now, and the end of the aerial silk performance was near. Any minute now, Rhona would deliver her final move—an excruciating version of the splits with each foot wrapped around a piece of ribbon—and the music would reach its climax before ebbing away to make room for applause.

When it did, the lights were cut and the performers swiftly disentangled themselves from their props, invisible to the audience. My breathing had become ragged; I knew we were down to the last few seconds before we were set to dash on, leaping onto the trapeze that would be lowered sometime in the changeover.

And then suddenly it came: the gentle pressure on my back from Silver's palm pushing me forward, acting as my cue to sprint into the ring with what had to be silent elegance. My heart skipped a beat as I spotted the center trapeze, and soon I was taking a running leap to launch myself up onto it.

I briefly wondered if Dave was one of the guys in charge of the equipment tonight as the trapeze was pulled into the air, carrying me with it. We were now floating above the crowd. Any second now the lights would make their return, the music would start, and my moment would begin.

And all at once it did, to a soundtrack of deafening applause. We were bathed in a dim red glow as the lights turned on, the crowd's wild noise washing over us like a warm wave. Seated on the trapeze, my hands gripping either string of rope, my gaze swept across the tent. The collective sound of fervent encouragement from every corner tugged my lips into a smile.

This, right here, was what I craved: the awe splashed across the face of every person in the stalls. They were here to watch us, to be transfixed as we waltzed across their vision, to question all possibility as our bodies transcended usual physical boundaries. Their energy was electric, and I wasn't sure I could live without it.

The music was due to start soon; I knew I should've been preparing myself. And yet somehow I'd let myself get distracted, my eyes on what they'd been skimming for a moment ago. A familiar, yet still remarkably unfamiliar, face in the crowd. A head of blond hair, deliberately messy. That charming smile, noticeable from a mile away.

My heart lurched.

He'd come to see me.

Our eyes locked for a fraction of a second, and he smiled. I didn't have time to return the favor.

The routine began, offering only one chance to catch my cue. I kicked my legs upward, remembering to keep my toes pointed, before curling myself into the rope.

A sequence of moves, strung together like a sentence. I forced myself to think of nothing else as I transitioned through the routine, one trick morphing into the next, exactly as I'd done it that afternoon. If I could just replicate the past perfectly, everything would be okay. Mind over matter.

It was fine. Everything was going to plan. Tonight would be yet another success for my restaurant superstition; Joe's fries had proven themselves. I was feeding off the crowd's raw, throbbing energy, riding out the buzz that seemed to vibrate through every fiber of my being.

This was what I lived for. Trapeze. The final piece of my own puzzle, the only thing that could make me feel truly complete. It was everything.

Until it wasn't.

The routine had come easily until then—almost too easily. I didn't even need Silver in my line of vision to calm me, which I'd always assumed necessary. This was my natural habitat, the most permanent home I'd ever have. And as I bent forward into the leg extension, coiling my foot around the rope for security, I was struck by the realization that in that split second, everything was perfect.

Until I saw the flames.

At first, it was nothing more than a flicker in the corner of my eye. I was frozen in position, my legs split into a continuous line along the rope, my gaze roaming the view behind me. I told myself it was a trick of the light, the misdirected glare from a spotlight as it circled the ring. I had to ensure I remained focused. A beat later and I would leap into the next move, and that was where my full concentration needed to be.

Until I heard the screaming.

It came from the far side of the circus tent, a place in the stalls farthest from the backstage door. There, it was a single sound, an earsplitting shriek, alone amid the thumping beat and wild applause. But as quickly as it died out, it returned, proliferating, the collective noise rising through the entire tent. As soon as I righted myself, head finally above my feet once more, I spotted the source of the distress. It took all I had not to let out a scream of my own.

The flames moved faster than anything I'd ever seen before. What started out as a single patch of fire was spreading by the second, morphing into a burning wave of heat that raced up the tent wall. The material crumpled like paper, disintegrating into blackened remains.

The shock turned my muscles to stone; I clung to the trapeze, dangling helplessly above the panicking crowd with absolutely no means to lower myself. All it had taken was a split second for the audience to flip, gripped by fear strong enough to transform them into a swelling riot. Figures scrambled in all directions for the exits, some even running into the ring itself, chaos burning all resolve. The flames advanced, closing in on the top of the tent, leaping onto the adjacent walls and threatening to consume the entire outer shell of the structure.

A glance to my left saw Silver and Kendra in exactly the same position, staring dumbstruck at the disaster that was rapidly unfolding beneath our feet. Another particularly loud scream hit my ears as the smoke billowed through the vicinity, its black musk obscuring view of anything and everything in its path. With the darkness of the evening, it was a lethal combination. In seconds, I was surrounded, the sooty fumes forcing their way into my lungs.

I snapped into action. Nothing was to come of hanging paralyzed above the calamity. Every second wasted increased the chance of the fire reaching the supports above, sending me toppling to the ground as it burned through the rope. I was left with no choice. To escape, I had to jump.

The fearless elation of several minutes ago had totally vanished; utter terror was all I had left. A tangible fear gripped me, squeezing the movement right out of my muscles. But I had to push past it. Unless I wanted to die here, to pass out from the toxic smoke already writhing inside me, I had to make an attempt to escape. So I lowered myself underneath the trapeze, shutting my eyes tightly to seal out the sting of the smoke.

And I dropped.

I hit the ground with a violent thud, a sound that seemed to resonate through every bone in my body. My odd landing was sure to have injured something, but I didn't have time to think about it. A clatter next to my head confirmed the trapeze had suffered the same fate, the fire ripping through the supports at the tent's pointed top. Though every muscle in my body was protesting furiously, aching with a strangling combination of fatigue and terror, I pushed myself to my feet. A dark mass of figures were heading in a direction that resembled an exit, so I stumbled after them. Anything. Anything to get out of there.

The fire was ruthless, tearing through anything that stood in its way—whether it be the wall of the tent, the stalls, or the skin of a human being. Only one coherent thought remained: *I just can't let it be me.*

CHAPTER FOUR

It took ten minutes for the firefighters to arrive, pulling up outside with their blaring sirens and hoses at the ready, by which point the tent had almost fully disintegrated. All that was left of the striped material was a smoking mess of ash that littered the field. Though its supports had, on the whole, been left standing, they were only in a marginally better state, and the tarnished metal no longer looked capable of holding anything up.

Everything we owned—everything we were—had been burned to the ground, in the most frighteningly literal sense.

I'd managed to escape, albeit by the skin of my teeth. My desperate dash for the exit had resulted in me being swallowed by the crowd, whose collective force had carried me in the right direction. The first gulp of clean air came as an unimaginable relief, and soon after stumbling into the nearest clear space on the grass, I found myself heaving huge breaths like my life depended on it.

Maybe it did. I couldn't be sure.

The chaos turned me invisible; nobody seemed to notice me, hunched over the ground several yards away from the entrance. The sheer volume of people made it impossible to spot anybody I recognized. Silver, Kendra, Aunt Shelby, even Luke—I couldn't see any of them, and the same was probably true on their end.

In that moment, as the fire behind me tore through our entire livelihood like it was a sheet of paper, I was completely alone.

Only when the firefighters had extinguished the last of the flames, about thirty minutes later, did the extent of the damage reveal itself. The fire had spread to several of the nearby trailers; entire homes and lifetimes of belongings had been destroyed in a matter of minutes. Like we hadn't suffered enough.

It was impossible to process, and yet the heartbreakingly obvious continued to stare me in the face: in the space of thirty minutes, everything I'd ever known had vanished.

Gone. Just like that.

Dave found me eventually and hauled me from the ground into his strong arms, while I flopped against him like a rag doll. The aftermath of the incident had robbed me of everything but horror and sheer exhaustion; I didn't have the strength to hold myself up. In a new world so terrifyingly stark against everything I'd ever known, I was willing to cling to the tiniest thread of familiarity and hold on for dear life.

I swung on either side of consciousness as he carried me away, my head too foggy to process what was going on. The commotion had dulled into one constant roar that continued even after I'd been lifted into the back of an ambulance, of which there was an entire fleet. It was white; that was all I noticed as I was lowered onto a stiff seat, my arms still circling Dave's neck.

When we arrived at the hospital, the emergency room was like a war zone. Neither Dave nor I was deemed an urgent case, so we were relegated to the waiting area, where we became spectators of the chaos. Unfortunately, it was there that the shock started to wear off, and reality came back into brutal focus.

Every person I saw stumbling through the ER was another knife through my chest. I didn't want to look, and yet at the same time couldn't tear my eyes away, which meant every horrific sight was seared into my mind. Unconscious children being rushed through the door, doctors scrambling to put oxygen masks over their faces. Patches of bloody, blistered skin where fire had lashed at exposed limbs. People screaming in white-hot agony, their faces contorted so intensely I could almost feel the same pain in the pit of my stomach.

I couldn't tune it out. No matter how hard I tried, the assault on my senses kept coming even when I resorted to leaning forward with my head in my hands, Dave's hand moving in soothing circles on my back.

If I thought the worst was over, I couldn't have been more wrong. Even the most earsplitting, agonizing scream from a stranger paled in comparison to the sound of one I recognized.

My head jerked up, following the sound in time to catch sight of Silver being wheeled through the ER on a gurney. She had no obvious trauma, though I could already see faint red-purple splotches over her skin where deep bruises would form later. It was the noise she was making that worried me most—a low, continuous wail, only broken by gasps for breath as she choked back sobs.

I couldn't stop myself. The doctors were already wheeling her toward a door across the room, but right then, no force in the universe could've kept me in my seat.

"Corey! What are you doing?"

Dave's voice faded behind me as I sprinted across the room. My head pounded, but it didn't matter if I collapsed halfway there; I had to get to Silver, and nothing could stop me trying.

Except the stern-looking doctor who blocked my way outside the door.

"Excuse me," he said, folding his arms, "what do you think you're doing?"

"They just—they took Silver in there," I forced out, suddenly feeling my lungs burn in protest. My throat caught on the last word, and the coughing fit came soon after. After smoke inhalation, running as fast as I could probably hadn't been the best idea. "I have—I have to see her."

"This is a private area. I'm afraid that's not possible."

"You don't understand," I said desperately. "She needs someone . . . she can't be *alone*—"

"Miss, I can assure you, she's in good hands. You'll be able to see her as soon as she's in a fit state for visitors. Are you waiting for medical attention yourself?"

"Yes, but—"

"Then please take a seat," he said. His voice had softened, from authoritative to sympathetic, like he'd picked up on my obvious sense of defeat. "I know it's chaotic in here tonight, but we'll do our best to have a doctor with you as soon as possible."

There was nothing else I could say or do. Without another word, I trudged back to my seat.

By the time I got back to Dave, the adrenaline from seeing Silver had subsided, making way for a throbbing ache that pulsated through every part of my body. The bright lights of the ER were starting to distort and swim in front of me. The pain must've shown on my face, because Dave stood up as soon as I got near him, and his hand was on my back to help me into the chair once more.

"Are you okay?" he asked, his voice tinged with genuine worry. I felt the warmth of his palm enclosing my arm, which helped keep me grounded while I struggled to focus. "Stay here. I'm going to get you some water."

I didn't argue, instead sinking back into the seat and letting my eyes flutter closed. It only felt like a couple of seconds had passed when I felt a presence in front of me, and I jolted when I opened my eyes to see Dave standing there once more. He held out a plastic cup. "Drink up."

I lifted the cup shakily and took a sip. As soon as the ice-cold water touched my lips, I realized how dry my throat was, and I downed the whole thing in one go.

"Thank you."

"Take it easy, yeah?" he said. "You've been through hell and back tonight. We all have."

"I just—" The image of Silver was back in my mind again, the echo of her wail ringing in my ears. Even the deafening chaos of the ER couldn't mask it. It felt like there should've been tears brimming in my eyes, had they not been so raw and dry from the smoke. "Did you see what state she was in? She's in pain, and there's no one in there with her . . . not even . . . have you seen Jack? Or Aunt Shelby?"

Dave shook his head. "I'm not sure where they were when the fire broke out. They will have got out, though—I heard the firefighters saying everyone did. They might have stayed behind to make sure everybody got help."

He was right, of course, but it didn't settle the churning in my stomach, or the way I was trembling all over. The physical impact of tonight had finally set in. But I couldn't let myself wallow in it; I knew I was one of the lucky ones. I couldn't focus on myself until I was absolutely sure everybody else was okay.

Dave and I were seen eventually. We were ushered through about three hours later, once the real emergencies had been dealt with. I insisted I felt strong enough to walk down the hall, but they gave me a wheelchair anyway. As I was pushed along, it was hard to believe that just hours ago I'd been strong enough to balance the weight of my body on a thin wooden bar. I didn't even feel like the same person anymore.

I got off lightly. Miraculously, the fall hadn't resulted in any broken bones—just some minor bruising. They were more concerned about the smoke inhalation, and so I ended up sitting around for a while breathing through an oxygen mask, which admittedly did make me feel better. By the time I was discharged, the ER was significantly less chaotic.

Dave met me out in the waiting area, where he shrugged off his jacket and offered it to me. It hadn't occurred to me until then that I was still in full costume—a tiny black leotard and flesh-colored tights, not to mention no shoes—and looked completely out of place in the hospital. Self-consciousness hit me all at once, and I took the jacket gratefully.

"Are you ready to go?" he asked. "I can call a cab."

I looked at him. "I'm not going anywhere. I'm staying here to make sure everybody else is okay."

"Corey, it's four in the morning," he said. "Don't you think you should get some rest?"

It was a sensible suggestion, especially as I could feel my exhausted body crying out for sleep, but at the same time, I couldn't think of anything worse. How could I leave now, when Silver—plus God knew how many other crew members—was still in the hospital, being treated for unthinkable injuries?

"I'm staying here," I told him. "I don't care if it takes all night. I have to see Silver."

There was also the painfully obvious, which both of us knew but didn't dare say aloud. What did we even have to go back to? The last we'd seen of the tent was a blackened pile of ash, and there hadn't been time to check how many trailers had been affected too. I didn't want to say it, but there was a very real possibility that we would return to the pitch and find nothing left of what we'd called our homes.

Dave seemed to sense I wasn't going to budge, because he nodded.

However long it took, we would wait.

~

Darkness gave way to early morning sunshine before Silver was allowed visitors. By then, Jack had shown up at the hospital, making his own scene at the front desk as he demanded to see her. When it came to her fiancé, the staff were a little more forgiving, and it only took a few minutes of back-and-forth before I watched him get taken to see her. After this, I relaxed a little, comforted by the knowledge that she wasn't completely alone.

It was later in the morning before I was finally allowed in, after Jack had headed back to the pitch to retrieve some of Silver's things from their—thankfully unharmed—trailer. But when the nurse came over to tell me, the news didn't bring with it the burst of energy I'd expected.

Rising from my seat, I glanced apprehensively at Dave. His expression was unreadable, and I knew there was a lot more behind his reassuring smile than was visible at surface level. "Go see her," he said quietly. "I'll be right out here if you need me."

I followed the nurse down the hall to Silver's room, the pace of my heart quickening with every step.

"I'll give you two some privacy," the nurse said when we reached the door, holding it open for me to step inside alone.

Silver was lying in the bed facing me, and when I got my first look at her, I couldn't help my sharp intake of breath. The bruises had started to develop properly now, revealing that she was covered in them; a particularly ugly one stretched across her forehead and down the side of her face, its bluish tone obscuring her features completely. Similar blemishes peeked out from under her hospital gown, blossoming across her chest as well as up and down one arm. The other I couldn't see, because it was trapped inside a thick white cast.

"Silver," I breathed. My voice cracked on the second syllable, which seemed to set the tone for the conversation to come.

Lying there, swathed in the sterile sheets of the hospital bed, she looked utterly broken, in all senses of the word. And when Silver— the one person who could keep me going when I had no strength left—had been sapped of all hope, I wasn't sure how I could avoid following suit.

She looked at me, not saying anything, her eyes glistening with tears. I was determined not to cry—I almost never did—but the lump in my throat made that incredibly difficult. I took a tentative step closer.

"Corey," she said, as a single tear breached her eye and rolled down her bruised cheek, "I lost the baby."

There was nothing I could say. There were no words that would make this better, nothing that would take away the crushing horror and hopelessness of the situation.

I'd seen the happiness in her eyes less than twenty-four hours ago, the excited twinkle that told me just how much she was looking forward to becoming a mom. She would've suited it too; the way she'd been like an older sister to me had proved that. But now it had been snatched away from her in the most brutal way, and I struggled to come to terms with how a single night could be so cruel.

Giving up on words, the only thing that felt right was to lean over her bed and wrap my arms around her. Instinct told me to hold her as tightly as I could, but she looked so fragile I was scared she'd shatter in my arms. So instead, I kept my touch feather light, hoping it conveyed everything I wanted to say and couldn't muster, silently letting her know that she wasn't alone in this heartless new reality.

For as long as I stood there, with my nose buried in her hair, it felt like I was doing something. Despite everything, there was a sliver of hope that—somehow—we might be able to make it through this. As long as we stuck together, like the circus had always done.

I knew, however, that that hope would be short lived.

And I was afraid of what I'd feel when I let go.

CHAPTER FIVE

Dave and I returned to Aunt Shelby's trailer that afternoon. To see it still standing was a huge weight off my shoulders; its location at the edge of the field meant it had remained safe from the flames. But this spot of familiarity didn't change the fact that the world had shifted around it.

For the next few days, time crawled by at a snail's pace. The minutes stuck to each other like glue, sliding past like bandages being pulled off agonizingly slowly. This refused to change, no matter how many hours I spent staring at the TV in the trailer. Wherever I tried to look, my eyes always found their way back to one thing in particular: the giant map of the United States on the wall, dotted all over with colorful pins. More specifically, one particular red pin stabbed on the northern coastline of California. I was seriously contemplating ripping the map off the wall altogether, but every time I got up to do it, something stopped me. Despite everything, it seemed wrong, as if traditions still stood when everything else had burned to the ground.

My exhaustion counted for nothing; sleep quickly became a rare phenomenon. Every time I closed my eyes, the flames were back, leaping toward me with incredible ferocity—and my only escape was jolting myself awake.

Aunt Shelby barely came home, and when she did, communication seemed to be the last thing on her mind. She'd retreat to her room to take a nap for a couple of hours at most, leaving for the hospital again as quickly as she'd arrived. Uncle Rodney—her husband—had been admitted as an inpatient, the smoke having exacerbated his emphysema, and the few hours she wasn't at his bedside were spent doing the rounds of the rest of the injured crew.

I expected nothing less. She was our resident nurse, though lacking the formal qualifications, and played the doting mother to almost everyone in the circus.

Even me.

Especially me.

The site cleanup had already begun. Through the trailer window, I could see the giant trucks that had moved in, as well as bulldozers ready to demolish the last of the dangerous structure. In theory, it should've been a good thing, as they took away the lasting reminders of that night—but the emptiness they left behind was somehow much worse.

It was for this reason that I started going for long walks, venturing out farther than before every time, willing to travel whatever distance necessary to shake off the uncertainty that plagued every thought. *One more step,* I'd tell myself. And then, when the suffocating sensation refused to let up, *one more. Just that little bit farther.*

But it was always one more step. It didn't matter how much distance I put between myself and what remained of the life I'd known since I was two years old, peace seemed always one step out of reach.

I just wanted to know what was going on, but when I tried to corner Aunt Shelby on her next brief visit to the trailer, my endeavor was unsuccessful.

"Aren't we going to talk about this?!" I ended up yelling when she'd brushed off my questions and hastened to her room. "I'm part of this fucking circus, aren't I? I deserve to know what's going on!"

All I got to show for it was a sore throat and yet more frustration.

It was on the fifth day—when I was sure I'd begun inching closer to total insanity—that things finally changed. I didn't know how much longer I could take it; I'd grown so used to being in constant motion, living a cycle of rehearsal, performance, and packing up. Now that we were stationed in one place, with nothing to fill the empty hours between dawn and dusk, I had no idea what to do with myself.

When Aunt Shelby emerged from her room, I expected her to rush off to the hospital as usual. I was lying on my bed in my tiny box-sized room, waiting for the slam of the door, which always rattled the entire trailer. I was doing nothing but staring at the ceiling, wondering on which number of my silent count Aunt Shelby's departure would come.

But it never did. What came instead was a knock on the bedroom door.

"Corey?" Her voice was tentative, edging through the crack with a tinge of hesitation. "Can we talk?"

I let a few second pass before getting to my feet. Part of me wanted to be angry about being kept in the dark, but the temptation of finally being given a sliver of information about Mystique's future was just too much. Pulling open the door, I found myself face to face with my aunt.

The sight was startling. I could count on one hand the number of times I'd seen her go out without makeup before, but now there was nothing to hide her pale face, worry lines carved deep into her forehead. Her usually immaculate hair looked like it hadn't been washed or brushed in days. And to top it all off, there was no strength in her expression; she looked like she'd had the life drained out of her, drop by drop.

"What is it?" I asked. "Are you finally going to tell me what's going on?"

"I'm sorry, Corey," she said quietly. "I really am. But there's something important I need to talk to you about."

I took a deep breath. "Okay."

She stepped aside to let me through, opening up my path into the compact living room. What usually was in order had fallen into complete disarray: takeout boxes were stacked on the dining table and countertops, the cream carpet was covered in grime and crumbs, and there were enough balled-up tissues laying around to fill a whole garbage bag. She gestured for me to take a seat, and I did, swiping away the junk before sinking onto the couch.

Sitting opposite me, she perched on the edge of the cushion, as if ready to leap up at a moment's notice. All we could do was stare at each other, wondering how this was supposed to begin.

"I'm sorry," was what she settled for eventually. "For leaving you sitting around here like this. Things have been so crazy, what with me being at the hospital, and . . . dealing with the police . . ."

"The police?" I echoed. "Why are the police involved? It was an accident, wasn't it?"

She didn't say anything.

"They *don't* think it was an accident?"

I watched her hesitate, as if choosing her words carefully. "We can't say for certain. It's so hard, now that everything's gone, to determine what happened . . . but it's a line of investigation, yes. They found traces of gasoline."

"What?" I breathed. I could hardly believe what I was hearing; this recurring nightmare only seemed to be getting worse. "Why would someone do that?"

"I don't know," she said. "We've always known there are people who have something against us. It's hard being an outsider in a small town. But nobody ever expected for it to come to something like this . . ."

"And what have the police found? Do they know who's responsible?"

Aunt Shelby shook her head solemnly. "No. There are no leads, traces, or suspects. Nobody seems to have any idea what happened that night. And honestly . . . it's not guaranteed we ever will."

"But they can't . . . surely whoever did this won't just *get away* with it?"

The anger simmered inside me, threatening to boil over. This had been no accident—and once that thought was in my mind, it wouldn't go away. Although our stops in most towns went off without a hitch, there was always the occasional frosty reception from people concerned we were spoiling their town's upmarket image. But they never actually *did* anything beyond throwing a few verbal obscenities our way. A thick skin was all we needed, together with the ability to pack up and depart for somewhere else with just a few hours' notice.

No one had ever hated us enough to try to kill us.

"We don't know, Corey." Aunt Shelby looked haggard; there was no other word for it. "We just don't know."

The wave of despair was already rising within me. I could feel it tightening my chest, hunching my posture, draining the energy from every muscle. All that was left was to ask the million-dollar question.

"So what's going to happen to us?"

It hung in the space between us for what felt like hours; expanding, morphing, inflating until it had squeezed itself into every corner. I could feel it in the air I breathed, the atmosphere in the room, the look on Aunt Shelby's face. It was inescapable.

"Well," she said quietly, "that's what I wanted you to talk about."

"It's going to be okay, though, right?" I was stammering now, the words gushing out with the force of a waterfall, but stopping myself was a whole other matter. "This is all going to work out? We'll be able to go back to how things were before . . . eventually?"

"Corey," she said. A single word. But it was the tone that terrified me.

"*Please* tell me it's going to be okay."

Her silent stare was enough of an answer.

"For God's sake, this can't be it! What the hell are we going to do? You can't be sitting me down here to tell me you've got *nothing*?"

"Everything's gone," she told me, and though I knew it already, hearing it aloud made it frighteningly real. "It's not just the tent, but all the equipment, the props, the stage, the lights, everything. It's all gone. There's nothing left."

"Well, we have to get it back," I said. I tried my best to summon up confidence, although I knew the hardest person to fool was myself. "That's all it'll take, right? We just need new equipment . . .

we just have to replace whatever we've lost. Then everything can go back to the way it was?"

"Corey, you know I want it to be that simple. We all do. But business hasn't been going spectacularly lately, and even if it had, we'd never have enough to replace everything."

"Surely we can find the money somehow. We have to. This can't be it. It can't be all over because of this."

"But that's not the end of it. It's not just the money. We weren't the only ones injured that night. People ended up in the hospital. People were nearly killed. We're under serious investigation right now. Even if we did have the equipment to pick ourselves up and keep running . . . well, it's looking more likely than not that we'll be shut down for good."

"But that wasn't our fault!" I was yelling now, well past being able to control myself. "Do people think we set ourselves on fire, or something?! It wasn't anything to do with us!"

"I know," she said. "I know that, you know that, and so does everybody else in this company. But it's not an easy thing to prove."

The fight was already seeping from my muscles; I could feel it as I sank back into the couch, overcome by a stinging sense of hopelessness that I'd been desperately trying to fend off.

"So it's done," I said quietly. "That's it. This is the end of us."

"It's too early to say for sure. We don't know yet what's going to happen. It's why . . . it's why I've had to make other arrangements for you, Corey."

And then, suddenly, the energy returned, a jolt of alarm that straightened my spine in an instant. "Other arrangements? What's that supposed to mean?"

"Listen to me," she said sternly. "Fifteen years ago, I took you into the circus. I swore I'd take care of and do whatever was best for you. At the time, we were in a good position. You were safe here, and you were safe with me. Now circumstances have changed . . ."

"No." The word was definitive, shattering the atmosphere in the room as if it were a pane of glass. "If you're about to suggest what I think you are, the answer's no. I'm not leaving the circus. That's final."

"Corey, for God's sake, just *listen*!" The interruption came as a shock, and was enough to force me back behind a wall of silence. "You haven't even given me a chance to say what I'm going to say! I know you want to stay, and I understand that, but we have nothing here. Absolutely nothing. I have no idea what the future of Mystique is even going to be. I made a promise to your mother and myself that I would do what was best for you. It's not fair to anyone involved to keep you in such an uncertain situation. You're still a child."

"I'm seventeen! I'm old enough to make my own decisions! I don't care if things are uncertain. That's what the circus is about, isn't it? Instability? Don't you think I'm used to it by now?"

"You don't know what you're talking about!" she yelled. "What do you think is going to happen? We have nothing. We can't perform, we can't bring in any money, and half the crew is in the hospital. We've got a hundred lawyers on our backs waiting to sue the hell out of our asses, not to mention a police investigation with absolutely no leads. Is that what you're used to?! Is that what you think you can handle?! Because you can't! You definitely can't handle it, because I can't either!"

The outburst left her short of breath; I could hear the aftermath in the silent room. I didn't want to shout anymore. Raised voices had lost their place in this conversation, and we both knew it. Instead, I swallowed hard and spoke, my voice shaky. "What's going to happen to me?"

She stared back at me with an expression of longing and regret. "You're going to live with your mom."

And there it was. The word a trigger, something that sent me stumbling backward, overcome by a wash of outdated memories I'd spent my whole life trying to uncover. There'd never been a complete story, at least not one that'd been told to me in full. My knowledge had been pieced together from fragments collected over my childhood: snippets of hushed conversations, photos in albums I'd only ever caught glimpses of, halfhearted answers to questions I'd asked over and over again. Aunt Shelby tended to avoid the topic, instead throwing me into a world of circus and trapeze to stifle whatever questions I might've been about to ask. I'd always known she was my aunt, but a life-sized question mark remained over the mother I couldn't remember.

"I never told you, but . . . I've been in contact with her for a few years now," Aunt Shelby said. She might've looked guilty had she not become so worn down over the last few days. "She likes to know how you're doing . . . to know that you're okay. I go see her when I can. To be honest . . . it's not just the sun that keeps bringing us back to this part of California."

"Wait," I said, "she lives near here?"

Aunt Shelby paused. "Probably a little nearer than you think."

"Oh my God," I said. "She lives in Sherwood, doesn't she?"

She nodded. "It wasn't coincidental that we came here. I knew Silver was retiring on lead, and that you'd have the opportunity to take over soon. You're not far off eighteen, and you know, taking on the lead role is a big commitment. I know it's what you've wanted for years, and I hardly expected you to want to abandon the circus as soon as you were old enough, but . . . I at least wanted you to have all the options on the table before you made your decision."

"You were going to let me meet her."

"If you wanted to," Aunt Shelby said. "I knew you had enough on your mind, so I was waiting until all the shows were over to talk to you about it, but . . . well. Things have changed."

I couldn't resist stating the obvious. "And now I don't get a choice at all."

When Aunt Shelby looked at me, I could see the pain in her eyes, but I couldn't find it in me to take it back. "I'm sorry, Corey," she said, and it was clear in her voice that she sincerely meant it. "I really think it's for the best."

I couldn't argue. For fifteen years of my life, I'd been blessed with the best guardian I could've asked for—one who'd truly helped me blossom in a world I'd come to love. It wasn't her fault that things had ended like this. Despite my unrelenting anger, and the heartbreak so intense it felt like every part of me was splitting in half, I couldn't take this out on her. It wasn't fair.

I had to find the inner strength that I'd prided myself on for so long, and face up to whatever came next.

My mom.

Throughout my whole childhood, she'd been shrouded in silence and secrecy, but I hadn't allowed myself to put up with it forever. The wondering had driven me crazy for long enough, and then it could no longer be stifled with an hour on the trapeze. So, about a year ago, I'd sat Aunt Shelby down and forced her to tell me the whole story.

No excuses. No lies. Just the answers I'd craved for years.

~

Hazel Ryder had been a teenaged mother, even younger than I was now. She was the youngest of two sisters, the other being eight years her senior. While Shelby had done everything right, going to college and graduating with flying colors, Hazel had conformed less to rules. At sixteen, a single mistake led to a pregnancy by her short-term boyfriend, who fled as soon as he heard the news. He was a coward, my father, and that was all I knew about him—even before his first name.

My mom dropped out of high school as a junior to take care of me; she'd been left with no other option. Maybe she'd been intelligent, a girl with a bright future. Maybe she would've gone far. But whatever she'd been aiming for, I'd well and truly screwed up her plans, and done it before even being born. I'd always thought that took a special kind of talent.

In the meantime, Shelby had shed her good-girl persona and announced to her parents that she was running off with a boy from a traveling circus whom she'd fallen head over heels in love with. They were shocked, but they didn't think it would last. They assumed it was just a fling, preparing to have her back home and heartbroken within six months. She proved them wrong.

Apparently, I went above and beyond to mess up my mom's plans, because taking care of me was a lot harder than she anticipated. Three months after I was born, she started drinking, a problem that slowly worsened until sobriety became a rare state. A spiral of depression caused this to intensify, until alcohol became drugs, and drugs became harder drugs. Before my second birthday, she was entirely incapable of looking after me.

It was then that Shelby stepped in, swooping down like my very own fairy godmother to rescue me from my own mom. Shelby was still part of the circus, now married to the love of her life, though they'd discovered they weren't able to have children of their own. At nearly two years of age, I was taken from my mother's care, thrown into the life of Cirque Mystique, and taught never to look back.

We'd had no contact. Fifteen years, and not a word had been exchanged between my mother and me. I didn't even know what she looked like, and I'd certainly never heard her voice.

Now, however, that was about to change.

CHAPTER SIX

The more Aunt Shelby told me, the more real the impending meeting with my mom became.

We spent hours in our trailer, talking things over, as if the more rigorously we went through it all, the smoother it would be later. I had no idea whether that was true. My world was about to be turned upside down anyway, and I wasn't sure any amount of preparation could make even the slightest bit of difference. At the very least, it fed my curiosity: a craving for information that had been fueled by years of not being allowed to ask.

Soon after two-year-old Corey was removed from the picture, Hazel Ryder hit rock bottom. She overdosed, almost dying from a dangerous cocktail of alcohol and narcotics. It was only luck that a neighbor stumbled across her just in time to call an ambulance.

Just in time. Everything had happened *just in time.* A few minutes longer, even the slightest delay, and she would've been gone.

While she was in the hospital, her parents decided they had to stage a severe intervention. They blew their entire life savings on a stint in rehab, the best they could afford. They were broke, but that didn't matter, as long as their daughter made a recovery.

I guessed it had been money well spent, because sure enough, Hazel began to get better. A year later she was out of rehab, and, sitting among the broken pieces of what used to be her life, she began to make plans to fit them back together.

She went back to high school, finishing up her last two years before moving on to night classes at the local community college. Several years later, a decent job came up at a marketing agency in Sherwood, which was pretty much a perfect match. A quiet, safe town, where the people were friendly and the beach was only a short drive away. She'd been there ever since, well and truly clean. Her life was finally back on track.

So why couldn't I shake off the feeling that, once again, I was about to send it careening off course?

Aunt Shelby gave me five days to get my things together, although if it had really been about just packing up my belongings, I would've only needed twenty minutes. Circus folk didn't come with a lot of baggage—at least literally. The five days were for something else entirely, and for that I really needed years.

When the time finally came, and my suitcase stood at the door of Aunt Shelby's trailer, the lump in my throat was harder to swallow than ever.

It was impossible to stay composed when my life was about to change beyond recognition.

Aunt Shelby wanted to come with me, right to the doorstep and across the threshold of my mother's house. She insisted to the point where it seemed likely she'd tail me the entire journey regardless. In the end, we compromised: she would drive me over, drop me off at the end of the street, and leave me to it from there. As strange as it sounded, I wanted to do this alone. Coming face to face with my mother after fifteen years would be a turning point in my life, however it turned out, and I felt the inexplicable need to prove I could handle it by myself.

"Are you sure?" Aunt Shelby asked once she'd parked in our agreed-upon spot and shut the engine off. "You don't have to do this alone, Corey—you know I'll come with you and introduce you, if that makes you feel better."

I locked eyes with her and smiled, even though it was the last thing I felt like doing. "Really, it's okay," I said. "I want to do it like this. For myself."

"You know I'm only doing this because I think it's the right thing for you, right?" she said. "That I don't want you to go as much as you don't want to?"

"I know."

"And your mom's wanted to meet you all this time," she continued. "I know it's happening in a different way than she and I imagined, but it doesn't change the fact that she wants you here."

"I know."

I was fully aware I was being emotionless, even as I saw the tears brimming in Aunt Shelby's eyes. There was so much more that I could've said, that I *wanted* to say, but it wouldn't change anything that was about to happen. There was no argument when she said it was best for me; I knew, deep down, she really believed that. And since she was the only one who'd actually talked to my mom about any of this, I wasn't in any position to speak for how my mom felt.

"Oh, come here."

She reached across the car to wrap her arms around me, pulling me in as tightly as she could in our awkward position.

"I love you so much, Corey," she breathed, gripping the back of my shirt like she didn't want let me go. "I know you can handle this."

Only in that moment did I let myself cling to her, letting a trickle of emotion break through my outer shell. I took a deep breath, inhaling the mixed scent of detergent and floral perfume that I'd associated with Aunt Shelby for years. It was perhaps the only thing more familiar than the feel of wood and rope in my palms.

Because while trapeze had always been there for me—an unfaltering comfort over the years—Aunt Shelby had too.

The time to break away came eventually, and when it did, I unclipped my seat belt quickly, so there wouldn't be time for second guessing. Aunt Shelby came around to help me haul my suitcase out of the trunk of the car. I didn't need help with heavy lifting, but it gave her an excuse to face me one last time, staring at me with a quivering lip, like she was trying to commit my face to memory, until it was really time to go.

I told myself this was only temporary, a quick-fix solution lasting only until Mystique was able to get back on its feet. It was the only way I could find it in me to put one foot in front of the other, turning away from Aunt Shelby's tearful expression and starting down the street.

The address was 42 Umber Court. It was printed in Aunt Shelby's neat handwriting on a slip of paper, which I'd folded four times and tucked into my back pocket, even though it had circled my mind so many times now there was no chance of me forgetting it. Every so often I would take it out, running my eyes over the lines again, just to make sure the letters hadn't rearranged themselves in the time I hadn't been watching.

For somebody who formed the sole reason for my existence, the few words seemed an oddly little amount to know. A name and address was all I had to show for half of my DNA.

But now I was here. Standing outside number forty-two with a churning stomach and a suitcase full of belongings. To some, it might've been remarkable, the fact that I could fit everything I owned into a single wheeled case. And yet to me it was the opposite; I couldn't wrap my head around how people could fill entire houses with their possessions.

I looked up at number forty-two, finally allowing myself to take in the building before me. I'd had no expectations, and yet it somehow still managed to come as a surprise. It was average sized: not intimidatingly huge, like some in a neighborhood on our way over, nor small and poky. In fact, it just seemed to scream *normal*, like this was even possible.

The place seemed to possess only one significant feature, which made it stand out against all others on the street. While Umber Court had clearly been designed in stark uniformity, with every house pretty much mirroring the next, there was no competition for the most impeccably kept property in the neighborhood.

Number forty-two was pruned and trimmed to within an inch of its life. Assortments of colorful flowers sat in straight rows in beds below the front windows, and the vertical-line pattern on the lawn looked stenciled into place. The stone driveway was edged with miniature hedgerows, every corner a clean cut. Even the windows looked like they'd been freshly scrubbed that morning.

Above the yard, the house stood tall, like a proud mother. Its eerie perfection was slightly unnerving; no matter where I looked, there wasn't a single feature out of place. It hardly looked like the house of a woman who'd lost control and her child, both at the same time.

But there was no mistake. This really was it.

Fifteen years of silence were about to be shattered, and it all started here.

I allowed myself a second of composure before starting up the front path. It seemed wrong to set foot on such spotlessness, as if my mere presence would leave a permanent stain. But I forced myself to swallow the feeling, pulled my suitcase up the slight incline, and approached the front door.

What happened next was entirely unexpected. My arm, already lifted, was inches away from ringing the bell when the door was yanked open.

And there she was. Right in front of me stood my mom.

She was tall—her height was the first thing I noticed—topping me by several inches. When my gaze adjusted upward, her eyes came second, and the realization was striking as soon as they locked onto mine. The gray color, swimming amid an expression I had yet to decipher, caused me to start. I was struck by the peculiar sensation that I was looking into a mirror; they were a perfect match to the shade of my own.

"Corey?" Her voice was weak and cautious, as if I were a wild animal she didn't want to startle. There was also a tinge of disbelief; I could tell the word hadn't passed her lips like this for a long time.

"Hi."

She stepped back, making room to open the door a little wider. Her hand gripped the edge of it, acrylic nails threatening to dig right into the wood. "How are you doing?"

"I'm okay," I said, though it couldn't have been further from the truth.

She paused, her gaze skimming over my face, studying my features like they were something she had to memorize. "God, it's

61

strange," she said. "You don't look anything like I thought you would."

I managed a weak smile. "Really."

She looked younger than I'd expected, though it was easy enough to do the math in my head. Her beauty was incredibly polished, in a sense not worlds away from what I'd thought about Luke. Shiny brown hair had been pulled back into a ponytail, the ends of which were brushing the back of her neck. It left her face exposed, which, at thirty-three, was still unlined. She could've passed as five years younger.

The beat of silence that lapsed between us was uncomfortable, though I wasn't sure what else I'd been expecting. She straightened a little. "Well, why don't you come on in?"

I took the cue once she moved aside, stepping over the threshold and into the house. With their first steps, my feet met a welcome mat, which kept the soles of my shoes safely away from the laminate. I only had to look up to see that the house's exterior perfection extended to the inside too; not only was the hallway empty of almost all furniture, but every surface seemed to gleam.

My mother's voice caused me to freeze before I'd even tried to move. "Would you mind taking your shoes off?" she asked quickly. I later convinced myself it was my imagination, but I thought I saw her wince at my scruffy sneakers. "I don't like shoes in the house."

I paused, taken aback. "Oh. Yeah. Sure."

I felt like I was under strange scrutiny as I tugged off my sneakers, lining them up on the edge of the doormat. Unnervingly, she watched my every move, though I wasn't sure she was aware of it.

"I haven't really had a chance to get your room ready," she said. "I've been so busy these last few days. I'm sorry that the house is a bit of a mess."

I stared at her, wondering if she was joking, but her straight-faced expression lacked even the faintest hint of a smile. I'd yet to notice a single item out of place in the immaculate house, but the way her eyes darted around nervously made it seem like she was living among hordes of clutter.

"It's fine," I assured her. "Really."

"I'm sorry," she said again, shaking her head. "Let me take your suitcase. I'll show you where your room is, anyway."

She reached out to take the case from me, but my hand instinctively closed over the handle. "Oh, no, it's fine. I've got it."

As soon as the words passed my lips, I regretted them. The last thing I wanted was to come across as rude, to make a bad impression on my mother when the foundations of our relationship were still so soft. And yet one habit in particular proved difficult to break—I'd never been one to readily accept help from other people. I didn't like to open myself up to dependency, to fall into the trap of trusting somebody and having it used against me. Witnessing it happen to other people time and time again had only made up my mind it wouldn't ever happen to me.

I followed her up the stairs, hauling my bag behind me, trying not to let the bottom of the suitcase clunk on the shiny wooden steps. As we moved through the upstairs hallway, my mother headed for one of the doors near the end. I ignored the urge to memorize the placement of her footsteps and ensure my own feet landed within the boundaries of each of hers.

She claimed she hadn't had the time to prepare my room, but it was—as expected—as pristine as any other area of the house. Painted white, the bright, clean color seemed to bleach the entire space. The bed was in the middle of the room, made up with pale blue sheets the exact shade of the drapes, while a huge window with an accompanying seat occupied most of the farthest wall. A fan on the ceiling pushed cool air around the room.

"Like I said, I haven't had much time," she was saying, scanning the room for any evidence of disarray, of which there was exactly none.

"No, it's lovely," I said. "Thank you."

It was convincing enough, and I managed to fool even myself until she left the room, telling me she'd let me unpack and get settled. Once the door had closed behind her, however, the illusion melted away. The sheer cleanliness suddenly became stifling, drawing up a tiny box and trapping me inside, while the combination of fresh white paint and shine was enough to bring on a headache.

How was it possible that I felt more suffocated in a room like this than in the tiny trailer I'd been squeezed into my entire life?

It was all too much; the pressure rose in my chest, the lump in my throat expanding by the second. Instinct told me to move toward the window, throw it open to let the outside air flood into the room. Maybe it was the sight of the cloudless sky—the same one I'd been looking at this morning—that calmed me down, or even just a momentary break from a view where everything had an exact place. I sat on the window seat for at least five minutes, inhaling and exhaling deeply, until the pounding of my heart eased up enough to let me feel like I was in control again.

I dragged out unpacking as long as I could, delaying the prospect of having to go downstairs and face my mother for a second time. Only once I'd transferred my clothes into the wall-length wardrobe did I realize they only filled a fraction of the space. I placed my leotard on the far right, pushed slightly apart from the rest of my clothes. Inside the pale room, the deep black and silver glitter couldn't have seemed more out of place. Maybe that was the reason it gave me a sense of comfort as I brushed my fingers over the velvet.

I placed my few other belongings inside drawers and lined up on the dresser, just to fill the space. I was about to slide my empty suitcase under the bed when I came across one last thing inside. Smoothing the glossy sheet in my hand, straightening out the worst of its creases, I realized it was one of the same flyers I'd handed to Luke on my first day in Sherwood. Not even two weeks had passed since that afternoon, and yet the time between then and now seemed to stretch longer than a lifetime.

Cirque Mystique, it screamed, the letters seeming to jump right off the paper. *The most spectacular show you'll ever see!* A collage of blurred snapshots from previous shows made up the background, spilling across the page, while computer-generated glitter made everything sparkle.

For a moment, seeing it made me want to burst into tears. But I'd decided long ago—even before the fire and everything that had come with it—that I was tougher than that. Though everything else had changed, I wasn't about to.

So, steering myself away from the sadness, I took a pin and stuck the page on the noticeboard above the desk, in plain view.

My surroundings may have shifted, but if anybody expected me to forget where I came from, they were in for a shock.

CHAPTER SEVEN

Everything was pitch black.

It was impossible to see anything else when the emptiness was staring me right in the face, consuming everything around me. The darkness had become tangible, strangely thick and impossible to penetrate, forcing its way inside with every breath so that it clogged my throat and blackened my lungs.

I tried to move, but my limbs weren't cooperating. Even turning my head was an impossible feat; the muscles in my neck had turned to ice, becoming irreparably stiff. There was no going anywhere.

All of a sudden, light flooded the room. It was peculiar, crackling and morphing before my eyes, spreading from a single dot in the distance to a wall on the horizon. It was also radiating an incredible amount of heat. Without warning, the feeling returned to my body—as if the warmth had melted away the temporary paralysis. I spun around, my eyes following the light, just in time to register the danger.

I realized it wasn't just light, but flames—scorching a path that had me surrounded in seconds. I was standing in the middle of a ring of fire, a lethal formation that stretched high into the air, like it was trying to snatch every last bit of oxygen. It was hungry, ferocious, uncaring. And I was trapped.

I went to scream, but surprise lodged the sound in my throat. Outside the ring stood a figure, their features indistinguishable, their face obscured by the wavering heat. I stepped closer, narrowing my eyes to make out their identity.

When I did, the sick feeling in the pit of my stomach proved even worse than the original terror.

It was my mom. Now that I recognized her, I noted the impeccable ponytail, each strand of brown hair slicked perfectly into place, and the gray irises that burned with an unnerving intensity. She stood tall behind the flames, their tips flickering just below her chin, but keeping enough of a distance to remain unharmed.

She smiled, then raised her hand.

In it was a can of gasoline.

When I realized what she was about to do, I couldn't stop myself from crying out.

"Are you trying to kill me?!" I screamed, my voice raw. "What's wrong with you?"

Despite my pleas, she remained silent, the ghost of a smirk curling her lip.

"Stop!" I screamed, louder this time. "Let me out, for God's sake! I'm your daughter!"

Every muscle in my body ached in protest, my brain foggy from the toxic fumes in the air, which were already pulsing through my bloodstream and choking me from the inside out. As my strength drained, I fell to my knees, casting one last desperate look up at my mother.

"Please," I begged, though I could barely hear my own voice anymore. "Please just help me."

Tears streamed down my face. With the heat intensifying tenfold, its sweaty pressure threatened to consume me entirely. My mother's lips parted; for a moment, I was fooled into thinking she was about to say something.

Instead, she lifted the can and started to pour.

And all I could do was scream.

Awakening with a start, I jolted into a seated position in the silent room. The ghost of a scream lingered in my throat and the air around me. I clasped a hand over my mouth, hoping to mask a sound that had clearly already escaped. My breath came in desperate gasps, and my entire face was soaked with sweat.

Eyes darting around the room, I wondered where I was. The sheets crinkled in my lap felt much too stiff, and the scent of detergent was stifling. Stark, white walls stared back at me from four directions, the emptiness of the room evident even through the strokes of paint. Several seconds passed before it all came back to me.

Early morning sunlight streamed through the gaps in the blinds, bathing the entire room in a soft glow. A quick glance at my phone told me it was five thirty. I froze, straining to hear any sound from the rest of the house, but could hear nothing.

For as long as I could remember, I'd been an early riser, but then again, that might've just come with the territory of Silver's strict training schedule. More often than not, she'd have me in the gym at six, panting on a treadmill or bench-pressing weights that seemed to get heavier every day. Even on my days off, I found myself awake at extraordinarily early times, through force of habit if nothing else.

Still, it didn't bother me. Morning was the best time of day, and

I savored those few precious hours when I had the world to myself. It sounded cheesy, but it was true; that one period of quiet was when my thoughts were clearest.

Going back to sleep was an impossibility, so I threw back the covers and got out of bed. My feet landed on a cool wooden floor, a mild relief when my body still felt like it was on fire. I wasn't sure what had come over me. There'd been nightmares about the fire, sure, but they'd never physically shaken me like this—and my mother had certainly never had a starring role.

I shrugged off my sweaty pajamas and pulled on an old T-shirt and running shorts. My gym shoes had been kicked under the bed sometime last night, so I fished them out and laced them up, already beginning to feel the tension seeping from my muscles.

The house was still as I padded downstairs and slipped out the door, and I finally felt myself relax when my feet started a familiar pounding rhythm on the sidewalk.

It had been another part of Silver's training regime, but running had also become one of my favorite pastimes, not to mention my most effective form of stress relief. With my heart pounding and muscles burning, running cleared my head like little else.

Right now, that was exactly what I needed. I'd spent all night trying to forget last night's dinner, but my mind kept wandering back regardless. When my mom had called me downstairs, I'd found her laying two plates on the dining table, though I could see no evidence of cooking in the spotless kitchen. She did her best to hold the conversation. We went through the motions, pushing the boundaries of small talk until they refused to stretch further, but neither of us could ignore that it felt choppy and awkward. Between every sentence there'd be a lingering pause, widening the gap between us another inch.

That half hour felt longer than the fifteen years we'd been separated.

I ran for almost two hours, eventually pulling out my phone for the last leg of the journey so I could find my way back to Umber Court. When I got back, pushing through the front door with my chest heaving, I realized I no longer had the house to myself. My mom was up; I could hear movement on the other side of the wall. For a split second I paused, considering whether it was worth making a desperate dash upstairs, but decided against it.

We couldn't avoid each other forever, and I only hoped that the more we talked, the less painful it would become.

She was balanced on a stepladder in the center of the living room, her entire body taut as she strained to swipe the ceiling with the duster in her hand.

"Hey," I said, later cringing at the sound of my voice in the quiet room. Though I didn't know what it was meant to sound like, I was also certain that I'd got it wrong.

"Corey." She paused, lowering the duster as her eyes swept over me. "I didn't know you'd been out."

"Yeah. I, uh . . ." I cleared my throat. "I went running."

It was a stupid thing to say; that much was surely obvious from my clothing and visible sweat. And yet, I felt compelled to explain anyway, desperate to be relieved of my mom's scrutinizing gaze. I already felt out of place in a house so tidy it seemed like a criminal offence to step out of line—where my scruffy postrun look probably deserved a life sentence.

"Oh," she said. "That's nice."

I wondered how much longer I could take this excruciating awkwardness without imploding. "Yeah. Well, uh . . . I'm going to take a shower."

She nodded, probably wishing as hard as I was for this conversation to end. "Okay."

I turned to make my exit, and as soon as I was back in the hallway, a huge breath of relief escaped me. I felt awful—with this opportunity for a fresh start, I really didn't want to be going to any lengths to avoid my mom, but it was impossible to find the right words to say. Though I knew we'd have to find a way to work it out eventually, for now, the easiest thing to do was walk away.

Unfortunately, before I'd even got past the first step on the staircase, my attempt to do exactly that was interrupted by a knock at the front door behind me.

The knock was followed by the sound of my mother's voice from the other side of the wall. She must've still been balanced at the top of the stepladder. "Corey—would you mind getting that?"

I couldn't exactly say no, so my disappearing act would have to wait. I turned back and went to the door.

The girl who stood there—a few inches shorter than me— appeared to question life itself when I pulled the door open, looking up from her phone so she could peer closer at the golden number mounted on the wood.

"Can I help you?"

"Sorry." The Australian accent was a surprise. She glanced down to check her phone again. "You know what? I think I've been a *complete* idiot and got the wrong house. This isn't number forty-two, is it?"

Only then did I notice the giant basket by her feet. Made of authentic wicker and covered in cellophane, it didn't look like a typical delivery, but the material made it impossible to see exactly what was inside.

"No, you've got the right place," I told her. "This is forty-two."

She was still glancing from her phone to my face, and back again. "I was looking for Hazel."

"She's here," I said, then paused. "I'm her daughter."

The girl's eyebrows shot up so far they disappeared behind her bangs. "You've got to be shitting me."

"Sorry?"

"No." She was already shaking her head. "You're screwing with me, aren't you? Hazel hasn't got a daughter. You've got to be, what? My age?"

Thankfully, my mom chose that moment to appear in the hallway beside me. "Hi, Kim," she said, her voice warmer and more at ease than I'd heard it since I'd arrived. "I see you've met Corey."

"I have," Kim said, "although I have to ask, what in God's name is going on here? Since when do you have a daughter?"

My mom smiled, the genuine expression softening her features completely. I only wished it would happen more often when she was around me. "About seventeen years ago," she said coolly, as if Kim didn't already look about to pass out from shock. "Corey's just moved back in with me."

Back in. As if I could even remember being there in the first place.

"Jesus, Hazel, you realize it's way too early in the morning for this?" Kim said, blowing her bangs from her face. Her black hair was impeccable: effortlessly sleek, without a single kink in sight. My own mousy waves, dragged back into a messy ponytail that running had loosened even more, felt animal-like in comparison. "I had no idea."

My mom shot a glance at me. "Kim's a junior at the local high school," she said. "You two will probably be seeing a lot more of each other."

Kim's face brightened. "Oh, you're going to Franklin?"

It was the first time I'd even heard of the school, let alone the fact I would be attending, but nodding along felt like the right thing to do.

"Amazing," she said, with a genuine smile. "It's always nice to see a new face in the hallway. And, hey—you've managed to choose the best person to meet first." She stuck out her hand. "Kim Senghaphan, student body president."

"Corey," I said, giving her hand a brief shake, and wondering if I was the only one who found it strangely formal.

"Now, I'll be representing you at Franklin for the rest of the year," she continued, the pace of her speech speeding up. "If there's anything you need, you can contact me at any time. I also advise everyone to stay up to date with the presidential work I'll be doing over the next year, so feel free to follow my Twitter, @KimSenghaphan. That's K-I-M-S-E-N-G—"

I interjected before she could get much further. "Sorry. I'm not on Twitter."

She looked at me like I'd just told her I was missing a vital organ. Then, a flash of realization caused her expression to change. "*Oh*. I get it. You're on a social media detox right now."

I frowned. "Uh . . . no," I told her, wondering whether to admit I wasn't even totally sure what that meant. "I just don't have it. Or any social media, really."

To say Kim looked horrified was not an exaggeration in the slightest. In fact, it took her a couple of seconds to recover, after which she gave her head a quick shake as if ridding herself of a nightmare. "Not a problem," she continued. "I'm sure we can find another way of keeping you in the loop."

I wasn't sure how much I actually wanted this to happen, but I nodded anyway. "Sure."

"Anyway." Kim's attention had moved swiftly elsewhere, and she turned to my mother, gesturing toward the wicker basket that was still on the front step. "I didn't just stop by for an early morning chat—I actually came to drop this off on my way to school."

She scooped the basket into her arms, its plastic crinkling noisily with all the movement, and passed it to my mom, who looked perplexed. "Uh, what is it?"

"Complimentary gift basket," Kim declared. "One of my parents' genius ideas. I'm supposed to be driving all around Sherwood this week, delivering them to members who've held cards for over a year. I've got a car full of them. You happened to be first on my list—so congratulations, I guess."

My bewildered expression must've been more conspicuous than I thought, because Kim looked over. "My parents own the gym downtown. Peak Fitness. Maybe you've heard of it?"

I shook my head. "Sorry. I'm not from around here."

"Oh right. Well, you're welcome to stop by sometime, if you're into training or anything. You could use your mom's membership card."

My grateful smile was genuine; it wasn't a bad idea. Kim seemed nice—even if she was also slightly overwhelming—and lazing around for over a week had left my body buzzing with pent-up energy. I would've given anything to get back on the bench press, building up the upper body strength I could already feel myself beginning to lose.

Then there was the added advantage that the gym could also be a sanctuary from a house that already felt stifling.

"I will. Thanks."

Kim hooked her thumbs behind her, gesturing toward the car idling at the bottom of the driveway. "I better go, or I'll be late for my first class. I'll probably see you around school sometime, Corey."

"Yeah," I replied. "See you later."

"You guys . . . enjoy your gift basket."

I stayed quiet as my mom bid her good-bye and closed the front door behind her, shutting in whatever icy awkwardness might've started to trickle away in Kim's presence.

I was thankful for the conversation, not to mention the added bonus that Franklin High would at least have one friendly face.

I only wished I could have said the same about my current address.

CHAPTER EIGHT

As it turned out, I couldn't stay away from the gym for longer than a day.

After meeting Kim, I spent the entire afternoon cooped up in my room, going back and forth with myself about whether to call Aunt Shelby. Part of me longed to hear her voice, to tell her I wasn't sure I could handle all this, but every time I found myself staring at her name in my contact list, I couldn't bring myself to do it. It wouldn't go the way I wanted. Never in a million years would she let me give up so easily, and no amount of conversation would get her to budge.

For now, at least, I was stuck.

The confinement was getting to me by the next morning, so I pulled on a pair of sweatpants and was out of the door by seven. My mother was already up; I could hear movement on the other side of the bathroom door, but I made sure to escape before there was any opportunity for conversation.

A quick Google search brought up the address for Peak Fitness; it was only a twenty-minute walk. My gym bag bumped against my hip as I set a rapid pace through the streets of Sherwood.

Though the houses of Umber Court were pretty similar, the properties seemed to increase in grandeur the farther I ventured out. This trend continued with a flourish at the end of one particular street; the house I found myself eyeing was huge, situated at the end of a lavish front yard. The oldest in the neighborhood, it stood tall against the others, authentic brick contrasting sharply against a street full of paneling. A large porch was supported by ornate stone pillars, while a couple of attic windows jutted out from the roof.

On the driveway sat a van marked with the words *Everett Real Estate*, but there was no evidence of any movement inside the house itself. In fact, everything was eerily still.

Then a figure appeared on the porch. I was jolted from my scrutiny by the tall man, somewhere in his late forties, who was dressed in a crisp suit and had a cell phone clamped to his ear. It didn't exactly look like a pleasant phone call; his creased brow quivered with the effort of not losing it altogether.

He marched down the porch steps and climbed into the van. The cell phone remained at his ear as he backed up quickly, turned into the street, and sped out of sight.

A short while later, I made it to the gym, pushing through the revolving doors before seven thirty. My mom had left her membership card on top of my dresser the night before, and it swiped easily through the automatic barrier, letting me in to the sound of whirring equipment that I'd been craving for almost two weeks.

I started with the treadmill, adjusting it to a setting that seemed frustratingly slow to ease myself in, before cranking it up several notches. The soles of my sneakers pounded on the rubber surface, which was all the soundtrack I needed. I wasn't one to run with music; it'd never been necessary among the crazy circus atmosphere.

I wanted to clear my head, but after meeting Kim, even running couldn't steer my mind away from one thing in particular: school. As if the past couple of weeks hadn't been enough to deal with, I was about to have another challenge thrown my way.

Circus life hadn't left me *entirely* uneducated. Most days, I was sent to one of the quieter trailers to spend several hours poring over textbooks. The other kids were forced to do the same, as insisted on by long-standing Mystique rules, though dedication usually started to waver by the time we hit fifteen or sixteen. I was the oldest who'd tried to maintain a commitment to studying, despite it becoming increasingly difficult as training intensified. Trapeze had a tendency to push everything else to the sidelines. So although I'd tried my best, I knew my knowledge would be shaky compared to any other student my age.

Of course, I'd never imagined it would matter. Until now.

Having picked up my speed, my legs were starting to ache, but I couldn't let myself quit. No pain, no gain—as had been drilled into me for so long. I'd spent so many years in intensive training that it was now a natural instinct to constantly push myself further, only stopping when it became physically evident I couldn't continue.

The bench press followed the treadmill. I could almost hear Silver's voice in my head, talking me through the schedule that clearly no longer applied. Upper body was always my main focus. When it came to trapeze, even the most basic moves were impossible without weeks of training—and it had taken years of work to get where I was today.

Midway through my workout, I felt the eyes of my neighbor wandering. Her sideways glances were less subtle than she thought.

When I completed my third set and shelved the weight, she seemed unable to contain her awe any longer.

"You're *really* good at that."

Perched at the end of her machine, she seemed to have abandoned her own workout in favor of watching mine. She was very pretty, in an obvious way, even with her dip-dyed hair pulled into a topknot and forehead glistening with sweat. Her slim build was admirable, but she lacked the serious muscle needed to be anywhere near a trapeze artist's caliber.

Her wide-eyed gaze had already sent a flush creeping up my neck, one that had little to do with the exercise. I slid out from beneath the bar, my legs still straddling the bench, and glanced over at her. "Oh," I said eventually, "I'm okay, I guess."

"Are you kidding? You made that look easy. You must train really often." She appeared genuinely curious, edging closer, like she was eager to learn my secret.

"Uh . . ." I couldn't work out why I felt so disarmed; it wasn't like this girl was mocking me. In fact, she was impressed, a feeling I'd come to miss in its brief absence. "Six times a week."

"Wow," she breathed. "Wish I could find that kind of time. Between school and everything else, the most I usually fit in is three."

I offered her a small smile, not really sure what else to say.

"So are you an athlete? I guess you have to be, with a schedule like that."

For a split second, I was about to tell her. The words were balanced on the tip of my tongue. Never before had I hesitated to reveal the way I lived, but those had been simpler times. I didn't know what this girl's views were on people like me, and now that I was trapped in Sherwood for the foreseeable future, any words I let slip had the potential to follow me around forever.

"Yeah," I said instead. "Something like that."

"You know, I haven't seen you around here before," she continued. "Everyone else is kind of a regular. Are you new in town?"

I cleared my throat, hoping it didn't sound too awkward. "Yeah. I, uh . . . just moved to town. I'm not from around here."

The moment the words came out, I regretted them. They'd left much too wide a gap, space for all the additional questions I was trying to avoid. I wished I could reach out and snatch them back, but the look of interest on the girl's face was enough to make me realize it was too late.

"Oh, where are you from?"

I hoped she would overlook the flicker of mild panic in my eyes, the way my mouth opened slightly before the words had a chance to find themselves. "I, uh . . ." *Think, Corey, think.* "Southern California," I said eventually, thinking back to where we'd last pitched up before things had kicked off in Sherwood.

Her face brightened. "Hey, I've got an aunt who lives down there. We've spent a couple of vacations in Santa Maria. What part are you from?"

My mind had suddenly gone blank. We must've visited a dozen towns in Southern California, but in that moment they all blended into one incomprehensible mess, their names hazy. All I had to do was think of one, and I couldn't even manage that.

"Oh, a bit of everywhere, really," I said, before I could stop myself. "We moved around a lot."

Curses flew inside my head before I'd even finished my sentence. I wanted to wince at my stupidity—or at least find an escape route out of this situation. I wasn't even sure how I'd got myself into it. All I'd been after was a simple trip to the gym, and somehow I'd landed here, squirming under the scrutiny of the first person I'd met.

She looked slightly bemused, but thankfully didn't keep pressing. "I'm Claire, by the way."

"Corey."

"Well, it was nice to meet you, Corey," she said, starting to gather up her things. "I've got to go, but maybe I'll see you around sometime. If I ever need some training tips, I guess I know who to come to, right?" Her smile was dazzling—there was no other way to put it.

I nodded, bidding her a good-bye I hoped was equally polite. As she left, heading for the locker room, I couldn't help but notice the back of her T-shirt. The bold text, white against the dark fabric, read *Franklin High Lacrosse Team*.

It seemed that I'd just met another classmate.

~

When I returned to the house, my entire body pulsed with fatigue but I felt far less agitated than I had in the last week. As soon as I let myself in, I came face to face with my mother, who was brandishing a thick brochure.

"I spoke to the admissions office at Franklin," she said matter-of-factly, like this was all business. Today, the polished black heels on her feet elevated her head even higher above my own. She was clearly dressed for work, minutes away from heading out the door; her white shirt harbored not a single wrinkle, and a pencil skirt finished just above her knees. "You start on Monday. They gave me a welcome booklet, if you want to look over it."

"Oh," I said. "Right. Okay."

I wasn't used to school being such an urgent priority. After all, what was the point of wasting time being hunched over a textbook when there was an evening show to rehearse for? No matter the time or the day, it could pretty much be guaranteed that we all had more important things on our minds.

"There's a bus that goes from down the street," she told me. "It should be pretty easy to get there . . . unless you want me to drive you on your first day?"

I thought of being trapped in a car with my mother, and the painful silence that would ensue as we struggled to fill the space. I shook my head quickly. "No, no, it's fine," I told her. "I don't want to inconvenience you. I'm sure I'll find it okay."

"Okay," she said. I wondered if I was imagining similar relief in her voice. "If you're sure."

I managed to give her a smile. "Definitely."

She left shortly afterward, snatching up her handbag and car keys while murmuring something about how she was going to be late, though I had a feeling "late" by her watch was nothing of the sort. I felt guilty for it, but I did allow myself a huge sigh of relief when the front door finally closed behind her. The atmosphere inside the house was a hundred times more bearable when I was alone. She wasn't a horrible person—not even close—and yet the unavoidable truth persisted: we were complete strangers.

I missed the circus so much that it had become a permanent physical ache in my chest, like a piece of my heart had been ripped out and left behind. I would've given anything in the world to turn back time, to be back there, to stop this horrific nightmare from playing out in the first place. But if wishing for change really worked, I wouldn't have been standing in my mother's hallway.

A chill went down my spine and caused me to shudder. I wasn't sure whether it was my imagination, or whether my mom had some kind of obsession with air conditioning, but the entire house had felt cold since I'd arrived. The late-August sunshine streaming through the windows didn't make the slightest bit of difference.

Cold and sterile. That pretty much summed up every room in the entire house, and after spending years among the cozy clutter of Aunt Shelby's trailer, I wasn't sure I'd ever become accustomed to it. There were no framed photos on the walls, no affectionate keepsakes on the counter, no photo albums stacked behind the couch. The house could have been the marketing suite for the rest of Umber Court.

A house where every bit of life had been wiped and dusted away.

I wanted to stumble across photos of me as a baby, my mother with her friends—even a yearbook of school days long since forgotten. There had to be something to fill the empty space, to prove that my fifteen years of absence hadn't left a gap stretched wide with nonexistence—some kind of evidence that life had gone on outside the walls of the circus tent, if only to give me hope that I might discover it myself.

And yet, I had a feeling that even if I turned the entire house upside down searching, I would never find anything close.

CHAPTER NINE

On Monday morning, I woke with a deep nausea in the pit of my stomach.

I considered getting up early, maybe trying to fit in a run before leaving for school, but for once things didn't feel curable by physical exertion. Even my recurring nightmares had been different: while they'd previously consisted of fire ripping through the fabric of Cirque Mystique over and over until I couldn't bear to watch, last night's had turned to something closer to home. A maze-like high school, where the corridors stretched on forever, the classrooms trapped me like a cage, and my stupidity made me fair game for constant ridicule.

Even waking up wasn't an escape; every dream took me back there. It got to the point where the last nightmare—in which the school burned down more ferociously than the circus tent had—actually felt like a relief.

I went through the motions of getting myself ready—stumbling into the shower, brushing my teeth, pulling on the clothes most likely to help me blend into the background. I'd never given it much consideration before, but it seemed there was a whole art to escaping notice. I only hoped I'd pick it up quickly.

The glittering black leotard hung in my closet, a hint of sparkle among everything else. For a moment, I let my fingers brush the material, reveling in its velvety feel against my skin, as if that would be enough to transport me back. Eventually, though, I had to force myself to step away, and shut the closet with unnatural purpose.

"Good morning," my mother said, glancing over her shoulder as I ventured into the kitchen. Standing at the counter, she was piling an odd combination of ingredients into a blender: spinach, an egg, and a weird gray powder. "Health shake," she explained when she caught me staring.

"Got it," I said, sliding into a seat at the dining table.

An array of food was already laid out on the tabletop, but my churning stomach didn't feel like it could cope with much. So instead, I opted for black coffee, hoping it made me seem calm and sophisticated—though I could never quite get used to the taste.

I wasn't sure what had happened to me. One month ago, I'd had no doubt in my ability to handle anything. I spent my days dangling over a live audience, clinging to a piece of rope with my bare hands, not even bothering with a safety net.

Corey Ryder was once effortlessly confident, and almost as strong as she made herself out to be. But in the space of a few weeks, I'd withdrawn into myself, threatening to crumble at the smallest upset. And I hated it.

"How are you feeling?"

I looked up, having not expected these words to cross the kitchen. At least not today. It was my mom's first attempt at a conversation deeper than "Is chicken okay for dinner?"—which I guessed had to come eventually, but didn't make it any less unnerving.

"Oh," I said awkwardly. "I'm okay."

"Did you do much studying while you were . . . ?"

Our eyes met, but her voice trailed off, dwindling into silence. A shot of defensiveness went through me before I could stop it. Why did she find it so difficult to say the words aloud? Was it really so taboo? We might not have talked about how I'd spent the last fifteen years of my life, but that didn't mean the whole thing had to be tiptoed around like the slightest disturbance would blow everything up.

"In the circus?" I finished, a little louder than necessary.

She blinked, perhaps not expecting me to fill in the gap so forcefully, before nodding. "Yes. That's what I meant."

I could've been imagining it, but her gaze seemed to have become more judgmental in those few seconds, like she was waiting for me to say something that would justify her opinion. I was determined not to give her the satisfaction.

"I did enough," I said simply.

Of course, I had no idea if this was true. How was I supposed to know what high school kids were learning nowadays? The textbooks I'd been studying from were years old, passed down through generations of students, and were painfully outdated and falling apart at the spines.

From then on, there was a definitive shift in atmosphere, and further conversation was frosty at best. It hardly made the rest of breakfast a pleasant experience, but it did have one advantage: regardless of how much I was dreading my first day at Franklin, and whatever it might bring, it gave me a push to get out of the front door.

True to my mom's word, the bus stop was at the end of her street, and the bus dropped me right outside the school grounds. As I stepped off, I got my first real look at Franklin: a huge, four-story main building that felt like it was looming over me, along with several smaller blocks that made up the rest of campus. Hordes of kids swarmed through the gates, and I soon found myself carried along with the crowd, whether I'd intended it or not.

The place was chaos. At first, I assumed this was just a regular high school atmosphere, but a few minutes of moving through the bustling crowd had me realizing maybe it was something more. The noise had become deafening, and as I managed to slip past a group of girls trying to record something on their phones, it became evident that the moving crowd of students was concentrated on one spot on the lawn.

Getting caught up in the crowd hadn't taken me to the entrance at all. Instead, I found myself in the middle of . . . *something*.

Angry shouts erupted from somewhere nearby. People behind me pressed into my back, eager to get closer to the action. I stood on tiptoe, craning my neck for a better look, but there was little else to see apart from the heads of people taller than me.

Then somebody moved aside and I found myself with a gap to peer through.

Two guys were having some kind of heated argument, both of them shouting furiously over one another. Through the gap, I could only really see one of them: the tallest of the pair, who was absolutely huge. He must've been at least six foot five. I guessed he was a football player, or at least that was what his blue jersey, stretched to the limit over his muscular torso, suggested.

Before I could get a look at the other guy, a collective gasp sounded around me, and a jersey-clad arm took a swing.

Its target moved out of the way at the last moment, into my line of vision. He turned, and a jolt of electric recognition went through my entire body.

"Luke!" I yelled, but my voice was drowned out by the crowd as the football player went in for a second swing, this time colliding with Luke's face with a sickening crunch.

Part of me wanted to close my eyes, to block out the horror that was unfolding before me, but every muscle had been rendered motionless. I couldn't do anything but stand rigid as the brawl escalated with frightening speed.

Luke went to retaliate, fist swinging for a punch of his own, but his opponent was having none of it. Bracing himself, he slammed into Luke with all the force he could muster, and they both went flying to the ground.

In the crowd, someone screamed.

The football player managed to pin Luke down, holding his limbs so he was completely incapable of self-defense. Then, he drew his fist back, preparing to land his most brutal punch yet.

My mind snapped into action just in time.

It was a stupid move, but the heat of the moment saw me push through the barrier of the crowd, screaming at whoever would listen to *Stop, stop, for God's sake*, ready to intervene by any means necessary. The football player was twice my size, but this barely crossed my mind as I stumbled forward into the heart of the chaos.

My hand enclosed his wrist just as he was about to land his punch. Whether it was his distraction or my strength, I wasn't sure—all I knew was that his fist didn't manage to get anywhere near Luke's face.

Thankfully, my action seemed to trigger the rest of the kids. Several others followed suit and stumbled forward, while a couple of burly guys grabbed hold of the football player's arms and yanked him back. It took all their strength to haul him off Luke, but they did eventually, restraining him for the few seconds needed for his target to get back on his feet.

The original punch had landed right across Luke's eye socket, and discoloration foreshadowed the bruise that would soon develop. It was noticeable even from a distance, before he pressed a hand to it, wincing in pain.

We didn't even have time to make eye contact before the first teacher of many pushed through the crowd, shouting orders. Grabbing Luke by the arm, he yelled, "Everybody clear out! Get to class *now*!" as several other teachers emerged in the vicinity.

The crowd dispersed over the next few minutes. I was one of the last to move; my muscles felt like they'd seized up from shock. All I could do was watch as the footballer was escorted by three teachers into the main building, kept firmly separate from Luke, who soon followed.

Everybody around me was talking about what they'd just seen, but there were too many voices to make sense of any of them. Even when I did manage to isolate a single few to listen in, they didn't reveal much more; from what I gathered, nobody seemed sure exactly what the fight had been about.

I was just as confused as anybody. When I'd met Luke at the diner, he hadn't struck me as the type of guy to get into fights, let alone ones with beefy athletes who looked as if they had more muscle than brain. He'd seemed normal, even sweet.

Had I been wrong? Or had I just caught him at the wrong moment?

The bell pulled me from my thoughts as it echoed through the school grounds. My heart was still pounding, high on adrenaline, but I managed to gather enough composure to head for the main entrance. I entered a blindingly bright hallway, lined for what seemed like miles with garish blue lockers. The mass of students had now started to dissipate, tailing off in dribs and drabs into classrooms all the way up the hall.

My own destination was the main office. Thankfully, it was clearly labeled, and I pushed through the door to see a couple of middle-aged women tapping away at computers, plus several fed-up-looking kids waiting on chairs outside the vice principal's office. Neither of these things held my attention, though, because that was when I spotted the girl leaning against the front desk, chatting to the receptionist.

"I've had just about every team captain in the school approach me, all demanding to be read out first." The familiar Australian accent gave her away. Sure enough, there was Kim, hovering by the desk and talking so fast it was like her life depended on it. "I keep telling them, you can't all be first, you know? The football team's the worst for it."

I'd said nothing since entering the room, but Kim seemed to sense my presence anyway, and spun on the spot. "Corey! Hey!"

"Hi," I said. "What's up?"

"Oh, just waiting to do the morning announcements," she told me, gesturing toward the microphone on top of the desk. "First few weeks of the year, it's a busy time, you know? I swear, it's going to take me about ten minutes just to read off all the tryouts."

I managed a small smile. "Sounds crazy."

"You have no idea. And then somebody comes in to tell me half the school's late because of some fight happening outside? *Just* what I needed."

"Yeah. I just saw that, actually."

"Well," she continued briskly, "I feel like it's my duty to apologize. That's probably not the greatest first impression of Franklin, witnessing some kind of teenage brawl right out on the front lawn. But I hope it hasn't put you off entirely. New students don't usually get mauled on their first day."

I thought back to Luke and the ugly black eye that had already started forming. The thought alone made my heart lurch, which seemed weird. We hardly knew each other, after all. There was only so much one conversation could mean, no matter how significant it had felt at the time.

But I wasn't about to stand by and watch him get pummeled without batting an eyelid.

"It's okay," I assured her. "I'm keeping an open mind."

"Thank God." She blew her bangs from her face. "I want to make sure your first few days go as smoothly as possible. And like I said before, if you need anything at all, just come find me."

This time, the smile that crept onto my face was truly grateful. "Thanks," I said. "Really."

Kim smiled back, and then noticed the clock on the opposite wall; it was almost eight. "Showtime," she said with a twinkle in her eye, before spinning on the spot and jabbing the button on the microphone. The next time she spoke, her voice was projected over the speaker set, so her Australian accent filled every room in the building. "Gooooood morning, Franklin High."

Part of me wondered if she was nervous, even just a tiny bit, at the prospect of broadcasting to the entire school. However, her confident stance and bright tone suggested very much otherwise. If there was anything that could faze Kim, it certainly wasn't this.

I watched, intrigued, as she scrolled through the notes on her phone as she talked. Running quickly over the generic morning announcements, she then moved onto a list of clubs that were running tryouts that week. I noticed, with slight amusement, that she purposely left mentioning the football team until the very last minute, adding them as an afterthought, like they'd slipped her mind completely.

When she finished, signing off with a cheery wish for everybody to have a good day, she turned to me with a grin. "I think I just pissed off Austin Murray—he's captain of the football team—but that was kind of worth it."

I didn't know who that was, but I found myself laughing along with her, drawn in by her easygoing charm.

"Anyway," Kim said, "I better get to homeroom, and you probably need to get your schedule sorted. Word of warning: when you're trying to find your way around, this place can be bigger than it looks. But we're a good bunch here—despite what you may have seen this morning—and people will be willing to help you out. So don't hesitate to ask, okay?"

It wasn't worth trying to explain that I usually went out of my way to avoid doing exactly that, so instead I just nodded. "Okay."

"And," she went on, "if you're looking for a friendly face in the cafeteria later, you know where to find me."

Her niceness was overwhelming; I couldn't believe she was so willing to go out of her way for somebody she didn't even know. My first instinct was to turn it down, to go it alone, like I would've done on any other occasion, but I couldn't bring myself to do anything of the kind. Things had changed, and perhaps it was a sign that I had to too.

"Thank you," I said again, aware I was starting to sound like an echo, but not totally sure how to stop. "I really appreciate it."

"It's no problem. Good luck on your first day," she said as she backed out of the office and headed for the hallway. "I'll see you around, Corey."

That was it. Somehow, with Kim's reassurance, I collected my schedule and headed off to find my homeroom classroom feeling slightly more optimistic than when I'd first stepped onto campus. While the place still seemed massively daunting, it felt like there was a chance I'd be okay after all . . . at least until the circus got itself back together. Then, of course, I would be willing to vanish at the drop of a hat.

CHAPTER TEN

The fight was only the beginning of life at Franklin.

I was starting to realize it had been but a glimpse into what the school was really like; the term "rowdy" didn't quite seem to cover it. Arguments would break out between groups of students in the hallway between classes, angry outbursts squeezed into the five minutes we were allotted to move between classrooms. Everywhere I went, somebody was shouting, whether it was a rebellious kid telling teachers where to shove it or someone asserting their aggression after being pushed in the hall.

When I stood at the front of my homeroom class, after the teacher insisted I introduce myself, I felt like a lion tamer, edging my way into a cage with thirty sleeping beasts—any sudden movement and they'd wake up to pounce.

I managed to keep my introduction limited to my name and a lame sentence about being new to Sherwood, and escaped to my seat before the lions had a chance to do anything but stare, uninterested.

I braved the hallways more times than I had strength for, trying to avoid getting shoved aside by some heavy-handed senior as they barged past. Things didn't improve much inside the classroom; it took no more than two periods to realize what I'd been afraid of all along.

I thought I'd done an okay job of keeping up with schoolwork between training sessions, but the gaps in my knowledge were far wider than I'd anticipated. In fact, in the past fifteen years, they appeared to have grown into one giant abyss, leaving me teetering at the crumbling edge and wondering how on earth I was supposed to leap across.

I was way behind even the worst students, barely able to keep pace with the teachers' spiels, though they all talked much slower than Kim. English, at least, was bearable—I could muddle my way through the likes of *Macbeth* and *Dr. Jekyll and Mr. Hyde*, both of which I'd skimmed before. Provided I rambled on for long enough, I could usually conjure up a point that proved valid.

The same, however, didn't stand for geography. I'd never heard of the technical terms all the other students were reeling off like they were fluent in a foreign language. It was one subject in which I'd assumed I would fare okay, since I could name just about any town in any state in the country. The poster on Aunt Shelby's wall had taught me well in that respect, but this class resembled nothing of the geography I'd built up in my head. While the girl next to me delivered a lengthy answer about the formation of some fluvial landform, I ducked my head, staring at my blank notebook and wondering how on earth I was supposed to get through this.

But I hadn't got through the worst yet. That came when I over-heard two girls gossiping in the back of my chemistry class. I hadn't been paying much attention to the teacher anyway, but my ears pricked up at the mention of one particular word I couldn't ignore.

"Wait, you didn't hear about it?" one girl said, her voice hushed. "It's been all over the local news."

"The fire, right? At that circus?"

"Yeah. But have you seen what the police are saying now? They found gasoline, and they think somebody might've done it on purpose. I mean, I know they weren't exactly welcome here, but I didn't think it would go that far. People almost *died*."

"Wait—was it the same circus? The people who caused all that damage at Clearview Heights last year?"

Suddenly, I was more tuned into their conversation than anything else in the room. "That's them. God, my parents were so pissed when they heard they were back in town. They'd just made the down payment on their new house in Clearview last year when all the vandalism happened. Smashed windows, graffiti everywhere . . . the whole place was a shithole when those criminals were done with it. The value dropped overnight, and my parents lost thousands on a house that wasn't even finished."

"That's awful," the second girl said. "I can't believe they'd do something like that."

Neither can I, I wanted to turn around and scream. *Because it didn't happen. And none of what you've just said is true.*

When the other girl spoke again, she'd lowered her voice, and I had to strain even harder to catch what she was saying. "I mean, I'm not saying arson was the answer, because whoever it was put a hell of a lot of people in danger that night, but . . ." She paused. "Let's just say a lot of people in this town probably didn't shed too many tears when they heard the news. Karma really is a bitch."

Fury bubbled inside me; it was mostly shock that kept me from reacting. I wanted to dismiss the story as a stupid rumor, but the more I thought about it, the more I realized the name Clearview Heights was familiar.

And then I remembered. Now that Aunt Shelby had explained why, it was easy to see how, despite this being our first time in Sherwood itself, we'd come close so many times. In fact, it was less than a year ago that we'd been in the next town over, a similar-sized place no more than twenty minutes away. A single mention of Clearview Heights, and it all came flooding back.

I remembered the development: a brand new neighborhood with an exclusive reputation before the houses were even finished. The sprawling billboards with artists' impressions of tranquil villages and breathtaking views, plus relentless invitations to *Come visit our showroom today!*, spoke for themselves. Clearview Heights billed itself as one of the most peaceful, safe, and desirable neighborhoods for miles—and the properties came with a price tag to match.

We'd driven past the site a couple of times, and it was impossible to resist trying to peek in; I distinctly remembered a conversation with Dave about which of the beautifully designed houses we'd buy if money was no object.

I had a vague recollection of hearing about vandalism on the site a couple of days before we left, but I hadn't thought much of it—and it certainly wasn't anything to do with us. I hadn't even known someone had made the link. We must've hit the road before any rumors started gaining traction, leaving us none the wiser.

Until now.

I wasn't sure how I kept my cool when every part of me wanted to scream at the girl behind me. How could she assume that we were responsible when there was no evidence we'd even been near the site at all? I wanted to challenge her right there, but I was pretty sure she represented a single voice in a collective opinion, and changing her mind would affect nothing.

I forced myself to remain in my seat, the tips of my ears burning, with the girl's words circling over and over in my head.

Chemistry class may have taught me nothing scientific, but I learned something more important: in this town, my circus roots were shameful. No matter how I tried to spin it, or how much I might try to convince people we weren't criminals, the rumors had had enough time to settle deep—and opinions in this town weren't likely to change overnight.

Still, at least I'd realized it soon enough. I had no option but to become a closed book and conceal my past from everybody I could. In that single moment, trapeze became taboo.

The only bearable part of the day was lunch. My mother had left me a packed lunch on the counter this morning, and I clutched it in my hand as I followed a bunch of noisy sophomores to the cafeteria. They led me to the biggest room in the school, which had white walls stretching up to an exceptionally high ceiling, and glaring blue tile that squeaked underfoot. Octagonal tables and their adjoining seats filled the room, with their occupants forming a well-established pattern. From what I could gather, seniors concentrated toward one end of the room, not necessarily the loudest, but clearly running the place. Juniors and sophomores stuck to the middle, while the freshmen squeezed into less desirable tables by the garbage cans.

Hovering alone at the door, I felt unnervingly exposed, with several people's eyes already on me. My gaze trailed toward the junior section. The first person I saw was Claire, the girl from the gym, but her table didn't seem like the easiest to approach; her friends were all exceptionally attractive and looked to be in the middle of some intellectual debate, which I'd surely have no part in.

It was a stark contrast to the table of jocks beside them, which included the football player who'd taken a swing at Luke this morning. They were all hooting loudly, cheering on the guy attempting to stuff as many fries in his mouth as possible.

When I finally spotted Kim, I was overcome with relief. She was seated at a table in the center of the room, deep in conversation with a group of several others. When she looked up, our eyes caught and she beckoned me over.

"Corey, hi!" she said as I approached. "Come sit down."

I lowered myself into the empty seat, setting my lunch down on the table. Several new sets of eyes trained themselves on me, waiting to be introduced. I tried to channel the confidence I'd always felt when in the air, watched by an audience of hundreds, but it proved much more difficult to muster with my feet planted on the ground.

"Guys, this is Corey," Kim announced, as if she hadn't already made this obvious. "It's her first day." She gestured around the rest of the table, reeling off the names of everyone there, as if I'd actually remember that many at once. Nick, Macy, and Jen blended into many others; the only one who stood out was the guy to her left, who had thick glasses and a head of brown curls, and whom she introduced as George.

"He has the great privilege of calling himself my best friend," she said, slinging an arm over his shoulder. "Right, George?"

"Wouldn't call it that much of a privilege," he mumbled jokingly.

On the whole, lunch turned out a lot better than I expected. I spent most of it listening to the story of Kim's endlessly complex nationality, which she tried to explain to the whole table. Her mom was Chinese, her dad Thai, and both of them were keen travelers. She had been born in France, then spent eight years of her childhood in Australia—picking up her accent in the process—and had lived in two Canadian provinces and three US states before settling in Sherwood. It was even more complicated than my own history.

Their chatter held most of my attention, but I couldn't stop my gaze wandering across the vicinity, skimming tables packed with juniors in the hope—or fear—of spying one face in particular.

Luke and I had connected a mere two weeks ago, but what seemed like an entire world now stood between us and that moment at Joe's. The fight this morning should serve as a warning—despite my first impressions, he didn't look like somebody I should be friends with.

And then, of course, there was the revelation that had come in chemistry. The gossip behind my back had put an end to my blissful ignorance; I now knew what people thought of me here, and I'd revealed more to Luke than I wanted anybody in this school to ever know. If they found out, I would be walking into a torrent of hate and constant whispers in the hallway, and my shot at settling in here would go up in smoke.

At that moment, I made my decision. Luke wasn't someone to get involved with, and I would be a fool to try. All I could do was keep my head down and move carefully through the minefield without risking exposure. It disgusted me that in such a short space of time I'd become so ashamed of what I'd once lived and breathed, but from the moment those flames had come into play, lashing at the walls of the circus tent, I'd known I was heading into something dangerous.

When lunch ended, I prepared myself for an uneventful afternoon. There were only two classes left in the day, a gentle slope compared to the mountain I'd faced that morning. As long as I could keep my head down and avoid drawing unnecessary attention, I could get through it.

~

Or so I thought.

The last class of the day was precalculus, which was the class I was dreading most. I'd never been good at math in general, and the thought of a junior-level class on my first day was enough to lodge dread in the pit of my stomach.

I slipped into a seat near the back of the room, hoping this would allow me to escape notice. As the rest of the class filed in, my attempts at maintaining a positive attitude started wearing thin— and as soon as Mr. Bronowski started writing up a list of different formulas on the board, I knew I was a lost cause.

Within minutes, I was lost in a blur of numbers and letters, all thrown together in a way that made no sense at all. I was usually able to stumble through simple equations, eventually finding my way to the correct answer after a few attempts, but this was in a whole other league. The sheer volume of random letters made it seem as if they comprised some foreign language, and I was trying to read an entire novel.

I gave up eventually, resigning myself to staring down at my blank page with a sense of panicked confusion. Occasionally, I'd look up and jot down an equation; even less often I attempted to solve the problems. Whichever way I looked at it, the obvious was staring me right in the face—I was entirely lost, with zero hope of muddling my way through.

As if that wasn't enough, the classroom was also heating up at an unbearable rate. I'd already peeled off my jacket, but my T-shirt was beginning to stick to my skin. Beads of sweat formed on my forehead and the stagnant air felt thick in my lungs. With the late-summer sunshine blazing through the closed window, turning the room into a greenhouse, I took a deep breath and watched the seconds tick away at an agonizingly slow pace.

Fifteen minutes into class, I surfaced from my sleepy haze—courtesy of the sudden opening of the classroom door.

"Luke," I heard Mr. Bronowski say, at which point my head snapped up instantly. "Nice of you to join us."

"Sorry, sir. I was with the principal." His voice was low, with barely a fraction of the confidence he'd possessed the last time we met. I watched as he handed something to the teacher. "My late pass."

A few seconds went by as Mr. Bronowski inspected the card in his hands. "Very well," he said, placing it on his desk. "Take a seat."

Luke wove through the grid of desks, heading for the only free one in the room. It was just my luck that it happened to be in the same row as mine, two desks over. I kept my head down as he swept past and slid into the seat just a few yards away.

I watched from the corner of my eye as he pulled a notebook from his bag, removed the pencil tucked into the outer cover, and flipped to the first free page. Only then did he seem to notice the temperature of the room, glancing toward the window to check if it was open.

Suddenly—as if sensing he was being watched—he looked over, and our eyes met.

There was a single beat of hesitation, before the flicker of recognition ignited in Luke's eyes. I could practically see the image of the trapeze artist flitting back across his memory, as the connection between then and this moment sparked unexpectedly to life.

I ducked my head so quickly I almost pulled a muscle. My heart pounded as realization sank in. Why had I even risked a look? It would've been safer to keep my head down, but I hadn't been able to resist temptation. I was stupid, led astray by a moment of impulse—and now I would pay the price.

I didn't dare look up for the rest of the hour, my eyes glued to the numbers on the page as if they made even the slightest bit of sense. Each time Mr. Bronowski swept around the classroom, craning his neck over shoulders to check our progress, I covered as much as my notebook as I could with my arm, shielding my work from view. The last thing I needed was for him to notice the nonsensical scribbles across my page and call me over to see him after class.

Relief of a new intensity surfaced when the final bell echoed through the classroom. There was a collective scramble as students hastened to shove textbooks and other belongings back into their bags, desperate to escape the stifling heat as fast as possible.

I was one of them—but of course, my reasons had little to do with the temperature.

I aimed to make a break for it, but being at the back of the room made it impossible to avoid the bottleneck at the door. Mr. Bronowski was yelling something over the chaos, a vague mention of the word *homework* heard in a window of quiet, but nobody was listening.

That was the least of my worries.

What *did* send a jolt of panic through me was the familiar voice that came from somewhere behind, calling my name.

CHAPTER ELEVEN

"Corey? Hey, wait up!"

Luke's voice was impossible to ignore, even amid the commotion of the hallway, but I was willing to try. I didn't want to *wait up*—with that came being forced into a conversation, and exchanging words I'd already resolved to keep silent.

But there was no quick escape route—students piling into the hallway from every classroom formed an impenetrable wall. The main doors were in sight up ahead, but Luke was catching up fast, and I could hear his footsteps advancing behind me.

"Corey!"

Once I felt his hand on my arm, I had no option but to stop, slowly turning to face him. He was slightly out of breath, chest heaving, his expression caught somewhere between disbelief and concern. "What's going on?"

The bruise that ringed his eye was an ugly reminder of that morning's events. It had definitely worsened since then, and the purple hue seemed even more prominent under the harsh hallway lighting. A split in his lip looked just as painful; the break in the skin was red and sore looking.

"What do you mean?"

"I just—" His sharp blue eyes flickered over my face as he struggled to find the right words. "What are you doing here?"

"What does it look like I'm doing?" I asked flatly. "I go here now."

"But what happened to . . . ? I mean, what about you being part of the—"

My heart lurched and I cut him off before the word had a chance to escape. "Shh!" I insisted, realizing too late that my voice was unnecessarily loud. "Keep quiet! Don't talk about that. Not here."

The hallway was bustling with activity, our voices drowned out by countless other conversations around us, so the chances of being overheard were slim—but I didn't want to take my chances.

Luke frowned. "What? Why?"

"Do we really have to talk about this?" I pleaded.

"Yes! Come on, Corey, you've got to tell me what's going on here. I bump into you at Joe's, this supercool trap—well, *you know what*—and I convince myself we'll never see each other again. Then all that stuff happens at the show, I'm out here wondering if you even made it out alive, then you show up two weeks later at my high school? Don't you think I deserve some kind of explanation?"

The retort quickly dissolved on my tongue. "Not here," I murmured eventually. "I don't want to talk about it here."

"Well, let me give you a ride home," he offered. "We can talk in the car."

The smart decision would've been to decline and get out of there as quickly as possible. It would've been mean to deprive Luke of an explanation, but I had to leave the circus behind if I wanted to fit in to a place like this. It had only taken a few hours at Franklin to realize that trapeze artist Corey had to go, to be banished to the deepest and darkest part of my mind, leaving only normal Corey on display to the world.

And yet already I could feel his piercing eyes chipping away at my resolve. Despite what had gone down that morning, and the gossip I'd overheard at the back of chemistry class, I couldn't shake the memory of the boy I'd met in the diner, the one I desperately wanted a chance to know.

If only for that reason, I agreed.

I followed him mutely to the parking lot, keeping up the silence as he approached his car and dug out his keys. Slipping into the passenger side, I clipped my belt into place and waited for Luke to do the same.

I spoke once when he asked where I lived, to recite my mom's address, hoping he was familiar enough with Sherwood to work out the directions himself. The radio was on in the background, saving us from complete silence, but my gratitude for that didn't last long. We'd just pulled out of the school parking lot when the local news started up, and the lead story was one that made my heart lurch.

"*Police are still investigating the fire that broke out in a circus tent on Sherwood Common two weeks ago,*" came the voice through the speakers. "*Investigations so far have pointed to the possibility of arson, but no major leads have yet been identified. The fire comes less than a year after the same circus was linked in the media to a spate of vandalism at luxury housing development Clearview Heights, although no prosecutions were ever made . . .*"

Luke quickly reached forward and shut off the radio, but the silence only drew more attention to what we should've been hearing.

"So," he began, clearing his throat, "how about telling me what's going on?"

My pause lasted longer than intended, but I didn't really know where to start. How was I supposed to condense the last two weeks into a matter of words? I felt like I'd barely pulled through, pouring every last drop of energy into surviving. I hadn't paused to take notes.

"Well," I said eventually, "you were there on opening night. You saw what happened."

"Saw it? I barely *escaped* it. Had my seat not been so near the exit, I don't even know if I'd have got out in time. God knows what it was like for you, up in the air like that."

I nodded slowly, keeping at bay the flashback that was threatening to take over. "I had to jump. There was nothing else I could do. We all managed to get out in the end, but . . . not everyone was lucky enough to get away unhurt."

For a moment I squeezed my eyes shut, seeing Silver lying crumpled in the hospital bed, sobbing over the baby the fire had stolen. When I opened them again, my vision quivered and fragmented before me.

I took a deep breath before continuing. "We lost everything. It was all destroyed, and of course the police are now involved. My aunt didn't want me staying when everything was so uncertain, especially as nobody knows if we'll even be able to pick ourselves up and keep moving. So she sent me here."

"To high school?"

If only things could've been so simple. "More than that," I told him. "She sent me back to live with my mom. I hadn't seen her in fifteen years."

For a fraction of a second, his eyes strayed from the road,

skimming over my face instead. I could tell he was searching my expression, trying to pick up on whatever trace of emotion might've leaked onto it. But, as always, I was doing everything I could to remain impassive. The easiest way out.

"You moved out of the circus?" His voice was quiet, tentative, as if coming on too abruptly would send me running for the hills.

"Yeah," I breathed. "No more trapeze, and no more Mystique."

He seemed to be struggling to absorb the new information. Running a hand through his hair, a ragged breath escaped him. "So, you were homeschooled before, I'm guessing?"

"Yeah. I mean, it wasn't like we've ever stuck around in one place long enough for me to get any sort of formal education. There were other kids too—we used to have a whole trailer set up as a school-type thing. But it wasn't serious, not like it is here. We had other priorities."

"Like trapeze."

"Yeah," I said. "Like trapeze."

I dared to glance across the car at the driver's seat. It was as if Luke's eyes had glazed over, an automatic focus on the road ahead, while his mind drifted miles away. His hair was disheveled from running his hand through it, and yet I could still tell it had been perfectly styled a few hours before. Luke was something of a marvel, I decided; even a fight couldn't stop him from looking put together. Meanwhile, my hair went flyaway after a couple of minutes on the trapeze.

"I still can't believe it," he said. "I can't even begin to understand what the hell happened. It's just . . . I met you, thinking it was just one conversation and one show, that you'd be halfway across the country within a month. And then you show up at my high school two weeks later, in the back of my math class, as if it's nothing out of the ordinary. As if you're just like everybody else. But you're not."

"I'm not," I said. "I know that, and you know that, but I don't want all the other kids at school to find out. Because apparently, everyone in this town thinks we're criminals."

I could tell Luke knew exactly what I was talking about, even though he tried his best not to show it. "That's not—"

"Please don't try to deny it," I said. "I've heard it all. We've clearly been scapegoated for something we didn't do, and we were gone before we had the chance to defend ourselves. It's not fair, but now I have to deal with the consequences."

"I never believed you guys were involved," Luke said. "Even when it first happened, way before I met you. My dad's real estate company is the one marketing the properties in Clearview, so I saw the damage up there after it happened—and it was clearly just some lowlifes trashing whatever they could, just for the hell of it. Why would some random circus be responsible? It didn't make sense. But the buyers in Sherwood were angry, and it was easier to be angry *at* something. Somebody made the link in the papers, some stupid editorial based on no evidence whatsoever . . . and since there were no other leads, everybody just ran with it."

I looked at him. "Well, that makes everything better, doesn't it?"

"I'm not trying to say it does. But just because a few people happen to believe some stupid rumor, doesn't mean everybody does."

"Well, this is my only chance. I don't have another mom I can be shipped off to if things go wrong here. I've got to stick this place out, at least until the circus can get back on its feet. If even a few people here believe that story, they'll think I'm a criminal. And there's no going back from that."

"Isn't that their loss?"

"Well, maybe," I said, "but I'm not brave enough to think that way."

He sighed then, a long, drawn-out breath that sounded loud even against the low rumble of the car engine. "People are stupid like that," he said eventually.

"You're telling me." I shook my head. "That's why I'd prefer to keep my mouth shut. There's no reason for anybody at school to know why I really had to move here, not if they don't need to. And I'd really, really appreciate it if you stuck to the same policy."

"Right."

"So do you promise you won't say anything?"

"Of course," he replied, and I watched as his features softened, the conversation finally shedding some of its weight. "I mean, it kind of sucks not being able to brag to my friends about the trapeze-artist chick I scored with, but, you know . . ."

"Hey!" I leaned over and slapped him playfully on the arm. It hadn't been a hard hit in the slightest, but Luke winced anyway, as if my palm had landed on a preexisting bruise. "You did *not* score with me."

He grinned, flashing perfectly straight teeth that were either the work of some kickass genes or hefty orthodontics. "What my friends don't know won't hurt them."

"*You'll* be the one getting hurt if you start telling people that."

"Ouch. Big threat there, Circus Girl."

"Circus Girl? That's your idea of an insult?"

"It wasn't meant to be an insult," he said simply. "Just a nickname."

I couldn't put my finger on it. Perhaps it was the fact we were now well clear of the school parking lot, speeding along the streets of Sherwood and moving farther away from Franklin with every second spent behind the wheel. Though I didn't quite have my bearings, nor knew how far we still had to drive, my mother's house felt farther away than it had ever been.

It was the space in between, the middle ground between two places that went against everything I stood for, that allowed a flicker of my confidence to return.

"All right, then," I said, undeterred. "What would your nickname be? How about Tough Guy? Seemed to be what you were trying to live up to this morning."

At that, the light atmosphere vanished, Luke's laughter drying up too quickly to be natural. Straight away, I could sense I'd touched a nerve. Part of me wished I could take it back, to return to the easy flow of conversation from moments ago, but the other part was far too curious. I'd yet to discover the reason behind this morning's altercation, and I hadn't forgotten it as the day progressed. Luke seemed too easygoing to get involved in anything more serious than a mild argument; I figured he was the type of guy to laugh things off, not pursue them to violence.

And yet, what I'd witnessed that morning suggested otherwise.

"Oh," he said eventually, just as I'd come to wonder if he'd stopped talking altogether. "You saw that."

"It was pretty hard to miss. I think the whole school was watching."

"Right." He swallowed. "I kind of forgot about that."

It didn't make any sense. How could it have escaped his notice that hundreds of people were closing in on all sides, eager to catch a glimpse of the action? How could the yelling not have drilled right through his head, like it had mine?

"So," I said carefully, edging my way into the topic, "you want to tell me what that was all about?"

"It was stupid," he said quickly.

"Was it?"

There was a lengthy pause before he answered again, shaking

his head. We'd stopped at a red light, only one of his hands on the wheel, the other tapping absently on his leg. "I don't know," he said eventually.

"Who was that guy, anyway?"

"Just some guy off the football team," he said, before adding, almost as an afterthought, "Landon Trafford."

"And Landon Trafford happens to be . . . what? Resident douche, or . . . ?"

"Cornerback," he said, "and part-time resident douche."

He hit the blinker and took a left; we were now moving through a residential area. It looked vaguely familiar, which had to mean we were close to my mom's place, and I tried not to feel disappointed. "So what happened between you two?"

"Uh . . ." I wondered if I was imagining the way Luke seemed to become nervous on the spot, shifting awkwardly in his seat. "It was just something I said. It was stupid, really. He overreacted and things got out of control. It never should've happened."

"What did you say?"

"Nothing. I can't even remember. It wasn't worth fighting over. I'm just lucky the principal didn't expel me, because then I really would've been screwed."

"It can't have been that stupid," I pressed, though by now I was wondering if it was wise to keep digging. Luke had suddenly snapped shut like a book, his fidgeting enough of a giveaway that he wasn't telling the whole story. Was it really my place to keep pestering him? This was only the second time we'd spoken. No matter how much it might've felt otherwise, we were pretty much strangers.

"It was, okay?" he snapped, causing me to jolt in surprise. "What he said wasn't important. I told you, it got out of control, but it's over now. There's no point in talking about it anymore."

I shrank back in my seat, deflated by his reaction. The car was slowing now, Luke's foot easing onto the brake until I realized we'd come to a stop right outside my mother's house. It was as pristine as ever, the entire place gleaming as if it had just been scrubbed all over.

"Anyway, this is you," he said. His tone was already softening, warming up from the cold that had blown across the car just moments ago.

"Thanks for the ride."

"That's okay. I'll see you tomorrow."

I unclipped my belt, hopped out of the car and felt my sneakers meet concrete. After returning the good-bye, I was already turning to make my way up the front yard when the sound of Luke's voice stopped me.

"Corey?" he said. "Just so you know . . . you can talk to me in school. I'm not going to blab about . . . well, you know . . . what you don't want to mention. I'm not going to spread gossip just for the hell of it."

Something about these words, or maybe his tone, made me believe him. He offered a gentle smile, one that twisted my insides slightly, which I was powerless to do anything but return. "Thanks," I said. "I really appreciate it."

This time we really did say good-bye. I hitched my bag over my shoulder and started up the path, all too aware of the fact Luke hadn't moved. Somewhere behind me, he sat watching as I approached the house, one hand on the wheel. It wasn't until I'd fumbled for my key, fiddled with the lock, and finally wrenched the door open that I heard him drive away, the rumble of the engine audible until he'd disappeared all the way up the street.

CHAPTER TWELVE

My first week at Franklin passed in very much the same way as the first day had.

Though there weren't fights breaking out between Luke and Landon every morning on the lawn, everything else remained pretty consistent. I moved from class to class in a permanent daze, wondering if there would ever come a point when I'd finally realize what the teacher was talking about. All I wanted was some kind of *Eureka!* moment, in which I had a sudden breakthrough about all the material I'd been struggling with.

No such thing occurred, and eventually I gave up wishing for it.

I was scraping by in English, mostly on common sense, occasionally drawing upon old books I'd found at the back of the school trailer. The only class that wasn't a hopeless struggle was gym; it was the one hour of the day when I didn't feel like I was lagging way behind my classmates. In fact, when it came to physical work, I excelled.

In my first week, we were put through fitness tests. Most of the others groaned, complaining loudly about how badly they were going to do, how it wasn't fair to spring this on them so soon after the summer. Claire was in my class too. She didn't protest as loudly as the others, but a quick glance behind me saw her pulling a face at her friends.

I expected something challenging, on the same level as my other classes, but the tests were surprisingly easy. They were enough to make gym my favorite subject in a matter of minutes. Four laps around the athletics track; that was easy enough, not a patch on the treadmill work I did regularly at the gym. With little effort, I found myself at the head of the pack, striding ahead of even the most athletic students.

I finished in fantastic time—or at least that was what the coach told me, clapping me hard on the back in what I assumed was a celebratory gesture. I hadn't run as fast as I could have, and my time definitely left room for improvement—but he was convinced it was golden.

The rope was undoubtedly the easiest of them all. Disappointment spread among everyone else when it was announced, but I secretly brightened. I'd been working on my upper body strength for years, but being in the right mindset was half the secret: you had to keep moving, to not think about stopping until you'd reached the very peak.

It was only how I'd spent the last few years of my life.

The first few students found it difficult. Some of them didn't even make it halfway before giving up and dropping back onto solid ground. Only a handful made it right to the top, but everyone saw the evidence of struggle in their faces. They might've made it, but it hadn't been easy.

I was one of the last people to take my turn, confidence sneaking into my step when I moved closer. Finally, this was something I could do. I had the opportunity to prove that I wasn't a complete lost cause.

Climbing the rope had to be the most liberating thing I'd done since being on the trapeze. I hauled myself up with ease, my legs coiling around the lower part, and didn't stop for a single beat. As I rang the bell, I couldn't stop myself from smiling, feeling lifted at last from the frame of hopelessness I'd been stuck in for the past week.

Once my feet were on the ground again, I realized everybody was staring.

"Brilliant!" the coach said, breaking into a round of lonely applause. "I haven't seen anyone do it like that in years. What did you say your name was again?"

"Corey," I told him, and my voice came out more confidently than it had since stepping through the school doors.

I glided through the rest of the fitness tests with much of the same ease. After all, they were designed for high school students, not athletes who'd spent most of their lives in training. The coach kept me behind after class, after everyone else had trundled off, exhausted, to the locker rooms.

"I haven't seen anybody perform so well in those tests for, what? Must be at least ten years. You did good today, kid."

"Thanks," I said awkwardly.

"You're new around here, right?" he asked, and I nodded. "You play any sport? Performance like that, you must do something."

I should've known it was coming. "I, uh . . . I've played a bit of everything," I answered, hoping my reply was sufficiently vague. "Bit of this, bit of that. I train hard, mostly."

For a moment, it seemed like he was looking me up and down, trying to determine if I was telling the whole truth. "Well, it's certainly paying off," he said. "You keep up a performance like that, and you'll have half the school teams begging you to join. You should really think about it."

"I will," I told him, though I had no intention of doing so.

Gym soon became my only spot of relief in a schedule that could otherwise be described as hell. I despised my classes, purely because they'd been rendered impossible by my poor homeschooling. However, there was one in particular that I dreaded most of all.

Precalculus was taught in the only classroom in the school with permanently broken air conditioning, so it heated up unbearably when packed with thirty students. Then there was the fact that, after a week, I'd yet to grasp a single concept. Needless to say, when faced with an announcement on Friday that we were being given a surprise quiz, it took all I had not to let my head fall into my hands.

Mr. Bronowski passed out the test papers right away. Without thinking, I shot a sideways glance at Luke, two seats over, and made a face. The returning smile was encouraging, looking like it was meant to convey a message along the lines of *You'll be fine!*, though I'd have been a fool to believe it.

Panic set in the moment the paper landed on my desk. I stared down at the symbols before me, the random words thrown in by way of instruction, hoping desperately that they would rearrange themselves into a logical sequence. The only thing I knew how to fill in was my name.

I cast a frantic glance around the room, wondering if anybody else felt this lost, but all around me pencils were scratching audibly on pages, answers taking form. My blank sheet looked more daunting than ever; all I could think about was the fact that this would be returned to the teacher at the end of class, who would discover how far behind I was.

What would happen then? Would I be kicked out of the class entirely? As much as that option had some appeal, I didn't want to go through the embarrassment of being put in some kind of remedial class—though that was clearly what I needed.

Panicked, I spent the remainder of the test scribbling down random equations and hoping they would magically transform into the correct answer. When my paper was returned to the front, I felt sick, certain in the knowledge that I'd flunked.

We got them back the following Monday. I'd been right.

The score of nineteen was scrawled on the front of my paper in patronizing red marker. Mr. Bronowski had added a comment in the same pen; it read *See me*, underlined several times.

Luke leaned over, craning his neck in an attempt to see my test paper. The girl who usually sat between us was out sick, so he'd moved across, though I suspected this had something to do with being nosy.

I moved my hand to cover the score just as Luke asked, "How'd you do?"

A moment's debate had me considering whether it would be easier to lie, but I decided there was no point. "I flunked," I admitted, moving my hand. "That test was crazy hard."

"Yeah," he agreed, his eyes flickering toward his own sheet.

"So what did you get?"

"Oh." He smiled sheepishly. "A ninety-eight."

"I thought you agreed that it was hard!" I protested, feeling my heart sink when I caught sight of his test paper, embellished with countless correct marks.

"It *was* hard," he said, "but I guess I knew the answers to the difficult questions."

"You are infuriating."

"Sorry." He smiled, looking torn between joking and being genuinely apologetic.

Sighing, I glanced back down at my test paper, flicking through the questions with only vague interest. On almost every one I'd made huge mistakes, and skipped some altogether. There was simply no getting around the matter: math was not a subject I would ever excel at.

Mr. Bronowski had launched into some dull lecture about our test grades. I wasn't paying much attention, and surprisingly, neither was Luke. Instead, he was still leaning toward me, making no attempt to break away from our conversation.

"You know, if you're looking for somebody to tutor you, I wouldn't mind," he offered.

I assumed he was kidding, which was why I laughed. "Yeah. Right."

"I'm serious," he said. "If you want some help, I really don't mind meeting up a couple of times a week to go over some stuff. Math is my favorite subject."

"I don't know how you can say that with a straight face," I replied, grimacing.

Still, Luke's offer got me thinking. Left to my own devices, I knew I would never improve. I was already far too lost, well beyond hope of catching up with whatever Mr. Bronowski was teaching. Perhaps all I needed was for Luke to explain things in a different way, and that would make it all click into place.

I knew it was a long shot, but it had to be worth a try.

"You're really offering to tutor me?" I asked, raising an eyebrow.

"Sure," he said, like it was that simple. "Why not? I like math, you clearly like spending time with me . . . it's a win-win for both of us."

It took a couple of seconds to realize exactly what he'd said. Shoving him in the side was a little too obvious for the middle of class, especially when Mr. Bronowski was still droning on up ahead, but I wished pretty hard I could've got away with it. "Pffft," I scoffed. "What gave you that impression?"

"Nothing," he said, but the smirk on his face gave too much away. "Just that little smile you get when you're around me."

"What?" I shot him a look. "There is *definitely* no little smile."

"If you say so."

"You cocky jerk," I muttered, though I couldn't help letting my own joking smile slip onto my face. "Maybe I don't want tutoring."

He raised a dubious eyebrow, and as if on cue, both our gazes dropped to the paper on my table, where the nineteen continued to stare us right in the face. He didn't need to say anything to make his point. "Okay, okay," I said, holding my hands up. "Maybe I do need tutoring. But it's *not* because I want to spend time with you. It's because I'm dumb as hell when it comes to math, okay?"

"Okay," he agreed, and there was something about the amused glint in his eye that made my insides flutter. "I'll tell you what—we can even meet up at Joe's to make it more bearable. You've got to be dying for a second round of those fries."

I definitely wouldn't pass up a second round of Joe's incredible food. Amid the chaos of the last few weeks, it'd been easy to forget the fries that had first brought us together that afternoon in the diner. Luke was right, that side dish did make tutoring seem easier to stomach, and if it didn't work out, at least we'd be set for comfort food.

With that in mind, I nodded. Luke grinned.

~

We arranged to meet the following evening, and I managed to scrape through the next day without failing any other tests. Gym involved a session of cross-country running, in which I streaked ahead of the pack, finishing my huge lap several minutes before the runner-up. One mistake I did make, however, was telling Kim and George about my plans to meet up with Luke later that day.

"Luke Everett?" Kim repeated, as if she might've misheard the name. "Luke Everett, as in the most popular guy in school?"

"He is?"

The more I thought about it, though, the more it made sense. It was something I'd come to notice over the past two weeks: Luke was well liked by most of Franklin's junior class and beyond. When he walked down the hallway, people who looked like they'd glare at anybody else couldn't help but smile. In the cafeteria, his table was the biggest of them all, surrounded by people who didn't just hang off his every word, but actually *talked* to him.

He wasn't a jock, definitely not one of the guys who lived in a football jersey, with muscles bigger than their heads. Instead, he was genuinely nice to his classmates, no matter their position in the social hierarchy. They all loved him for it.

It was obvious he had natural charisma, but apparently I'd underestimated it.

"You're kidding, right?" George cut in disbelievingly. "Everyone knows Luke—and, well, Luke knows everybody."

"He's right," Kim said, pulling open her locker. "If I wasn't president right now, it would definitely be him. He ran against me last year. We were neck and neck the entire running. I'd like to say it was my Australian charm that won the school over, but Luke dropped out at the last minute."

"Why?"

She shrugged. "Beats me. He didn't tell me, and I'm pretty sure he didn't tell anybody else either. I guess he's always been kind of secretive about anything outside school. He's just one of those private kind of guys, you know?"

"Like me," said George.

"You've got to be joking." Kim rolled her eyes. "You share way too much. You'd do well to be a little more private."

He turned to wink at me. "We're close."

"*Way* too close," she corrected, but I could hear the affection in her voice. "Still, with Luke, everybody loves him. It's probably got something to do with how he seems like the nicest person ever to walk this Earth, but, you know . . ."

"*Seems like?*" I echoed. "What's that supposed to mean?"

"Well, I don't know. Like I said, he's kind of secretive about stuff. I'm just not sure you can trust somebody like that fully."

"Maybe he just doesn't want to share his personal life with the whole school."

"Maybe. Or it could be that he's got something to hide. You just never know," Kim said, shaking her head, as if delivering some kind of profound wisdom. "Don't get me wrong, he seems like a nice guy, and everybody else obviously thinks so too. I just don't know if it's a good idea to get too close."

"Who said we were getting close?" I asked, immediately regretting the defensive edge to my voice. "It's just tutoring. He's helping me with math a couple of times a week. It's not like we're about to become best friends."

"Hey, don't worry. I'm not telling you what to do." Kim closed her locker, the metal clinking as it locked into place. "I'm not saying he shouldn't be your tutor. I just thought you should know that there's a lot of stuff he doesn't like to talk about. Not to mention that fight last week—I mean, what was that about? It's all anyone's been talking about, and yet nobody seems to know what actually happened."

I thought back to the conversation in the car, and the way Luke had expertly dodged my questions, dismissing each probe with the vaguest answer he could get away with. I'd been determined to get to the bottom of why he'd got into a brawl with somebody twice his size, and yet my attempts had fallen flat under Luke's refusal to cooperate. His actions only served to back up Kim's warning, as much as I didn't want to believe it.

"Somebody told me Landon took a swing for no reason," George said, "but that doesn't seem likely, does it? He's not the brightest guy in the world, but I don't think even he would start a fight unprovoked. Especially not with somebody like Luke."

"It was probably just a misunderstanding," I said.

"Probably." Kim offered me a smile. "I'm not trying to cause trouble, Corey, I swear. It's just something I thought you might want to know."

"Okay," I said. "Well, thanks, but he's still going to help me with calculus."

There was no doubt about it—at this point, if *Landon* offered me the slim chance of improving my grade, I probably would've seized it.

"Got it." She glanced at her phone, eyes widening slightly as she noticed the time. "Shit, George, we better get going. Physics is all the way across campus, and changeover's going to be over any second. See you later."

"See you," I returned, as Kim grabbed George's arm and they hurried off together.

As much as I wanted to forget about this whole discussion, I couldn't quite bury it in the back of my mind. There were, of course, those few snippets of odd behavior I'd witnessed myself, but had chosen not to dwell on. Who was I to say Luke shouldn't keep some parts of his life secret? It would make me a total hypocrite. I was keeping an entire world hidden from those at Franklin, flat out lying to everyone I met but him. We were still essentially strangers; he couldn't be blamed for not wanting to spill everything to me.

I wanted to believe there was nothing more to Luke than the nice guy he made himself out to be. And yet the more I tried to discard Kim's words, the more they stuck in my mind.

I couldn't get rid of the doubt even if I wanted to.

CHAPTER THIRTEEN

Whatever reservations I had about Luke were forgotten once I arrived home from school.

Like most weekdays, my mother was still at work, meaning I had the house to myself for a couple of hours. She didn't seem too happy with this arrangement: each day, she would burst through the door looking panicked, like she'd spent the entire journey worrying about me trashing the place. Part of me wondered if I should be offended, but when it came to my mother, I was learning it wasn't personal.

Her obsessive habits had taken a while to start grating, but now they were truly getting on my nerves. She seemed to have a talent for appearing from nowhere the moment I stepped off the mat with my shoes on, and every time she walked into my bedroom she had to suppress a grimace. I wasn't an overly messy person, but my room looked like any other teenager's: sometimes I threw my clothes over the back of a chair instead of folding them, I kicked things under the bed to put them out of sight, and I didn't dust all the surfaces daily. To my mother, all of the above were criminal offences.

It was clear we were both happier with our previous lives, but neither of us could undo the sudden turn of events that had forced us together. We were just going to have to live with it.

Perhaps it would've been more bearable if we'd bonded gently—if the foundations had been allowed to solidify before we were pushed into something as intense as living together. We were strangers despite the familial bond that linked us, and trying to pretend otherwise wouldn't change the truth. Our personalities clashed; they were shapes that just didn't fit together, forced to find some way to connect.

Luke and I had agreed to meet at Joe's around five; he'd bring his textbook and class notes, and I an open mind. I scribbled a message to my mother and stuck it to the fridge.

Getting dinner with a friend, it read. *Be back in a couple of hours. Corey.*

I slipped out of the door at four forty-five, confident in my ability to find my way to the diner without major problems. So far, figuring out my vague bearings in Sherwood had gone pretty well, and it wasn't like making my way through unfamiliar places was new to me. So how hard could it be?

The answer came twenty minutes later: extremely. I got lost at least three times, on each occasion having to backtrack once I realized I'd walked past the same set of houses a few minutes before. Eventually, after asking for directions from a weary-looking woman with a double stroller, whose children's screeches nearly drowned out our voices, I found my way downtown and somewhere I recognized.

I rocked up at Joe's fifteen minutes late, but I'd made it.

"Get lost?" Luke asked amusedly as I slid onto the stool beside him at the counter.

"Maybe a little," I admitted.

Stepping inside the diner came with an odd sense of déjà vu. The Elvis clock was still on the wall, clearly a treasured feature, and all but a couple of the leather booths were occupied. A waitress in the same flared skirt flitted between tables, alternating between carrying menus and teetering plates of milk shakes and burgers.

Nothing had changed since the first time I'd visited. And yet, outside the walls of the diner, my entire world had shifted beyond recognition.

"Maybe I should've given you directions."

"Hey, I got here, didn't I? And in one piece. Don't ask for more."

"How about an enthusiasm for calculus?" he asked, a smile tugging at the corners of his lips. "Or is that totally unreasonable?"

"It's pushing it," I said, but pulled the textbook from my bag anyway, my test paper slipped inside the front cover. His books were already on the counter, notes for several other subjects piled underneath his math work. "Hey, have you been here a while?"

"What?"

I gestured toward the other books and the page in his notebook already covered in handwritten prose. "You came here to study?"

"Oh." He looked down as if they'd only just caught his attention. "Yeah. I sometimes come here to get schoolwork done. I like this place."

"You don't study at home?"

"I do," he said, but the words slipped out too quickly, and a vacant glaze appeared over his eyes. It was what told me to stop pressing, that this was territory not to be ventured into. "But like

I said, this place is nice. And of course, the food's way better than anything I could ever cook myself."

He smiled, but there was something off about it that I couldn't put my finger on. Had it been the mention of home? My mind flickered to Kim's words from just a few hours ago: *I guess he's always been kind of secretive about anything outside school.*

Whatever it was, I certainly had no business prying. So I smiled back, cracked open the textbook and tried to listen intently as he talked about calculus.

I wanted to stay focused. For the first few minutes, I forced myself to hang on his every word, refusing to let my attention slip. This became increasingly difficult as we waded through the first equation, Luke's handwritten notes becoming lengthier until they'd stretched half the page and become little more than incoherent squiggles.

When he looked up, I couldn't hide my confusion. "You didn't understand a word of that, did you?"

"Sorry." I shook my head, trying to clear the junked-up thoughts that had accumulated. "I'm trying, I swear. It's just when I did this before . . ."

"Who taught you? You know . . . before?"

"Oh, uh . . ." I paused. "Me, pretty much. We'd occasionally have someone come in and check we were doing okay, or I'd get one of the older ones to explain something, but for the most part I taught myself."

"You're kidding."

I studied the surprise etched into his face, wondering why this had come as such a shock. "No. Is that weird?"

"It's not weird, it's just . . ." He stopped, shaking his head. "Pretty admirable, I guess. I don't think I could ever teach myself any complicated mathematical concepts from scratch."

"That's probably why I'm flunking," I said miserably.

"Hey, that's why we're here, isn't it? Other than the fries, of course. When we're through here, I'm telling you, you're going to be kicking *my* ass in precalc."

I couldn't help but laugh, my gaze drifting back to the textbook from which they'd strayed. "Don't worry, there's no danger of that happening," I said. "I just want a passing grade, if that's not too much to ask."

"Okay, well, why don't we start with going over your test? Maybe we can see where you went wrong, and that might help you learn."

We started with the first question, on which I'd achieved nothing at all. At the top was a fat red cross, its lines emphasized by several strokes of the marker. Luke started with the basics, drawing out the underpinning formulas with painstakingly detailed explanations. He went slow enough for even me to follow, though that didn't stop me interjecting every couple of steps, requesting that he go over something again.

It must've taken at least twenty minutes to get through one question, but it proved worth it—when we reached the end, some of the fog in my head had cleared. I needed hours more practice to really grasp what I'd just learned, but progress had been made. And after struggling in class for over a week, it felt like we'd just moved a mountain.

The next ninety minutes consisted of more of the same. Every so often Luke would push the paper toward me, letting my pencil move across it in a scrawled attempt at what he'd just explained, before moving to correct it with a colored marker. When the time neared seven, however, we both slumped somewhat in our stools.

"God, that was way too much concentration so soon after summer,"

Luke groaned, plucking two menus from the stand and passing one over. "I need fries—and fast."

We spent a while looking over the menu, though Luke hardly needed to. I soon realized he was a real regular, more so than anybody else in the diner. The waitress gave him a smile every time she passed, and kept refilling our drinks without charging extra. Luke hadn't been kidding when he said he came here often to study. Honestly, Joe's looked like it was his second home.

"You already know exactly what you're getting, don't you?" I asked, peering over the top of my menu.

"Yep," he said, letting his eyes skim over the list for a moment longer before slapping it shut. "I just do that for old time's sake."

I laughed. "You're so weird."

"You think I don't know that already?" He grinned, catching my eye. The bruise was still prominent across the side of his face, purple-brown shades harsh against the pale skin, though it had definitely faded. I had to stop myself from wincing each time I saw it. I didn't like the constant reminder of my first day, more specifically, the jolt of pain that went through me after realizing Luke was about to get hurt. It kept coming back, each time as vigorously as the first, thrusting me back to the moment when the scream had died in my throat.

He noticed me looking, a frown creasing his brow. "You okay?"

I snapped out of it at once. "Yeah, I'm fine."

"So what's the verdict?" he asked, nodding toward the menu in my hands.

"Oh, uh . . ." I trailed down the list again, my eyes scanning the vast selection on offer, which I was convinced would take ten years to sample entirely. "You know what? It worked out for me last time, so I'll go for whatever you're having."

"Wise choice," he said, winking, before flagging down the waitress.

The food arrived in remarkable time; it was almost as if the kitchen had been preparing all evening for Luke's imminent order, because our burgers were plated and on the counter in about ten minutes flat. I'd remembered the food being good, and this time certainly didn't disappoint, especially on the fry front. They were every bit as delicious as I'd remembered them being.

"So," Luke said, breaking the comfortable silence halfway through dinner, "tell me. What's your take on Sherwood so far?"

I looked up, having not expected the question. "What do you mean?"

"I'm just curious." He shrugged. "You've traveled the entire country, right? You must've shacked up in more places than you can count. I'm intrigued to know how little old Sherwood stacks up against the rest of them."

"You want an outsider's point of view."

"Something like that," he told me, with a smile. "So what do you think?"

He was right in saying that I'd lost count of the number of empty fields we'd pulled up in as we worked our way across the entire country. Only a handful were memorable enough to stick around for long in my mind. There was Bedford, Wisconsin, with its seemingly constant stream of thugs ready to shout insults as we left our trailers. Crescent Bay, Florida, home to the most beautiful beach I'd ever come across. Not to mention Bellmere, Illinois, where Dave finally found a bar that would serve him—and I spent the night helping him stagger home.

And now, there was Sherwood. A place I already knew I would never forget.

"It's definitely something," I answered eventually. "But I suppose when it's the place where everything goes disastrously wrong and your entire life falls to pieces, it kind of has to be."

He was looking at me curiously now, his brow crinkled in a frown. "If this is you falling to pieces," he stated, his voice perfectly level, "then you've got to be the most together person I've ever met."

It was such a strange comment to make—at least not one I'd ever heard before—that at first I assumed I'd misheard. I might've pretended to be strong, working all hours of the day to maintain a tough exterior that rarely faltered, but that didn't mean I felt that way on the inside. In my head, especially recently, I felt like I was constantly teetering on the brink of emotional collapse, one step away from falling. It didn't exactly seem like the mark of someone who had things together.

"That's what you think of me?" I asked incredulously.

"Yeah. I mean, I know we only met once before it all happened, but you don't seem all that different to me. Before, you were this . . . how do I even put it? This constant smile, a breath of fresh air, talking about what you loved. I know you're not performing anymore, but . . . well. You don't seem to have changed that much. You don't strike me as unhappy."

"Really?"

He paused. "*Are* you unhappy?"

I was about to give him a straight answer, but something stopped me.

Given the situation, I should've been at my darkest point, stuck in a hole that only the light of Mystique could get me out of. How could I be anything *but* unhappy, when everything I'd ever known and loved had been snatched away in a single night? My mother and I weren't on great terms, and I couldn't see that changing any time soon. I was lost in the majority of my classes, and was sure I'd be shoved into a set of remedial placements designed for hopeless cases. I hadn't touched a trapeze in weeks.

But I was still here. Sitting across from Luke in his favorite diner, accompanied by a pile of precalculus work, absorbed in a conversation that questioned where my loyalties lay. Even I couldn't work out why.

"I don't know," I said honestly, in response to the question that still hung in the air. "It's just so complicated, and everything's so different that . . . I honestly can't tell how I feel about it." Said aloud, I could tell the words sounded stupid, and I grimaced. "I know that doesn't make any sense at all. I'm just trying to figure everything out right now."

"No, I get it."

"It's all just got so crazy," I said. "I'm beginning to wonder if I'll ever get past this stage of feeling completely lost."

"You will," Luke assured me. "You're still here, aren't you? Obviously your instinct's telling you there's something here worth staying for."

"But is it?" I asked. "If the circus suddenly got back on its feet, I know I'd abandon everything and leave without looking back. Maybe the problem is that I'm still waiting for that to happen."

He looked at me then, this time with an expression I couldn't quite decipher, his blue eyes sharp as they locked onto mine. It surely wasn't the intended reaction, but I suddenly felt exposed, like the inner workings of my mind had been laid bare for him to analyze. I quickly looked away.

"So what about you?" I said, spearing a fry with my fork and doing my best to steer the conversation away. "Planning to stay in little old Sherwood forever, or have you got plans for bigger and better things?"

Slumping in his seat, he shrugged with an air of true indecision. "Honestly? I've got no idea."

"What about college?"

I wondered if I'd imagined the way he seemed to wince at the subject, an almost physical reaction to the word. "I don't know. My dad wants me to shoot for the Ivy League—you know, aim high and all that. I'm trying to keep my options open at the moment, but I'm not really sure if it's for me. Yale, Princeton . . . I don't know. I always figured I'd end up somewhere more low key."

"Well, you've got to make a decision based on what you want, right?"

"Yeah," he said, but it hardly sounded like I'd convinced him. His mind was already wandering, moving on to something way beyond the conversation we were having. He ran a hand through his blond hair, disheveling the messy waves. "I guess."

I sensed this was the end of the discussion, at least on the college front. Luke's gaze had turned almost vacant as he finished up the last of his food. It was strange—in the space of a few moments, his natural charm had disappeared, ebbing away like something stronger had come rushing in.

When I finally packed up my belongings, piling them into my bag and forcing it closed, a strange weight had descended on the pair of us. Though I may have made some progress up the mountain of calculus that still loomed before me, I was struck by a sudden feeling of incompletion.

Something had been uncovered, a loose end making itself known—and as I walked away from the diner to begin my journey home, I couldn't shake off the odd sensation that I'd left something behind.

CHAPTER FOURTEEN

When it came to seeking out gossip, Kim didn't waste any time. She cornered me the next day before first-period English lit.

"So how did it go last night?"

I knew exactly what she was referring to—especially since I'd thought of little else since arriving back home yesterday—but I decided a slight charade wouldn't hurt either of us. "What happened last night?"

At the front of the classroom, our teacher, Ms. Taylor, rose to her feet. She tried to settle the class so she could begin her spiel about what we'd be covering that day. It was at this point that most of us tuned out; she wasn't the world's greatest teacher, and we were used to being left to our own devices. Provided we kept our voices somewhere below screaming across the room, it was generally possible to hold a conversation at the back of class without attracting attention.

"Don't give me that," Kim snapped as Ms. Taylor began writing page numbers on the board. I flicked absently to the instructed scene, though it was likely that little reading would get done that morning. "You know exactly what happened last night. Your tutoring session with Luke."

"Oh," I said. "That."

"Any major breakthroughs? Did you have a stroke of genius and realize you're a calculus prodigy?"

"I wish," I said miserably. "I guess I made some progress, but I won't be getting an A anytime soon."

"Well," Kim continued, cracking open her copy of *Macbeth*, "if anyone's going to make it happen, it'll be Luke. You might not be a calculus prodigy, but he sure as hell seems to be."

It was then that something occurred to me, and once it had, the realization seemed so obvious I wasn't sure how it had never crossed my mind before. "Wait," I said. "If Luke's so good at math, why is he even in the same class as me? You took precalc last year, didn't you?"

She paused, her eyes fixed on the front of the room like she was concentrating on what Ms. Taylor was saying, but I could tell there was more to it than that. "Yeah, I did," she said. "And Luke was in that class last year too."

"What?"

Finally, her eyes found their way back to me, uncomfortably meeting my gaze. "Look, it's really not my business to speculate," she said. "I don't know much about it. All I know is that he was in precalc with me last year, so he must be retaking it."

"But why? He wouldn't have failed, would he? Like you just said, he's pretty much a calculus prodigy."

"I'm not sure," she said. "As far as I know, he was doing great in the class last year, but for some reason he missed the final. He wasn't in school that day. I guess he never got the opportunity to take it, so they must be making him take the whole class again."

It didn't seem fair, to be made to repeat an entire year of content to make up for a single absence, but perhaps that was just the way things worked at Franklin. I hadn't been there long enough to find out.

"I'm not trying to make out like it's suspicious," Kim continued, when I didn't give her a response. "He was probably just sick that day, and the school board decided to be assholes and not let him make up the final. I wouldn't put it past them."

"Yeah," I said, nodding, like the action would make it easier to convince myself. "Probably."

I tried to remain present, but my mind felt like it was miles away, and the conversation soon trailed off into nonexistence. I attempted to focus on the open book before me, twiddling the highlighter pen I was supposed to be using to highlight key passages—but the letters on the page blurred, as I could concentrate on nothing but the new Luke-related information that was rattling around in my head.

He'd taken precalc before. That alone wasn't a crime, nor automatically indicative of something suspicious. It was more the way things didn't add up—how every time I thought I'd slotted a new piece into the puzzle, I realized the previous one didn't fit. I was beginning to see a pattern. And the more I discovered about Luke, the more I realized how much I didn't know.

~

Heading to the gym after school quickly became part of my routine. I would catch the bus home, or walk if I was up to the trek, stopping off at my mom's house to grab my gym bag and dump the evening's homework. That was a problem left to later hours of the night, when I usually allowed myself to fall asleep on top of my books after accepting the fact it was work I could never manage.

Kim's parents' gym soon became a kind of haven. Intensive exercise had always been a constant, one stable thing in my life to provide an outlet for stress. What once was merely a session Silver penciled into my schedule had turned into my saving grace.

Maybe it should've been a concern. Was it normal to want to escape the swarm of thoughts inside my head by working my muscles until they ached? Was it delusional to revel in the moment I began panting for breath, a physical sign I was coping under pressure? I wondered about it sometimes, but no answer would change my routine.

The week after my tutoring session with Luke, Thursday afternoon was unfolding as per my new schedule. I showed up at the gym thirty minutes after school let out, swiping my mother's membership card at the barrier, though I should've just got my own. Kim sometimes worked the reception desk after four, a part-time job she balanced atop countless other commitments, but today was her day off. This was too bad, as she usually finished her shift about the same time I abandoned my workout, and it was nice to have someone to head back with.

That afternoon, I'd been on the treadmill for about ten minutes when somebody stepped onto the one beside me. When I glanced over, I recognized the slim brunet and her neat ponytail immediately.

"So," Claire said, looking over at just the right moment for our eyes to lock, "looks like we meet again, huh?"

I nodded, maintaining my steady pace, my sneakers pounding beneath me. My lungs were already heaving, the air moving in thick and fast to accommodate the need for more oxygen, but it was a feeling I'd come to know like the back of my hand. "Looks like it."

Our conversation stretched no further while we ran. Claire had her earphones plugged into the phone in her pocket, and the music was turned up so loud I could hear a faint tinny beat. It was only later, when we were both finishing up our sessions and had moved on to stretching, that she had the chance to say something more.

"So how's Franklin treating you?"

Half of me wanted to search for a trace of sarcasm in her tone, because surely it had to be there somewhere. Maybe nobody was perfect, but Claire Delaney, I'd quickly noticed, was as close as humanly possible. Naturally pretty, I'd never seen her have a bad day, and even with minimal makeup she could turn heads. She was smart too—she was placed in all honors classes and could hold an intelligent conversation.

It was only natural, I thought, to expect her to be a bitch. Wasn't that the way it always worked out? The girl who was beautiful, smart, and popular could not possibly be nice as well. To this idea, Claire took a baseball bat. She had to be, almost annoyingly, one of the sweetest people I'd ever come across.

"Yeah, it's treating me okay," I answered vaguely. "I'm still settling in, really."

"Of course." She nodded. "It's a nice place, once you get to know it. Still, I don't think you need to do any more settling into gym."

I was waiting for the biting tone in her voice, convinced that Claire had to possess some kind of ulterior motive for striking up such a casual conversation. And yet it seemed that I'd be waiting forever; her entire face had broken into a smile, brightening her already radiant features.

She was trying to joke with me, I realized, just before it became too late to laugh.

"Oh," I said, smiling. "That."

"You know exactly what I'm talking about," she said, switching legs so her arms were leaning on the opposite one, her torso bent forward. "And don't even think about being modest. Coach has been raving about you since you started. He's desperate to sign you up for every school team there is, and he's never even seen you play a single game."

"Really?" I asked. "He said that?"

"Only every minute of the day." She grinned before shaking her head. "Seriously, though—you've got to tell me your secret. I really don't know how you do it. I've played lacrosse since freshman year, and I started playing basketball as a sophomore, yet I can't run for half the time you do on that treadmill."

I shrugged, though the truth stood that being on two high school teams paled in comparison to training for years. I was working for my future, after all, which was a little more than most people had at stake.

"Should've known you'd keep quiet about it," Claire said, straightening up and leaning over to jostle my arm.

"Sorry."

My voice must've sounded a little too sincere, because she looked over in surprise. "I'm just kidding. You're really good, though, Corey. I'll think of you climbing that rope every time I have to get up at five thirty for a run."

I couldn't help but laugh. I'd relaxed into the conversation now, finally settled in the knowledge that it wasn't Claire's mission to humiliate me or uncover anything I wanted to keep hidden. "Thanks."

Her bright green eyes seemed to flicker then, sparking with a shot of realization. "Hey! I know what I've been meaning to ask you."

I didn't know whether I should be wary, but I was.

"I'm having a little get-together at my place Saturday night. Well, I say get-together—some people might call it a party. Only a small one. I'm trying not to have the entire school show up to gate-crash, but I guess there's always that risk, right?"

I nodded knowingly, as though having dozens of teenagers burst into my house uninvited was something I had to deal with all the time.

"Anyway, it should be pretty fun. Kim's coming—you guys are friends, aren't you? You can come, too, if you want. No pressure, but you might want to check things out if you find yourself with nothing better to do."

Had I heard her right? Girls like Claire Delaney shouldn't have been handing out party invitations to people like me, let alone acting like I might have something better to do. Clearly, she wasn't aware of the fact I spent my evenings cooped up in my room, poring over textbooks I'd never understand and trying to avoid awkward interaction with my mother wherever possible.

If there was anything considered "better" than attending the biggest party in school, I was certainly not doing it.

I only remembered I'd yet to give her an answer when she asked, "So what do you say?"

"Oh!" I said, with a pause. "Yeah, sure. I'll be there."

"Great!" The news looked like it had made her day, though I wasn't sure why. "I'll get Kim to text you my address. I'll see you there!"

That seemed to mark the end of our conversation, and as

I watched her hop up from the mat and head toward the locker room, I couldn't quite believe it had even taken place.

I'd never experienced anything like this before. And that was just the thing. For everybody else, this was all they'd ever known. The same routine—waking up, stumbling through the high school minefield in a vacant daze, repeating it over and over—was the normal way to live.

I'd seen more. I'd made my way across the entire country, thousands of miles away from this small town, making a living from what I thrived on. The energy was constant, our community abuzz with excitement and anticipation. When I was on the trapeze, twirling through midair, I felt alive in a way that nothing else could replicate.

Perhaps it was the daily repetition of this new life, the stifling regularity I was desperate to break away from, that tempted me into going to the party in the first place.

~

"So, Kim," I said slyly, as I slid into my usual seat at our lunch table, "I heard something *very* interesting yesterday."

This captured her attention right away. She paused with her fork in midair, her eyes drifting slowly toward me. "Okay," she said warily. "And what would that interesting thing happen to be?"

Across the table, George leaned in, just as keen to hear what I had to say. Wearing a sweater-vest Kim had spent the entire morning ridiculing, and with his curly hair ruffled, he pushed his glasses farther up his nose and tried to inch closer without making it too obvious.

"Oh, nothing in particular," I teased. "I just didn't know you were planning on going to Claire Delaney's infamous party tomorrow night."

Her dark eyes flickered in surprise, and the fork in her hand dropped to the tabletop with a noisy clatter. I could tell she was about to say something, the stream of words already on the tip of her tongue, but was beaten to it by her best friend.

"You're *going* to that party?" he repeated incredulously. "You never said anything about it!"

"I *definitely* mentioned it," she countered, but the raised eyebrows from both George and me made it clear she didn't have us convinced. "Okay, okay, maybe I didn't, but nothing was definite anyway. There's that big French test on Monday to study for, and I really should stay in, but I thought—only if I had time—I might pop in and show my face for a couple of hours."

"Really?" I asked, amused. "Funny you say that, actually, because I bumped into Claire at the gym, and she seemed *pretty* confident you were going to be there."

Kim struggled to string together an explanation on the spot, although she knew I was only teasing. Any other minute of the day, she was the most collected person I knew, constantly occupied with something to do with one of her countless extracurriculars, managing to maintain a sharp tongue on top of it all. Moments like this made her seem more human, instead of the superwoman we'd all begun to view her as.

"I have to go to these things!" she settled for eventually. "In fact, I'd even go as far to say it's my *duty*. I'm student body president. How can I do my job properly if I don't even understand the students I'm representing? It's research, really."

"Research," George stated, his voice half flat, half tinged with amusement he couldn't quite contain. "You're going to one of

Claire Delaney's famous house parties, full of popular people having an amazing time, for *research*."

"Well," Kim said, "when you phrase it like that, it sounds stupid."

"It sounds stupid any way you put it," George said. "I can't believe you didn't invite me along!"

"And me," I chipped in. "When were you planning on telling us about this? How were you going to explain it when you magically appeared in the background of everybody's photos?"

"Photoshop," she deadpanned. It was the serious tone that had George and I bursting into simultaneous laughter.

When we sobered up, he shot her a pleading look. "Come on, Kim. Can't we at least come along? Surely we won't embarrass you that much?"

"Speak for yourself, George," I said. "I'll have you know I've already been invited. I don't even need Miss Research here to get in."

His expression of disbelief intensified. "You're kidding."

"Nope."

"Wait, are you telling me I'm the only one here *not* popular enough to qualify for the ultracool party where everybody's going to be?"

Kim frowned. "Why are you suddenly so bothered? I thought you hated all that clichéd high school stuff. That's why I didn't tell you in the first place—I thought you'd make fun of me for being a walking stereotype and actually going to these things."

"That was before you two decided you were going!" he protested. "Now I feel like I'm missing out on something."

I laughed, shaking my head as I opened the plastic box that contained my lunch. With not a word spoken by my mother or me, it had become a routine in the house. Every morning I would find lunch already packed—one of her prepared boxes, of which she had dozens in the freezer—and waiting on the counter as if the gesture spoke for itself. I guessed it kind of did. I was more than capable of making lunch for myself. But it didn't stop my mom from doing it every day, always making the effort, never just leaving a few dollar bills on the table instead.

Mostly, I remained convinced it was just another part of her obsession with regularity and order. But there was a small part of me that took comfort in the fact it might've been a little more.

"It's okay, George," I told him. "You can be my plus-one if you want."

"Thank you, Corey," he replied pointedly, shooting a look at Kim, though it was clear he didn't mean any of it. "Though I still think I deserve to be Kim's." He turned to her. "I've been your best friend for, what? Two years now. And I was the *only* one who didn't laugh at your accent on your first day. Does that count for nothing anymore?"

"You may not have laughed that day," Kim muttered, "but you've sure as hell made up for it since."

At this, he gave me a mischievous look. "Sorry, with a voice like that, how can you not? Back me up here, Corey—she sounds like she's been hanging about the Australian bush all her life."

"I'm not getting involved," I told him.

"She *does*."

Kim stared him down. "Just because I'm more cultured than you, California Boy."

I picked up my fork and dug into the vegetarian stir fry my mom had prepped for me, thoroughly entertained as Kim and George continued to throw jabs back and forth.

It was only when he asked about her pet koala, and she responded in a ridiculous American surfer dude voice that sounded absolutely nothing like her best friend, that I felt compelled to step in.

"Come on, guys," I said, raising a hand to pretend to separate them. "We're all going to the party now. No need to ruin a friendship over it."

Though both looked disappointed to have their bickering cut short, they sank back into their seats, resigning themselves to having to pick it up at a later date. That was fine by me. For now, I had more important matters to think about—and all of them involved the party we'd just worked our way into, which was just over a day away.

The main reason I'd agreed to it was the opportunity to break away from the monotony, to throw myself into something new.

But in hindsight, I probably should've been careful what I wished for.

CHAPTER FIFTEEN

"Corey?"

I winced at the sound of my mother's voice ringing out across the hall. Undoubtedly, it'd been the last step that had given me away, due to its irritating tendency to creak at the slightest movement. It really wasn't designed for slipping out unnoticed.

As much as I wanted to grab my shoes and make a dash for it, this would only lead to trouble later, so I forced myself to call back. "Yeah?"

Moments later she appeared in the doorway, one hand resting on the frame, eyes sweeping over me. I'd chosen to dress down; my jeans were more than suitable, I decided, and it wasn't like I owned any sort of tight dress anyway. Still, the fact that I was intending to go out was pretty plain. I'd blow-dried my hair so it lay flat on my shoulders, removing its usual kinks, and the purse slung over my shoulder definitely didn't hold any of my usual sportswear.

"You're going out?"

I nodded, hovering awkwardly on the final step. "Uh . . . yeah."

I braced myself for an interrogation, but the look on my mother's face betrayed no hint about what was to follow. Her face was as perfectly sculpted as marble. The ponytail secured at the back of her head was tight, not a strand out of place, and I realized then that I'd never seen her wear it any other way. Perhaps this was the only way she could function: safe in the knowledge that every aspect of her life that could be controlled was perfectly so, and hoping the others would merely fall into place.

"Where are you going?"

"A party," I said. "Nothing big. Just with a few friends from school."

"Oh. What time are you planning to get home?"

"I don't know. I probably won't stay too long. Maybe somewhere around midnight?"

"I see." The word passed her lips, but she looked unsure of herself, like she wasn't used to playing this new, motherly role. "Well, make sure you don't stay out too late. It's not safe for you to be wandering around the streets at night. You can always call me for a ride."

"No," I said, much too quickly. "I mean, I'll be fine."

"And make sure you're sensible," she told me. "I know how things can get at house parties. They can spiral out of control. I know you won't do anything stupid, Corey, but just in case."

"I won't," I said.

Stepping onto the wooden floor of the hallway, I made to pull on the shoes that were waiting on the rack, hidden out of sight by a convenient arrangement of furniture. I hoped at this point she'd take the hint and move back into the living room, trusting that I could leave the house without making some terrible teenage mistake, but her feet remained firmly in their original spot.

She called good-bye as I moved through the front door, but her voice was almost flat, unburdened by the presence of emotion. I returned the gesture out of courtesy, but as the front door closed behind me, the tie that held us together had never felt so frayed.

~

Kim's house was only a few streets away, and naturally the directions she'd provided left out no details, so I found it easily enough. She was already half in her car when I walked up the driveway; one leg was inside the door, the other hanging out as she yelled something to a George-shaped figure standing at the front of the house.

"Corey!" she said exasperatedly, as I approached. "Please tell him to hurry the hell up and get in the car."

I looked over at her best friend, who was still hovering in the doorframe. "What's going on?"

"He can't decide which *tie* to wear," she informed me, sounding like she was struggling to keep her head from falling into her hands. "And, quite honestly, I can't believe I just said that."

"You're wearing a tie?" I asked, frowning.

"See! I thought it might be a bit much." Reaching up, he yanked it from his neck, letting the fabric fall in one long strip into his hand. "I'll go without, then."

Beside me, Kim groaned. "I've been telling you that for the past thirty minutes," she said, though her look of impatience softened as George shut the door behind him and ambled up the driveway toward the car. "Are we finally ready to go?"

"Shotgun!" I said without thinking, as George closed in on the passenger side.

He shot me an incredulous look. "No way," he said. "You're not getting the front seat. I was just about to get in!"

"She *did* call shotgun," Kim chipped in from behind the wheel. "As much as I hate to conform to superficial American teenage rules, I have to side with Corey on this one."

"You're kidding me!"

I shot George the most innocent smile I could muster, pulled open the door and slid into the seat beside Kim. "Sorry," I told him, as he resigned himself to the new seating arrangement and clambered into the back. "Better luck next time."

"I underestimated you, Corey." I could see him shaking his head in the rearview mirror. "I didn't think you'd have the nerve to call shotgun over somebody who's been best friends with Kim for two years. The *only* one, I'll add, who didn't make fun of her accent . . ."

"Oh God, that one again?" She grimaced. "I'll have you know my accent wasn't *that* bad. Much less ridiculous than your surfer dude voice, anyway."

"I don't even surf."

"Really?" Kim was grinning now, and I could tell the remainder of George's annoyance had melted away too. He wasn't the type to hold any kind of grudge, and it seemed no petty argument between him and his best friend would ever last. "You're a disappointment to the state of California."

Claire's house was farther than I anticipated; we must've driven through residential patches of Sherwood for twenty minutes before finally pulling up near a house that appeared to be vibrating with a musical pulse. The entire road was gridlocked, blocked with cars I recognized from the school parking lot, and it took a fair amount of maneuvering for Kim to squeeze into a gap between a beat-up Chevy and some flashy convertible. On first impression, it looked like I'd been right in assuming Claire's "small get-together" was nothing of the type.

Some great blundering guy shoved past me before I'd even got the car door shut, staggering toward a nearby bush just in time to throw up into it. It was barely nine o'clock.

"I think I just remembered why I don't go to high school parties," I heard George murmur from somewhere behind me. The guy was now swaying on his feet; if not careful, he'd topple headfirst into his own vomit.

The pounding beat of the music intensified as we got closer to the house. Claire's front door was wide open, security obviously wildly overlooked in the midst of free-flowing alcohol and the promise of a crazy night. Once inside, however, my expectations of total destruction and chaos were significantly downgraded. The house may have been packed with people, but its sheer size did wonders to reduce the potential for claustrophobia.

We elbowed our way to the kitchen, where the effect of gleaming white tile had been somewhat dimmed by stacks of plastic cups littering the countertop. Bottles and cans were stacked at one end; it looked like it was a help yourself kind of deal.

"Do you drink?" I asked Kim.

She shook her head. "I have a strict no-doing-anything-stupid policy, and alcohol usually doesn't go down too well with that."

"Fair enough."

"What about you?"

I had to admit she had me considering. The entire setting was new to me. Before, there'd been small parties involving parts of the crew when events called for celebration, but nothing like the state of the house I found myself in. Over the years, I'd witnessed on too many occasions the destruction that alcohol could cause;

the violence that broke out between drunken gangs and the circus guys would never have taken place had it not been for the beer cans clutched in their hands.

"No," I said. "Not tonight."

Kim didn't stick with us for long. As expected, everybody who stepped into the kitchen seemed to notice her, and came over for a chat—and soon enough, she disappeared into the living room, claiming it was her presidential duty to go and mingle. George and I were left to our own devices in the kitchen.

After mine and Kim's dual resolutions to stay away from the alcohol, I was surprised to see George help himself to a can of beer.

"What?" he asked, when he caught me staring.

"Nothing." I shook my head. "I just didn't expect you to be drinking, since Kim said you were opposed to the whole high school party thing."

"I'm here, right? I suppose I might as well try it out."

"Maybe it'll give you the courage to go and talk to those girls looking at you over there," I said, nodding behind him at the three giggling girls who were huddled together, talking in hushed tones. When George glanced over his shoulder, they all ducked their heads at the same time, making it spectacularly obvious that he'd been the topic of conversation.

He went red in the face, the tips of his ears flushing with color. "I'm not really interested," he told me, cracking open the can. "I, uh . . . I've kind of got my eye on someone else, anyway."

I shot him a look. "You have? Well, what are you waiting for? Go get her."

"You can't be serious."

"Why not?"

"I don't think—"

"Come on, George. Don't be a chicken."

"She'd never in a *million* years—"

"You don't know that for sure."

"I don't even know *how*—"

"Here's a wild idea," I cut in, smirking. "You could go find her right now and talk to her."

He'd started chewing on his lip, evidently nervous, but I could see him beginning to consider it.

"I mean, the plus side of being at a party," I went on, "is that if it all goes hopelessly wrong, you can pretend you were drunk and didn't know what you were doing."

It was these words that seemed to ring loud and clear; no sooner had they left my lips than he brought the beer to his lips and took a hearty swig. I couldn't help but laugh as he grimaced, fighting the urge to shudder at the taste.

"Dutch courage?" I asked.

"Tastes God awful, but I think I need it."

"Go get her, buddy."

The returning smile was nervous, but he made for the living room nonetheless, leaving me alone in the kitchen. I leaned against the counter and took a deep breath. The thick stench of alcohol was overpowering, and once in a while I'd catch a whiff of some girl's sickly perfume as she brushed past me to fetch another drink. At least the kitchen was cool; I could hear the whirring of an air conditioner somewhere in the room, and the granite countertop was cold to the touch. There were worse places to be.

Claire bustled into the room several beats after this crossed my mind, her high heels clattering noisily on the tiled floor. In a beautiful striped jumpsuit, she was miles off looking like a mess, but her skin had lost the edge of its powdered finish, and her smile was a little too lopsided to be totally sober.

Her grin widened when she saw me. "Corey!"

"Hi," I said meekly.

"You came!"

Without warning, I was pulled into a hug, though this would've been more accurately described as Claire throwing her arms around my stiff form. I laughed awkwardly as she pulled away, still smiling. "Yeah, I did. You invited me, didn't you?"

"'Course! Like I'd forget!" She leaned over me to snatch a cup before filling it with a hearty helping of something from a bright-blue bottle. Taking a swig, she looked back over me before heaving a strange little sigh. "You look so pretty tonight."

"Uh . . . thanks," I said, slightly disarmed by the unexpected compliment. "You too."

"You are having a good time, aren't you?" A second swig and she'd already downed half the cup. I suppose I had to admire her determination. "God, I really hope everyone's having fun."

"Looks like it," I assured her. "It's a fun party."

I had no idea how true this was, having ventured no farther than the room we were already in. However, I gathered that the mass of sweaty, dancing figures in the next room were all enjoying them-selves, judging by the amount of noise they were making. I had a feeling Claire wasn't about to check my sources, though, because my assurance saw another wide grin spread across her face. "Oh good!"

Suddenly, her sharp green eyes were drawn behind me, flicking to the kitchen window, with its perfect view of her backyard. "Oh God, *please* tell me they're not about to . . ."

I swiveled as her sentence trailed off, catching sight of two people who'd found their way outside. Halfway down a gravel path sat a sprawling fountain lit by a backlight that made the water gleam in the darkness, which was what both adventurers seemed to be heading for.

"They better not be thinking of going for a swim," she said, suddenly much less giggly. "My parents will kill me if they touch that fountain."

"Maybe you should go scare them off before anybody else gets any ideas."

"Yeah." The plastic cup was returned to the counter, and Claire's eyes remained fixated like a hawk on the people outside. "I'll be back. Make sure you enjoy yourself, okay? Have fun tonight."

I watched her retreating back as she slipped outside to the yard. She had remarkable balance, even in staggering heels, her footing only faltering once as she tackled the steps down to the grass. The pulse of the music drowned out any trace of her voice, but I could tell when it rang out, because the two guys near the fountain stopped abruptly under her command.

I'd become so absorbed in watching what was going on outside that I barely noticed the guy who'd been lingering in the corner, inching his way over. By the time I became aware of his presence, he was almost beside me at the counter, and a jolt of unpleasant recognition shot through me as soon as our eyes locked.

Before I could say anything, he reached out a hand, offering a cupful of a liquid I neither recognized nor trusted. "Want a drink?" he asked, the corner of his lip twitching, threatening to spread into a smirk. "You look like you need livening up."

He towered over me, well over six feet, so that I had to crane my neck to make eye contact. Not only was he tall, but large in every other sense of the word; huge muscles strained against the sleeves of his T-shirt. A mop of messy black hair looked as if it hadn't seen a brush in weeks, and as hard as he tried, his smile was miles off charming.

Landon Trafford. Even his name left a sour taste in my mouth.

"No, I'm okay," I said, shaking my head.

"You sure?"

"Positive."

"You know," he continued, sidling up closer, "I think I recognize you from somewhere. Have I seen you around before?"

All I wanted to do was walk away, and in any other situation I wouldn't have hesitated to do so. Landon was repulsive; though we'd never had a face-to-face conversation, a couple of weeks at Franklin had taught me more than I needed to know. His favorite pastime was terrorizing freshmen in the hallways, and his persistent flirting with anything female often bordered on harassment. Seeing him in a fight outside school wasn't out of the ordinary—only Luke's involvement was.

By now, it was obvious I wasn't going to get a straight answer from Luke about what had happened that day. However, there was another chance to find out the truth—and it involved the guy who was inching closer.

"I don't think so," I said, forcing my face to relax so I could hide the repulsion I felt inside. "I'm new in town. I guess you could say I'm still finding my way around."

"No, I definitely know your face." Landon's face twisted in concentration, and it looked like it was taking all his brainpower to place me. Then the lightbulb moment occurred. "Hey, I know why. You're that chick who tried to stop the fight."

Judging by his furrowed brows and narrowed eyes, it didn't seem like he'd made a positive association—and if I was going to achieve anything here, I had to find a way out quickly.

"Yeah, that was me," I told him, purposely making my voice high and simpering in an attempt to soothe his ego. "It's not my usual style, but that day I couldn't help it. You're just so strong . . . you looked like you could cause some serious damage. That kid didn't stand a chance."

This seemed to have been the right thing to say, because a smirk curled Landon's lip, as if he was pleased with himself. Apparently, I had more talent for flattery than I'd thought. He was now looking at me like I was a piece of meat, but I decided the discomfort would be worth the information I received. "Maybe you're right," he said. "What's your name?"

"Corey."

"Landon," he said, and I had to swallow my distaste as our eyes locked. "How about you give me another chance at making a first impression?"

"Well, I'll have to see about that," I said, holding his gaze. "You looked pretty angry at the time. Must have been a serious fight."

Shaking his head, he took a swig of the cup he'd offered me a moment ago. The strong alcohol had no visible effect; he downed the contents in remarkable time, knocking them back like water. "Not really. The guy's just a dickhead. I don't know why everybody thinks he's so great."

"Sure seems like he's got a lot of people fooled."

"Yeah, well, he must be a good actor. I never liked him. Saw straight through him, in fact."

"What did he do?"

The question rolled off my tongue, but it was carefully calculated. I was taking a risk that Landon would get defensive, but I couldn't quit without getting the information I wanted.

"I don't know," he snapped. "He was just being an asshole like usual. I can't remember what he said exactly. Made some comment about my girlfriend, I think. I warned him, you know. He could've backed off. But it was like he was looking for a fight. Wouldn't quit until I'd punched him. Asshole. He deserved it."

I watched as Landon crumpled the cup in his hand, the red plastic giving way under the strength of his fist. Then he tossed it across the room so it hit one of the kitchen walls and fell to the floor with a clatter.

"What did he say, though?"

Landon's head snapped around. I'd gone too far. "Jeez, why are you so interested in that guy? I already told you he's a dickhead. What does it matter?"

"It doesn't," I corrected, shrinking back into the counter. I cleared my throat, all too aware of the way my voice had cracked on the last word. "I was just curious."

"Well, don't be. I've got better things to do than talk about Luke fucking Everett."

"Right. Of course."

My chance was gone. Though a glimmer of light may have been shed on what I was looking for, I couldn't work out whether it illuminated the bigger picture at all. Landon's story didn't add up. Nobody in their right mind would pick a fight for no reason, encourage him, keep pushing when it was obvious he was getting riled up.

It was like Luke was looking for a fight. But why? And why did it have to be with the toughest guy in school?

It seemed Landon's drink had started working its way into his system, because his earlier temper had dissolved, and a nauseating smile crept onto his face as he nudged my arm. "Hey," he began, in a low voice, "how about we get out of here? Maybe find someplace a little more . . . private?"

I couldn't hold it together any longer. His arm brushed against mine, the contact vile, and I immediately jumped away.

"Don't you have a girlfriend?" I asked, dodging out of the way of the arm that had been threatening to slip around my shoulders.

"Yeah, well. That's just a technicality, isn't it?" He smirked. "What she doesn't know won't hurt her."

"No, thanks," I said, backing away. "I just remembered I have to go."

"Oh, come on," he protested, in a tone that was bordering on whining. "Don't be such a tease."

I said nothing as I turned on my heel, approaching the living-room door with Landon's lingering stare hot on my back. Inside, the air was thick with a combination of perfume, perspiration, and alcohol, while a dense mass of people jumped along to the beat. It wasn't exactly where I wanted to be; it was too dark to make anyone out, and I needed to find somebody I recognized. But each step into the room put more distance between Landon and me—and that alone had to be progress.

~

It was my first real high school party. And, with any luck, it'd also be my last.

I couldn't see what all the fuss was about. I couldn't have been the only one in the house not having the time of my life, but it was starting to feel that way. One bonus was that the dense crowd in the living room had thinned, as newly formed pairs migrated to the upstairs rooms. In the corner, three couples were squashed on a two-seater couch, so close together they looked in danger of accidentally swapping partners. Music pulsed through the building, but well-known hits had long since been pushed aside in favor of crappy dance tracks.

I'd assumed I would get into the swing of it eventually, but two hours had crawled by and all I wanted to do was leave. Most of my time had been spent tailing people I thought I recognized, trying to cling to some sense of familiarity in the house that was brimming with strangers. I could've sworn most of them didn't even go to Franklin.

Kim cropped up every now and again, but I hadn't managed to catch up in time to latch back onto her side. Though sober, she had an incredible knack for tolerating the tipsy antics of our classmates, which of course made her a total hit. Next to her, I'd never felt more antisocial.

Eventually, I decided there was nothing to do but give up. The fact things hadn't picked up already seemed like a sign they never would. I couldn't stick around much longer without going out of my mind. I pulled my phone out of my pocket and started tapping out a text to Kim.

This party blows. I'm gonna head home.

Before I could hit send, however, a staggering figure came my way and crashed into me from behind.

"Shit, sorry!"

I spun around to see Claire, quickly regaining her balance. After a few seconds, I realized why she'd dropped a few inches in height; she must have abandoned her shoes at some point in the evening. Specks of mascara had flaked off beneath her eyes, and her dark pink lipstick was slightly smudged.

"Corey!" she yelled, her voice straining to be heard over the stereo. "I've been looking for you!"

"You have?" I asked, but she couldn't hear me. I gestured toward the kitchen, to which she nodded.

Once the door had closed behind us, blocking out the worst of the noise, I couldn't help but breathe a sigh of relief. I'd almost forgotten what it felt like to hear myself think.

"Thank God I found you," she sighed.

"What's going on?"

"Luke," she said. "Luke's what's going on."

I could already feel my heartbeat quickening, thumping beneath my shirt. It was possible he was one of the people I'd been looking out for all night, much as I hated to admit it. There was no doubt he'd be here; the most popular guy in school wasn't about to miss Claire Delaney's party. And yet somehow the hours had slipped by with no sign of him. It was almost like he'd been hiding.

"What about him? Did something happen?"

"If by *something*, you mean he's drunk out of his mind, then yes," Claire clarified, running a hand through her hair. "Thankfully, I managed to coax him into my room before he got too crazy. Still, now he's up there asking for you. He wouldn't say why. I had to promise I'd come get you."

"*Me?*" I echoed. "He was asking for me?"

"That's what he said."

"Oh." I couldn't find any other words.

"You should probably head up there. I don't want him coming out to find you himself and falling down the stairs or something. My room's the second door on the left. Please don't let him do anything stupid."

"I won't."

"Look, I'm really sorry to dump this on you," she continued. "I feel bad. I'd be keeping an eye on him myself if he wasn't so insistent on speaking to you. I'm sorry."

I could barely stay long enough to answer, already itching to move across the kitchen and head for the stairs. Some force was tugging at my limbs, pulling me toward Luke with a strange insistence.

I had to find out what was going on, and it felt like nothing in the world could stop me.

CHAPTER SIXTEEN

The room was dark.

When I pushed the door open, light from the hallway met the darkness at a sharp edge. All the lights were off, but the drapes were pulled back to expose the window, letting soft moonlight filter through the glass.

The space was so still it felt miles away from the downstairs commotion. My voice was tentative. "Luke?"

Several beats of silence passed before there was a stirring from the middle of the room. Pushing the door open a little more, I realized the movement had come from a figure laying flat on the bed.

I dared to take a step inside, trying my voice again. "Is that you?"

Louder movement came this time as the figure sat up. "Who's there?"

My hand fumbled for the light switch, and light flooded the room.

Luke groaned. I could see him properly now; he'd become more than just a silhouette. We were in a pink-and-white-striped room, and he was laying on top of a huge four-poster bed, tangled in fluffy pink blankets. Matching drapes fluttered in the slight breeze that blew softly around the neat bedroom.

"Who's there?" he repeated, holding a hand to his head.

"It's me," I said quietly. "Corey."

He blinked rapidly, eyes still adjusting to the light. "Corey?" The tone was tinged with confusion, as if the name was distantly recognizable, but he couldn't quite grasp the meaning. Then, all at once, it clicked. "Corey."

"Are you okay?"

"I don't know," he said, his voice wavering. "I feel really, really weird."

"Have you been drinking?"

"No!" he protested quickly, almost cutting me off, before deciding against the lie. "I think so. Help me."

I stepped closer to the bed. When his face came into the light, I couldn't help but frown. The past few weeks had seen the bluish ring around his eye fade, as time healed the battered skin. Now, however, it seemed darker again, as if the clock had been reversed on the healing process.

"What happened to your eye?"

Clumsily, his hand moved up to his face, fingers brushing against the bruised skin. He winced as they pressed a little too hard, inflicting more discomfort than intended. "Got punched," he told me. "Outside school."

"No, I know that," I said. I'd approached the bed now; there was nothing to do but climb onto it and sit down beside him. Up close, the new bruise looked worse, angry blood vessels peeking at the surface more ferociously than before. "I was there, remember? I saw it happen. But that was getting better. It looks like it's . . . like it's coming back, almost."

I lifted my own hand, leaning in to inspect the bruise, but Luke snapped to his senses with bizarre urgency and swatted me away. "Don't," he said. "It's fine."

"It doesn't look fine," I pressed. "Maybe you should get that checked out."

"I told you, it's fine."

His voice had hardened along with his expression, and I sensed I shouldn't press any further. Instead, I steered the conversation back to where it had been heading before. "So what's going on? Why did you want me to come up here?"

He fell back against the covers, the comforter crinkling beneath his body. The longer of his blond curls were splayed across the fabric, and a dazed look returned to his features. "Did I?"

"Yes," I said. "Claire told me you were upstairs and you'd been asking for me."

"Claire said that?"

"Jeez, Luke, how much have you had to drink?"

I couldn't work it out. At some points he was hopelessly confused, barely holding a grip on what he'd done in the past few hours. And yet as soon as the conversation had turned to the black eye, the vicious bruise spreading across fair skin, his sharp tongue didn't seem to be under the influence at all.

"I can't count that high," he said.

"You got a ninety-eight on the last calculus test. You're also my tutor. If you really can't count the number of drinks you had, you should've died of alcohol poisoning by now."

"I got a ninety-eight?" He managed a lopsided smile. "That's pretty good."

"*Pretty good?*" I snorted. "Try the best in the class."

The smile remained for a good few seconds before it drooped. He groaned, putting his head in his hands. "Ugh, Corey, I don't feel so good."

"You want me to take you to the bathroom?"

He shook his head vigorously. "No. Not like that."

I peered at him, confused. "Then what's the matter?"

He looked up, our eyes locking above the crumpled bedsheets. His hair was ruffled from lying down, tufts sticking up in every direction, while his piercing eyes remained wide and unblinking.

His next words were perhaps the most unexpected of all. "Can you give me a hug?"

I blinked. "What?"

But he was already moving closer, not waiting to hear my answer. Before I knew it, he'd wriggled near enough to throw his arms around me. It caught me by surprise, but after several seconds, I relaxed into the hug and wrapped my own arms around him.

He's drunk, I kept telling myself. My heart had shifted into over-drive, threatening to pound right out of my chest. He'd nuzzled so close his bruised face was buried in my shoulder. *He's drunk. He won't even remember this in the morning.*

But I couldn't shake off the heartwarming comfort that came with being enclosed in Luke's strong arms.

I wasn't sure how long we stayed like that before he shifted against me, lifting his head so our eyes met once more. I dropped my arms back to my sides, but he seemed more reluctant to let go.

"Can I ask you something?" he asked quietly.

It took all I had not to hold my breath. "Yes."

The space between us, as little of it as there was, seemed suddenly charged; I could almost feel it crackling with electricity. My thoughts toppled over one another and tangled themselves until I wasn't sure I'd be able to pull them apart.

"Could you maybe . . . drive me home?"

The moment came crashing down on us all at once; I wondered whether Luke could feel it too. I didn't even know what I'd been expecting—but it had to be something that made being asked for a ride home feel like a crushing disappointment.

"Oh!" I said, failing to keep the surprise out of my voice. "Uh, yeah. Sure."

He fumbled in his jeans pocket, digging around for a set of keys. "You can drive, right?"

I nodded. I may have been a little rusty, but driving was one skill the circus hadn't deprived me of. Anyone in the company over the age of sixteen could drive. Dave had been my main instructor; I couldn't count the number of times he'd taken me out in his trusty Chevy, guiding me through the basics until I was confident enough to hit the road on my own. During a month or so in which we'd been unusually settled, I'd applied for my license and passed the test the first time.

Helping Luke down the stairs was tougher than I'd anticipated. Supporting his weight wasn't the issue, it was maintaining our stability that proved tricky. Even with his arm slung over my shoulder and one of my own wrapped around his waist, his steps were undeniably shaky. When we safely reached the bottom, I released a breath I hadn't known I'd been holding.

We bumped into Claire in the hallway. "You guys are going already?"

"Yeah," I said. "Luke, uh . . . doesn't feel so good."

"Oh no." She looked genuinely concerned. "Are you going to be okay? I'd give you a ride home myself, but I've had a couple of drinks . . ."

"It's fine," I told her, already beginning to step toward the door. "I don't mind giving him a ride."

"Oh, okay. I guess I'll see you Monday, then! Have a safe ride home." After a small pause, she added, "And I'll see you tomorrow, Luke."

Curiosity gnawed at me as we headed down Claire's driveway toward Luke's car on the other side of the street. I wanted to ask, to find out exactly what they had planned, but it felt like that would be overstepping some kind of boundary. What gave me the right to pry, anyway?

Still, it didn't stop me thinking about it.

Luke clambered into the passenger side once I'd unlocked the car, and I climbed in after. Making a mental note to send that text to Kim, I twisted the key in the ignition.

"You're not drunk enough to forget where you live, right?" I asked, casting a sideways glance toward Luke that was only half joking.

"Not quite."

In fact, his directions were surprisingly coherent as we set off down the street, though his face paled a few shades as we drove.

When I noticed his fingers were curled around the edge of the seat, nails digging into the fabric, I had to ask, "Are you okay?"

"Yeah," he answered shakily. Then, as the car rounded a particularly sharp bend, sending us both tipping toward the edges of our seats, he groaned. "No. I feel really sick. Can you pull over?"

His expression conveyed the urgency of the situation; I hit the blinker as quickly as I could and pulled up on a grassy verge at the side of the road. As the car ground to a halt, Luke threw open the passenger door, stumbling out just in time to bend over and throw up into a bush.

I hovered awkwardly behind him once I got out of the car, not knowing if it was appropriate to do something like rub his back. Thankfully, he straightened up soon enough, his legs trembling beneath him.

"Oh God," he groaned quietly, his back still turned. "I knew drinking so much was a mistake. I should've stopped way before . . ."

He'd grown even paler, a luminous face in the evening darkness, when he turned back to face me. A sickly sheen of sweat had formed across his forehead, and his skin was pasty. He looked so defeated that it felt wrong to do anything other than throw an arm around his back.

He slumped against me as I led him to the edge of the sidewalk, taking a seat on the concrete together. His entire body was trembling now, and I moved closer, holding on to his arm like this would steady him.

"I knew it was a mistake, drinking in the first place," he said. "There hasn't been a party that I haven't regretted it, and every time I do it anyway. Now I just feel like shit."

"Come on," I said coaxingly. "Once you get home, you can sleep it off and you'll feel better."

But Luke was shaking his head, drooping as if my words brought no reassurance at all. He looked as if he was about to say something, but before he did, we were both jolted by a ringing from his pocket.

After a few seconds of fumbling, he had his phone in his hands, swearing loudly once he caught sight of the caller ID. "Shit," he said. Then, more forcefully, "Shit!"

"What's the matter?" I asked, but my voice went unheard as he cleared his throat and put the phone to his ear.

"Hello?"

I could hear a deep, booming voice on the other end. Though

crackling with electrical interference, this didn't detract from how intimidating it sounded. At once, the sorry-for-himself Luke disappeared, replaced by one with a creased brow and visible pulse in his neck.

"Dad," he breathed. "Look, I'm okay, I swear. Calm down."

From what I could hear, Luke's father seemed to be doing anything *but* calming down, as he continued to shout down the line.

"It's only twelve," Luke said, trying to reason with his dad. "I'm on my way home now."

I sat awkwardly, hardly daring to move. A heavily loaded truck rolled past, engine roaring. As it faded into the distance, Luke was saying, "I'm fine. I've just been at Claire's."

It was like the mention of her name had a calming effect; his father's yelling ceased, and Luke breathed a quiet sigh of relief.

"No. No, Dad, it wasn't a party. I swear."

His lie was effortlessly convincing, to the point where I was actually taken aback. If I hadn't known the truth, I would've believed him myself. And it got me thinking—if it came this easily to him, had I been duped by one of his lies too?

When Luke hung up, a huge sigh escaped him, and he put his head in his hands.

"Angry dad?" I asked, when he looked over at me, as if he'd forgotten I was still there.

"Something like that," he replied vaguely. "I thought he was going to be out of town until tomorrow afternoon. He got home earlier than expected and he wasn't all that happy to come back and find me gone." He sighed again, as if the whole conversation had exhausted him. "Look, change of plan. Things aren't going to go down too well if I turn up with you driving me home. He'll know I've been drinking and, well . . . it's better not to go there. I'll give you a ride back to your place, but I can get home on my own."

"Are you kidding?" I would've laughed at the suggestion had Luke not looked so serious. "You're drunk. You can't drive yourself home; you'll end up getting killed."

He got to his feet, swaying slightly on the spot as the momentum threatened to tip him over. "I'll be fine," he insisted. "I haven't had that much to drink."

He was holding his hand out for the keys; I grasped them more firmly. "No," I said. "I'm not letting you do this. It's not safe. If you don't end up killing yourself, you'll kill somebody else."

"Corey, I'm not kidding."

"Neither am I!"

He groaned in exasperation, running a hand through his messy hair. "Why are you making this so difficult?"

"Because what the hell am I supposed to do, Luke?" I yelled, louder than I'd been intending. "You think I'm about to hand over the keys and let you drive down the street knowing you're at risk of seriously hurting somebody? You think I could live with myself if you did? I don't even know why we're having this argument. For God's sake, just let me drive you home."

"No!" he shouted back. "I already told you, it won't end well if my dad finds out I've been drinking."

"He's sure as hell going to find out when you get arrested for driving under the influence!"

"What does it matter to you, anyway?"

I could barely believe what I was hearing. "What does it matter to me?" I echoed incredulously. "Of course it matters! Do you think I'm about to stand by and let you get hurt?"

"You're treating me like an idiot! I'm fine! Just give me the keys."

"No!"

He made a swipe for them, but my sober reactions were quicker than his, and I darted out of the way before his hands could enclose the cool metal.

"You can stand here and argue with me all night," I told him, "but I'm not handing over these keys. Now get in the car and let me drive you home like you asked."

We stood facing each other across the empty space, both breathing heavily in the aftermath of our yelling match. Cars roared past us, drowning out what might've otherwise been silence, but Luke's piercing stare was as intense as ever. We stayed like that for several seconds, neither of us daring to say anything.

Luke moved first. A wave of relief washed over me as he broke eye contact, ducking his head and returning to the passenger seat. My chest was still heaving, breaths coming thick and fast.

I'd never expected to have an argument like that. Not with Luke. What might've been sparking between us now seemed well and truly extinguished.

The rest of the ride passed in silence. Luke remained still beside me, his eyes fixed straight ahead, refusing to focus his attention on anything inside the car. It was like the awkwardness had become tangible, something I could physically shatter if only I packed a hard enough punch.

The only time Luke spoke was to direct me; every so often he'd mutter something along the lines of, "Next right," or "Left at the stoplight." I couldn't bring myself to do anything more than nod, while his instructions led us to a residential area clearly reserved for the high and mighty. The houses towered above us, most of them three stories, some adorned with ornate pillars, and I realized then with a jolt that I recognized the place.

We were on the same street I'd mistakenly walked down on my

first visit to the gym. I hit the brakes when Luke mumbled a quiet direction from beside me, stopping in front of a house with a gold number five emblazoned on the front door. I shut the engine off and was hit with an urgent sense of recognition when I spotted the Everett Real Estate van parked in the drive.

"Take my car home," he said, already hurrying to unclip his seat belt and jump out of the car. "I'll come by sometime tomorrow to pick it up. You can go now."

I frowned as he fiddled with the door handle, his fingers trembling against the catch before he was finally able to wrench it open. "Wait, hold on," I said. "What's the rush? What's going on?"

"Go home, Corey. Seriously."

"I'm not going to drive off," I said. "I at least want to make sure you get inside your house and don't spend a night on the sidewalk."

"I'll be fine," he insisted. "Just go. Please."

The crease in his brow was etched deeper than I'd ever seen it before. Something was going on—and I didn't know if I wanted to find out what.

A noise from across the yard drew our attention. Then we saw the source: a figure striding from the open front door, approaching the car with alarming speed.

"Shit!" Luke swore loudly, the panic now seeping into his voice. "Shit, shit, shit."

"What is it?"

"My dad," he answered, as if this spoke for itself. "Oh God. He's going to know I'm drunk. He's going to kill me." He shot me a warning look. "Go on, Corey. Just go home. Please. It'll be better for you to stay out of this."

I knew what he wanted me to do. And yet my hands remained frozen on the wheel, my feet unable to move. The moment I heard footsteps pounding on the sidewalk, I realized it was too late.

"You've finally decided to come home, I see," I heard a voice say. Then, as if noticing the car and its unexpected driver, he paused. "Who's this?"

He bent down to peer in the window, our eyes locking as an icy chill went down my spine.

I felt compelled to do something to break the excruciating silence that had settled, so I managed a weak smile. "I'm Corey," I told him. "A friend of Luke's."

"Mr. Everett," he said coldly, as if hoping I'd never have to address him again. "Luke's father."

He straightened, turning slowly toward his son. He was wearing a crisply pressed suit, his graying hair slicked back. "May I ask why this young lady is driving you home, Luke? And in your car?"

"I, uh . . ." His desperate stammer was hard to listen to. "It was just that I didn't feel well, and Corey offered to give me a ride back from Claire's . . ."

"Have you been drinking?"

The ensuing silence made Luke's answer pretty obvious. It took all I had not to wince; the stillness that followed was almost painful. I jumped in my seat when Luke's father bent down again, his head appearing at the car's open window, the same gaze piercing me.

"You're welcome to drive home in Luke's car," he said. "He'll stop by sometime tomorrow to pick it up. Provided, of course, you haven't been drinking yourself."

"God, no! Of course not," I answered quickly, unconvinced he wasn't about to pull out a breathalyzer and force me into a test. I hadn't touched any alcohol, and yet under Mr. Everett's disapproving stare I felt as disoriented as Luke.

"Thank you for bringing him home, Corey," he said, but his

voice betrayed no emotion, rendering the words cold and meaningless. "How lovely to meet you."

"You too," I replied automatically, though it was clear neither of us was being truthful.

There was a something strange in the air between us, a peculiar feeling that had my foot hesitating over the gas as I went to pull away. As I started up Luke's street in the direction of Umber Court, it proved difficult to shake off the notion that I shouldn't have left Luke alone with his dad.

At the intersection, it hit me full force. I glanced back, to check if everything was okay, but the front door of Luke's house was already closed.

CHAPTER SEVENTEEN

On Monday, I was called into the guidance counselor's office. I should've seen it coming.

I didn't even get to homeroom before I was pulled into the meeting, ushered into a small room with a strange burnt smell and motivational posters plastered across every spare inch of wall. The guidance counselor herself was a very small woman with a rosy complexion and what looked like the world's largest collection of hair beads. Huge glasses were perched atop her nose, the thick lenses magnifying her eyes so that she looked almost like some kind of insect.

She introduced herself as Ms. Osenberg, and followed this with a swift invitation for me to take a seat. I glanced over at the cushy chair opposite her desk, the worn fabric of which looked like it hadn't been cleaned for fifty years, before reluctantly lowering myself onto it.

"So," she began, as the chair creaked threateningly under my weight, "what can I do for you?"

I stared blankly at her. "I don't know. I was told to come here."

"Oh!" She tried her best not to look perturbed, though I seemed to have thrown her slightly. "Well. Is there anything you wanted to talk about?"

She was stalling, trying to collect her thoughts as she tapped madly on her keyboard. I guessed she was looking for my file, though I wasn't even sure I had one. "I don't think so."

I was wrong, because after a few moments she seemed to find what she was searching for, leaning closer to the screen to read the text more clearly. "Corey Ryder," she muttered, more to herself than anything. "Yes, here you are. Let's have a look at what's going on."

"I've only been here a few weeks," I pointed out. "I really don't think there's going to be much in that—"

"Oh dear," she interjected. "You haven't been doing so well in your classes, have you?"

It wasn't exactly shocking news. I'd sat tests in every class and failed nearly all of them, the exception being gym. While the coach might've taken a shine to me, the same couldn't be said for any other teachers. It wasn't that they were angry—just concerned, which in some ways was even worse. The decent ones were the most irritating, always lingering a few feet from my desk, ready to pounce at any opportunity to discuss my progress. And yet the more they tried to help, the more I shied away from it, determined to keep to myself.

But there was only so long I could be kept in a class I was hopelessly failing before somebody stepped in. My schedule had been constructed as a standard junior's, with room for adjustment, but I didn't want that to mean being held back. It would be even more humiliating if I was struggling to keep up in freshman placements, surrounded by a bunch of fourteen-year-olds.

The meeting dragged on longer than I hoped; I ended up missing homeroom completely, along with half of first period. Only one thing lived up to my expectations: the meeting was every bit as dull and awkward as predicted. Ms. Osenberg tried her best to make me feel comfortable, reeling off stupid anecdotes about her time at high school, but still I wouldn't budge.

Everything was a *why*. *Why* did I feel like I wasn't achieving my potential? *Why* didn't I feel settled at school? *Why* wouldn't I just give in, for crying out loud, and answer the questions properly so it would be over quickly for the both of us?

Some of the teachers wanted to switch me out right away, but I protested hard enough to buy myself some time. My insistence that I was being tutored in precalculus seemed to sway her a little, though I wasn't even sure where Luke and I stood after the weekend. Eventually, we reached a compromise: I would stay put for another couple of weeks, but my progress would be closely monitored. If my marks didn't improve, they'd step in.

When I slipped into English lit, Kim looked like she'd been waiting for me for years.

"What's the matter with you?" I asked, approaching my desk to find her practically bouncing on the spot.

"Where have you been?" she asked. "I've been waiting to talk to you all morning, and you didn't even show up to homeroom."

"I got called in to see the guidance counselor."

"Oh." This, at least, seemed to give her pause. "What for?"

"Gee, I don't know," I muttered, my gaze lazily flicking over the work on the board so I could make a better attempt at pretending to do it. "Maybe the fact that I'm failing almost every class I'm taking? Turns out the school is actually pretty concerned about things like that. Who knew?"

She shrank back in her seat, something I'd never imagined Kim would do. "Okay. I was only asking. You don't need to bite my head off."

Guilt swept over me. "Sorry. Bad morning."

It wasn't just spending forty-five minutes with the counselor that had dampened my mood. Thoughts of Saturday were as fresh in my mind as ever. I'd spent most of the morning wondering what I was supposed to say if I bumped into Luke sometime before pre-calculus—that was, if he even spoke to me at all.

I wasn't sure exactly how drunk he had been on Saturday. For all I knew, he may not even remember what went down between us; it was his dad who'd arrived to pick the car up yesterday morning. And if Luke did remember, he may not have meant the things he'd said in the heat of the moment.

There was also something else niggling at me, though I was ashamed to even admit it. After everything that had happened that night, it shouldn't have even made my list of concerns, but my mind kept wandering back there regardless. No matter how many times I told myself it was stupid, I kept hearing what Claire had said as Luke and I were leaving the party.

And I'll see you tomorrow, Luke.

What did they have planned? It was probably nothing—and yet, when considering an entire catalog of possibilities, my brain instantly went for the worst. Luke had never given any indication that he liked Claire as more than a friend, but what if I'd misread the situation? While it seemed like something could be blossoming between Luke and me, whatever history they had could trump an instant connection anytime.

"It's fine," Kim said, appearing to forgive my attitude. "I just wanted to find out what happened after the party. I've been texting you all weekend."

"Sorry." I thought briefly of the messages that had popped up on my phone most of yesterday, and how I hadn't been able to find the words to respond. "It was a bit of a crazy day."

"I got your text when you left the party. I was too busy rubbing George's back while he puked his guts out in the bathroom. Turns out his wild high school experience got a bit *too* wild when he discovered vodka." She shuddered. "Who did you leave with, anyway? You didn't exactly say much. I was worried you'd run off with some random hookup who'd kidnapped you."

I raised an eyebrow.

"I know, I know. It sounds crazy, but your mind wanders when you're stuck in a toilet with your vomiting best friend," she said. "Once he fell asleep on the floor, there wasn't much in the way of conversation."

"Didn't sound like he had much luck with his mystery girl, then."

She gave me a strange look. "What do you mean?"

"Well, I convinced him to go after the girl he had a crush on. It seemed to sway him when I pointed out he could pretend he was drunk if all else failed."

"Huh." Kim shrugged. "He must've chickened out, then, because he spent the whole evening with me. You'll have to talk him into it again next time. So what *did* happen to you?"

"I left with Luke," I replied, bracing myself for her potential reaction. "He asked me to give him a ride home, but we kind of got sidetracked on the way."

"Sidetracked as in . . . hooking up?"

"No!" I hissed, the volume of my sudden outburst causing several people to turn around in their seats. I smiled sheepishly, waiting until their attention turned elsewhere before I spoke again. "I was actually doing the same thing as you, if you swap Claire's bathroom for the side of a road."

She grimaced. "Nice."

"Not exactly the word I'd use."

"Well, I think we can agree that both of our nights weren't fabulous."

"You can say that again." I let my gaze fall back to my blank notebook, torn between resigning myself to getting started and confiding in Kim. Eventually, temptation got the better of me. "Luke and I argued on the way home. It didn't end well."

She peered at me curiously. "What happened?"

"I don't even know," I sighed. "One minute he was fine, and then the next. . . . He got a phone call from his dad, saying that he'd come home early, and after that Luke just sort of freaked. Started telling me he was going to drive home on his own, even though he was drunk."

"What?"

"Of course, I wasn't going to let him. He kept insisting, though, asking me why I even cared. I don't know what got into him." I shook my head, remembering how his dad's furious voice had boomed through the phone. "That's just normal dad behavior, isn't it? To call and find out where you are?"

My lie was expertly crafted, the words slipping out so easily I almost believed them myself. Of course, I had no idea what was considered normal for dads; the closest I'd ever come to one was Uncle Rodney, Aunt Shelby's husband, who'd looked out for me since I'd joined the circus.

"Yeah," Kim agreed. "Mine would probably go a little crazy, too, if he got home and I was nowhere to be found."

Nodding, I ducked my head, finally making a start on the day's work. My hand moved across the page, but I was barely present. All my brain wanted to do was transport me back to that night, to force me to stand by and rewatch the events that had unfolded between Luke and his dad.

Mr. Everett had a right to be worried, even if he had let his anger get the better of him. He'd arrived home to find his son gone; any father would have been concerned. I went over this so many times, it was like I was trying to convince myself of something. Strange as it was, I couldn't shake the feeling that there was more. Something that maybe warranted worrying about.

But after the argument Luke and I'd had, I wasn't sure I even had the right to worry.

~

Precalculus came both too quickly and not soon enough, all at the same time.

When the bell rang after fifth period, I packed up my belongings with painstaking care, zipping up my backpack only once everybody else had passed through the door. But once in the hallway, my footsteps sped up of their own accord, like I couldn't get to class fast enough.

The class was still piling in when I arrived, and Mr. Bronowski had yet to appear at his desk. Despite my resolve to act as cool as I could, my eyes went instantly to the seat on the back row—and my heart lurched.

Luke was sitting with his head slightly ducked, looking at what I assumed was his phone under the desk. I moved quickly, trying to head for my seat as silently as possible, but my bag clattered against the chair leg as I set it down. He looked up, and our eyes locked—

but by this point Mr. Bronowski had already waltzed through the door, commanding everyone to get their textbooks out and turn to page eighty-three.

The book on the desk—filled with complicated formulas I'd yet to grasp—didn't do much to capture me, but I was willing to try. Desperate to take my mind off Luke, I attempted to throw myself into the realms of integration, undeterred by the fact I had no freaking clue what the process entailed.

I had ground to a hopeless standstill on the first question, my brow creased, when my phone buzzed in my pocket. Figuring it was probably another notification from Kim, who'd forced me to sign up for a Twitter account so I could follow her every update, I fished it out.

But the name on the screen wasn't Kim. It was Luke.

You free for some tutoring tonight?

I glanced over in surprise, coming face to face with Luke's questioning look. He didn't, as I expected, show any signs of leftover bitterness; in fact, I could detect the faintest hint of a smile.

I tapped out my reply quickly.

Yeah. If you're still talking to me, that is.

I tried to discreetly gauge Luke's reaction as his eyes scanned his phone under the desk, but it was difficult when I could feel Mr. Bronowski's eagle eyes watching me. When he turned around to write on the board, I had just enough time to catch sight of Luke's frown and his mouthed, "What?"

> Can you really not remember what
> happened at Claire's?

His reply came fast:

> Not really. You gave me a ride home, right? Did I do
> something wrong?

I hesitated long enough for him to look over, obviously keen to hear what I had to say.

> We'll talk about it later. I'll meet you at Joe's.

It hardly seemed to satisfy his curiosity, but he nodded and returned to his textbook.

The class, like all those before it, seemed to drag on for an eternity. When the bell finally rang to signal the end of the school day, I felt as if I was being woken from a deep stupor. I gathered my books and slipped into the dense throng of students already making a beeline for the exit, ignoring Mr. Bronowski's reminders about that night's homework.

I half expected Luke to come after me, like he had done just a couple of weeks ago, but I made it all the way down the hallway without feeling his hand on my arm. I would be seeing him later, of course, over a pile of textbooks and a plate of fries, when we could finally straighten out what had happened at Claire's party. So why did I still feel disappointed?

Later that evening, I set out on the walk to Joe's. I'd left another note on the fridge for my mother, although I wasn't sure why I even bothered. The atmosphere between us was becoming icier than the Arctic, with neither of us willing to slow the incoming frost. Sometimes I wondered what it would be like if we failed to bond at all, if we kept up this sterile act for years and years, the tie we'd once shared losing all significance. The way Aunt Shelby had talked, she'd assumed we would click in a matter of days, that we'd establish a relationship like those I'd built among the members of Mystique. As it stood now, she couldn't have been more wrong.

Luke was already at the diner when I arrived, perched on his usual stool at the counter. Surrounded by an array of textbooks, he was scribbling notes on a pad, earphones blasting music loud enough to drown out the noise of my arrival.

He only looked up when I lowered myself onto the adjacent stool and glanced over with a half-formed smile.

"Oh!" The sudden eye contact appeared to startle him; he jumped in his seat, one of the earphones falling right out of his ear. "Corey! I didn't hear you come in."

"I'm not surprised," I said, nodding toward the single bud that now lay on the counter, the tinny beat audible even from where I was sitting. "Are you trying to deafen yourself, or something?"

He smiled sheepishly. "It helps me concentrate."

We lapsed into silence, awkwardness taking immediate effect. I could almost see the text message in the air between us: *Did I do something wrong?* Neither of us dared to ask the question aloud, and yet it was already there, hanging in the air.

Luke was chewing nervously on his lip, a sign I took to mean he wasn't up for initiating the inevitable. So, drawing a deep breath, I prepared myself to take the plunge.

"So . . . you really can't remember what happened on Saturday?"

His eyes flickered with something I didn't recognize. The bruise around his eye was starting to heal, but purple was still inked worryingly across his pale skin. "I can remember some of it," he told me earnestly. "It's not like I blacked out. It's just . . . everything's kind of fuzzy. I don't know exactly what I said. But from your text, I guess it must've been something out of order."

I went to say something, but Luke continued.

"I remember getting a phone call from my dad," he said, "and me telling you I was fit to drive home. I wasn't, really. I can't thank you enough for stopping me from making what could've been the stupidest decision of my life."

A faint heat was rising to my cheeks, despite the diner's air conditioning being on full blast. "It was nothing," I said dismissively. "I wasn't going to let you drive off drunk, was I? That would've been an even stupider decision on my part."

"I really don't know what I said. I just can't remember." He held his head, squinting his eyes, as if that would somehow help the memory come back to him. "Did I say something to upset you? I mean, I remember shouting . . ."

The words still rang out as clear in my head as the moment they'd been spoken: *What does it matter to you, anyway?* As if I was the sort of heartless person who wouldn't bat an eyelid at the news Luke had been involved in a drunken car crash.

And yet, I realized then, they were just words that had broken the surface of a haze of alcohol; Luke hadn't known what he was saying. We'd both been caught up in the moment, as well as the panic induced by his dad's call, and I couldn't blame Luke for something said in the midst of that. Nothing would come of repeating it now. I shook my head.

"No," I told him. "It's fine. It was just a stupid argument. It doesn't even matter."

"Well," he pressed, eyes shining in a way that made my heart leap, "whatever I said, I'm sorry. I wasn't thinking straight."

It was right in front of me, the chance to put this all to bed, to cut short the weird atmosphere that had settled between us. Of course I was going to take it.

"Really, it's okay," I told him. Then, as his expression softened, an amused smile crept onto my face. "I'm guessing you didn't spend yesterday feeling so fresh, huh?"

Almost instantly, he pulled a face, like the mere mention of it was enough to turn his stomach. "Oh God, don't remind me."

"That bad?"

"Horrific," he said, shaking his head. "I may have spent the early hours of Sunday morning sleeping with my head in the toilet. And then, to make things worse, I had to sit through a two-hour brunch with Claire and her dad. I'm not going to lie—there were a few times I had to run for the bathroom. Not my finest hour."

The image that sprang to mind made me laugh out loud—although I couldn't deny a touch of relief may have had something to do with it too. His plans with Claire had been a family thing and nothing more. It shouldn't have even bothered me in the first place, but now that I knew for sure, I could breathe a little easier.

"You're a mess," I told him, but I was smiling as I shook my head in disapproval. "A total and utter mess. I hope you've learned your lesson."

He grimaced. "Trust me, I have. Never again."

The tension between us had dissipated, and it was easy to relax into conversation. We couldn't erase what had happened at the party, and all that I'd seen as a result, but this was the best resolution I could've asked for. Things were already starting to feel normal again.

I reached into my bag to pull out my textbook, followed by my calculator and pencil, and laid them on the counter.

"So," I said, "calculus, huh?"

CHAPTER EIGHTEEN

The following week slipped by almost without me noticing. Every day followed the same monotonous routine, my mother and I continued to keep each other at arm's length, and I couldn't see a way out of either any time soon.

Thankfully, the spots of brightness in my day also ran on a consistent schedule. The gym continued to be my haven, Kim and George's playful bickering never failed to lighten my mood over lunch, and I now looked forward to afternoons spent at Joe's with my calculus textbook, and, of course, Luke.

My grades were on the rise, albeit very slowly. Mr. Bronowski continued trying to corner me at the end of each class, but on the one occasion he succeeded, mentioning that I'd landed myself a tutor in the form of his best student seemed to appease him. When I made it home from the diner, I was finding myself more and more motivated to crack another textbook, determined that my grades in other classes would follow suit.

I was never going to be accepted into any Ivy League colleges, but it was progress, and that was all that mattered.

Aunt Shelby called occasionally, and each time I answered with frantic urgency, like the opportunity to speak to her would slip through my fingers if I didn't answer within two rings. In my first few days with my mom, our conversations had consisted solely of me begging for her to change her mind and let me come back. Things had since changed. Part of me reasoned it was because I knew she wouldn't budge, and I was just wasting my breath. But deep down, I knew there was more to it.

Now, my time was spent firing questions, trying to find out what I wasn't getting elsewhere. Whether everyone was okay. How things were going. What the investigation had uncovered—and whether the sick, twisted person responsible was behind bars yet.

Everyone was fine. They were coping. And the investigation was still ongoing—which of course meant the culprit was getting away with it.

And there was nothing any of us could do about it.

"I'm sorry, Corey." Crackling through the line, Aunt Shelby's voice couldn't have sounded farther away. She never told me their exact location—probably for fear of me finding my own way there—but I sensed they'd been moving around a lot, likely ushered along by the authorities when it was revealed they had no permit to stay anywhere. "As soon as I know more you'll be the first to hear."

And that was it. That was all I had to cling to. For the foreseeable future, at least, my world was confined to Sherwood.

Despite my complaints of monotony, something new was on the way; two weeks after Claire's party, Luke invited me somewhere other than Joe's for the first time. Granted, it was only his father's open house event, but it seemed like it counted for something.

"It's usually kind of dull," he told me honestly, during one of our tutoring sessions, "but if you're there, we can hang out."

"Way to sell it," I answered, grinning.

"He does these kind of things all the time," he said. "Trust me, it's just going to be a bunch of middle-aged people having a nose around our house, drinking too much champagne, and having hours-long conversations about hardwood floors and en suites. I won't pretend you're going to have the time of your life, but my dad will be so busy schmoozing potential buyers he won't even notice if we slip off at some point."

I had to hand it to him, that did sound more appealing. "Sure, I'll come," I told him, which put a smile on his face. "When is it?"

"October first."

For a while, I kept it to myself, a tiny secret I'd slipped into my back pocket. At surface level, it didn't *seem* significant, but the more I thought about it, the more I convinced myself it had to mean something. An open house event was hardly going to make for the most exciting evening of my life—which meant he wasn't inviting me for that alone. There had to be something more. His offer left space for interpretation, and apparently my mind was more than willing to fill in the gaps.

It would've spared me some embarrassment if I'd managed to keep it quiet, but I should've known that would be impossible with friends like Kim and George.

"So, Corey, how's the tutoring going?" George asked me one day over lunch.

"God, is he still calling it tutoring?" Kim piped up, shooting me a look from across the table. "I thought he would've given up the game by now and just asked you on a date."

"He's not trying to *date* me," I told them. "You do realize I actually

191

suck at calculus, right? Just because you two are both math geniuses doesn't mean we can all be. I need help."

"Okay, okay," Kim said, "so he *is* actually tutoring you. But are you honestly telling me he hasn't asked you out on a real date yet?"

I was fully intending to deny it, but my mind went to the open house—and all its potential implications—before I could stop it. And under Kim's discerning gaze, the involuntary flush to my cheeks gave me away.

"I knew it!" she said triumphantly. "That is *not* the look of someone who doesn't know what I'm talking about. He's asked you, hasn't he?"

"Not on a *date*, per se . . ."

She raised an eyebrow. "Then what?"

"Just to his dad's open house," I said, and the look of disappointment that crossed her features didn't go unnoticed. "He warned me it was going to be super boring, but I think we're going to hang out."

Kim glanced sideways at George, searching for a second opinion, and clearly the look on his face supported whatever she was thinking. "Yeah, that doesn't sound like a date," she said. "But I guess it *does* prove he wants to hang out with you more often. When is it?"

"October first."

There was a pause as the pair exchanged another look. This time, though, it seemed to convey something more urgent.

"What?" I asked. "Why are you looking like that?"

"October first," George said. "You know that's his birthday, right?"

"His birthday?" I echoed. "Wait, how do you guys know that?"

"He's only the most well-liked guy in this whole school," Kim said. "Ask anybody in this place and I'll bet they can tell you straight off. I remember him throwing a party in freshman year, although nothing big has happened since."

"And it's his eighteenth this year," George added. "It seems strange that he's not doing at least *something*."

"Eighteenth?" I repeated, feeling increasingly like a parrot. With this sudden overload of information, I couldn't help myself. My birthday had been a couple of weeks ago, but I'd only just turned seventeen. "But he's a—"

"A junior, yeah," Kim finished for me. "I guess he must've been held back a year somewhere before. Must've been a while back, though, because he started at Franklin the same time as us."

"He's never mentioned that before."

I could feel Kim looking at me; though I couldn't bring myself to meet her gaze, I had a clear enough idea of what she was thinking. The unspoken *What did I tell you?* hung in the air between us.

The bell rang then, cutting our conversation short, but I knew it would linger in my mind long after we'd stacked our trays and left the cafeteria. Why hadn't Luke told me it was his birthday? Perhaps he didn't want to make it into a big deal—but if so many people at school were familiar with the date, like Kim had said, he couldn't have expected it to stay hidden. And why would he agree to attend something as tedious as a business event on his eighteenth birthday?

One thing was clear—I had to do something to make the day more than just an open house. There was no way I could act like I didn't know it was supposed to be a special day.

And though I didn't know yet what my plan was going to be, there was sure as hell going to be one.

~

"Good afternoon, may I take your . . . ? Hey! Corey!"

I paused, taken aback by the sight of Luke at the front door, assuming a straight-backed, soldierlike stance. In a pressed shirt that had certainly never seen the inside of Franklin High School, his blond hair gelled back into a style that was every bit as calculated but neater than usual, he was more dressed up than I'd ever seen him before.

"Whoa, what's this? Have you been put on butler duty, or something?" I asked, stepping across the threshold into the hall.

"Something like that," he said, but a smile tugged at his lips, like my arrival had brightened his day. Then again, maybe I was reading too much into it. "I'm outta here now, though. I swear, I can't take another comment about what a *nice young boy* I am."

"That's a shame," I added with a wicked grin, "since I was just about to mention that myself."

"Very funny. Do you want me to take your jacket, though? I can, if you want to make full use of my services."

My right hand instinctively went to the pocket, brushing over the gift-wrapped box inside. I planned to give him his birthday present at some point tonight, but there was something else to check off the list before I could hand it over. "That's okay."

He led the way through a door to the right; this turned out to be the living room, which had been transformed into a reception area. Several plush couches had been pushed back against the walls, widening the space in the middle of the room so it felt twice the size it actually was. Huge windows, affording a view of the front yard, let more than enough light into the room, bathing the space in late-afternoon sunshine.

One step inside and I was greeted by a suited waiter, who bent to brandish his platter with a flourish. "Swedish meatball?"

I looked over the plate, my initial *No, thank you* dissolving the moment I caught sight of the food. I had no idea what made the meatballs Swedish, but they looked so good it was hardly a matter of concern. The offering was accompanied by a branded napkin, then the waiter scurried off toward the rest of the guests, all eyeing him hungrily.

"Good food," I told Luke appreciatively once I'd taken a bite of the meatball and discovered they were every bit as tasty as they looked.

"Good caterer," he said with a smile. "Shame about the napkins."

Frowning, I looked down at the square piece of tissue in my hand. On closer inspection, the writing was in fact a bright green logo for Everett Real Estate, complete with their incredibly cheesy tagline: *Leading the way home*.

"They're not that bad."

"Really? I've been avoiding the meatballs just to boycott them."

"Bad decision," I said through my second mouthful. "You're missing out."

As it turned out, the waiters bearing canapé platters were the only tolerable part of the event. I soon realized we were being closed in on all sides by middle-aged property investors, who didn't make for the most exciting company. Once or twice I caught sight of Mr. Everett laughing good naturedly with several people dressed in suits, his expression unrecognizable from the one I'd seen the night of Claire's party. He flitted past occasionally, most of the time only pausing to bark various instructions at his son in a tone that bordered on rude. I expected Luke to talk back—or at least do something more than shrink in the face of such treatment—but all he ever did was nod and fulfill his father's requests without complaint.

I hadn't known that Claire would be here too; I only realized when a short, stocky man bustled over and pulled Luke into a one-armed hug.

"Luke, my boy!" he declared once they'd broken apart. "How are you?"

Claire stood beside the man, whom she topped by several inches. With her hair pulled back into a tight bun and a smart dress fluttering just above her knees, she looked every bit as professional as anybody else in the room.

Luke barely had a chance to answer before his father appeared at his side, his presence having more effect than anybody else's in the room. Every time Luke looked at me, his eyes seemed to narrow, though not obviously enough to give away his displeasure to anybody else.

"I see you've met my business partner, Corey," Mr. Everett told me, gesturing toward the smaller man. "Robert Delaney. Robert, this is Corey, a . . . friend of Luke's."

Within moments Mr. Delaney seized my hand, giving it a vigorous shake. "Nice to meet you! One of Claire's friends as well, yes? I'm sure she's mentioned a Corey before!"

"Franklin's very own elite athlete," the girl herself chipped in with a smile. "Honestly, I'm just concerned for my spot on the track team this spring."

"Yes, I've heard you've been giving everyone a run for their money!" Mr. Delaney said cheerfully. "Lovely to finally meet you. I'm assuming you're not here to buy one of our houses, though?"

I forced myself to laugh. "Not exactly. I'm more like Luke's plus-one."

"So, Claire," Mr. Everett cut in, looking toward the brunet with pointed interest. "You're going for track this year? Not considering the swim team again? I know Luke was going to try out, and you two certainly had your successes last year."

Luke cast him a look. "What are you talking about? I already told you I'm not trying out."

His father laughed as if Luke had just told a hilarious joke. "Oh come on, Luke! We already talked about this, remember? It's college you've got to start thinking about."

"I am thinking about college. That's why I've been focusing on studying."

"Nothing wrong with being an all-rounder, though, is there?" his father said, in a tone that suggested the matter wasn't open for debate. "Still, I'm sure you and Claire can find time elsewhere. I'll make sure of it."

Claire was still smiling pleasantly; I wondered if she could sense the uneasiness that had fallen upon us all, or the friction between Luke and his father. It was pretty obvious what Mr. Everett was trying to achieve; his business partner's daughter was a perfect match for his son, as far as he was concerned. It had to be difficult to consider anything else when the girl on offer was Claire, after all. I took comfort in the fact that Luke seemed to be resisting the pressure, but I had a strange feeling that whatever his father wanted, he got.

We played at being good guests for a couple of hours, toward the end of which I was growing tired of putting on a fake smile for Luke's father's clients. There were only so many times I could talk about how wonderful the meatballs were, or how lovely Luke was, without wanting to tear my hair out. By the time we extracted ourselves from a sticky conversation with a woman firing questions about what Luke was like at school—questions that didn't seem to have a correct answer, whichever way I responded—it was nearing six thirty, and I could tell Luke was fed up too.

"Hey," I murmured quietly when we managed to retreat to a free corner of the room, "do you think your dad would notice if we got out of here?"

His gaze followed mine across the room, landing on the man himself, who was deep in jovial chatter with Mr. Delaney once again. "Maybe not," Luke answered quietly, his tone suggesting his thoughts were following a similar track to mine. He looked over at me. "You never left if I didn't."

"You were here the entire time," I said. Then, purely on impulse, my hand grabbed his. "Come on. I've got something I want to show you."

Though it was obvious he was confused, he let me lead him toward the hallway. "If you're going to show me something inside my house, I'm pretty sure I'll have already seen it. You know that, right?"

"Shut up. Just follow me."

I led him into the hall, scooting around a large group of people to ensure our exit escaped Mr. Everett's notice. Emerging on the porch, my gaze drifted to the sky, where the sun was beginning to sink lower on the horizon. It would be another hour or so before the real darkness set in. A cool breeze tugged at the hem of my jacket, but it was more of a relief from the day's sunshine than anything else.

"Where are we going?" A note of curiosity stood out in Luke's voice.

"I'm not telling."

"What are you going to do, put a blindfold on me? Are you forgetting that I know Sherwood like the back of my hand?"

We'd barely made it off the porch, but I couldn't help it; I spun around to face him, my stern expression already being pulled apart by laughter. "I'm not the one who's forgetting something here," I told him, aware that we were standing a little closer than necessary.

He frowned. "What's that supposed to mean?"

"You know full well what it's supposed to mean, Luke Everett," I said, "and don't try to pretend otherwise. You didn't even think to tell me that it's your birthday today. Your *eighteenth* birthday, and you were going to keep it a secret."

He knew I'd foiled him; his mouth moved, though no words emerged as he tried to work out how to defend himself.

"So when were you planning on telling me?"

He bit his lip, managing a sheepish smile. "Tomorrow?" he tried, preparing to wince at what he was expecting to be a fiery reaction.

"This," I said, jabbing him in the chest, "is why I'm never leaving anything to you again. I had to go and find this out for myself."

"Who told you?"

"Kim," I replied. "But apparently, it could've been anybody in the entire school."

"What do you mean?"

"Hey, don't ask me. All I know is that you were trying to keep your birthday on the down low, and you were content with staying at your dad's open house for the whole day. So, naturally, I felt the need to step in."

"Should I be scared?"

"No," I said, before adding, "Well, only a little. I do have the upper-body strength of a trapeze artist and could pin you to the ground if I wanted to, so you should probably be permanently scared of that."

He grinned. "Good to know."

"Come on, then. Follow me."

I expected him to protest, but he let me take his hand once more and lead him down the steps of the porch. Gravel crunched underfoot as we headed down the driveway, and it seemed to surprise Luke even further when I stopped beside the driver's side of his car.

"What are you doing?" he asked.

"I need your car keys," I told him, motioning for him to throw them my way.

He looked wary, but his hand was already wandering toward his back pocket, and I could tell it wouldn't take much to convince him. "Why? Where are we going?"

"Well, I'm not going to tell you that, am I?" I said, catching his eye mischievously. "That would ruin the surprise."

In a weird way, it was kind of flattering that he trusted me enough to press the set of keys into my palm, when I'd given him precisely no information about what I had in store.

Not wanting the GPS to give away the destination, I'd memorized the route as best I could beforehand, but the real test wouldn't come until we were on the road. If everything went to plan, it would take us less than an hour to get there. We were heading out of Sherwood, almost to the next town over, but I was convinced it would be worth it in the end.

And when eventually I pulled into the parking lot—which really wasn't more than a makeshift setup in a muddy field—that conviction only intensified.

Because now, in view, stood exactly what I'd been intending to show him.

"Whoa," he breathed.

It was exactly the kind of reaction I'd been hoping for. A short distance away from our parking spot we should've just been looking at the other end of the field. And yet tonight it had been transformed into a whirling array of color: bright lights spanning all shades of the rainbow, a tangible atmosphere that seemed to reach

right out and pull us in, and stalls of food, games, and other novel-
ties lining the edge.

What stood before us was a traveling fairground, and while the
sight made my heart lurch, I hoped it affected Luke in a different
way.

"Think of it like a circus," I said, breaking the awestruck silence
that had settled in the car as a smile crept onto my face, "without
the supercool trapeze artists."

He looked over then, his eyes brightening in a way I hadn't seen
for a while. To have it back was such a relief that I almost sighed out
loud. "You're here, aren't you?" he said. "That's all I need."

Since I'd first come across the ad for this place, I'd known it
would be a bit of a risk. I wasn't sure exactly how Luke would react;
for all I knew, he could've thought it was lame. But as our eyes
locked somewhere above the center console, I realized it had all
fallen into place.

We got out of the car and I walked over to Luke's side so I could
hand his keys back. He kept his eyes trained on me as he slid them
back into his pocket, and for some reason, that single look had my
breath catching in my throat. I was half-convinced he was about to
lean in when another type of contact jolted me, and I realized he'd
taken my hand in his.

A small smile curled the corner of his lip, but it seemed to convey so much more than muscle movement. His laced his fingers
with mine. "You ready?"

I nodded. "Yeah."

And with that, like the idea had occurred to both of us at exactly
the same moment, we were off, breaking into a full-speed run
toward the fairground. Churned-up grass squelched beneath my
clumsy steps, clinging to the soles of my sneakers, but that wasn't

going to slow me down. In fact, with the wind whipping through my hair and the muted evening heat warm against my skin, it seemed almost like we'd keep going forever.

CHAPTER NINETEEN

I was heading back across the field, a paper carton of fries in my hand, when I spotted Luke lounging on the grass. He'd chosen a spot some distance away from the main attractions, where the ground was considerably less trampled and sitting down didn't feel like sinking into some kind of bog. My sneakers were already caked in mud—a sight I was sure would recur in my mom's nightmares if I tried to enter the house—but I was more than used to muddy fields, having spent most of my life living on them.

Settling down beside him, I waved the fries in his direction. "You want some?"

He grimaced. "No, thanks. My stomach still hasn't recovered from the Gravitron."

"Oh come on." Already digging into the fries, I glanced over at the ride we'd been on about ten minutes ago. I still couldn't see what was so intimidating about it. While I'd been joking—okay, half joking—when I'd offered Luke my hand to hold, he'd actually taken me up on it, and I'd come off the ride feeling like the bones in my fingers had been pulverized. "That was nothing. Wasn't even scary in the slightest."

"Well, of course you'd say that," he shot back. "You're a trapeze artist. You've spent your whole life dangling at crazy heights from a little bit of rope. Excuse me if I prefer to keep my feet a little closer to the ground."

We'd been at the fair for about an hour, and in that time had managed to ride everything at least once. By now, the night had already taken hold, inking the sky in a dark shade broken only by the wispy rim of the moon. Neon lights from the fairground contrasted sharply against the backdrop, the flashing lights of the Ferris wheel the most striking of them all. The air was electric with the fair's atmosphere, and yet an undeniable feeling of peace had descended upon Luke and me, as if this had been all we needed to unwind.

"Gravitron? Easy. Heights altogether? Piece of cake."

"All right, Miss Invincible," he muttered jokingly.

"See, now *there's* a nickname I'm a fan of."

"Don't let it go to your head."

I grinned. "Too late."

His attention drifted toward the carton in my hand, giving the fries the once over. "Any good?"

"Obviously not a patch on Joe's," I said, "but I can live with them."

He reached over and swiped a few from the carton. "Sorry," he said, though it didn't sound like he meant it at all. "Couldn't resist."

"What happened to your recovering stomach?"

He shrugged, stuffing a fry into his mouth. "I got over it. Just consider it my birthday present, okay?"

"Oh! That reminds me." I passed the carton over for him to hold, freeing up my hand to dig around in the pocket of my jacket. "I did actually get you something better than fries."

Judging by his expression, this came as a surprise, though it really shouldn't have. What did he think I was going to do? Go through all the trouble of dragging him to the fair only to come up empty handed on the gift front? Of course I'd thought of something. Granted, it had taken more effort than stumbling across the ad for the fairground, but I thought it was worth it. And hopefully, Luke would feel the same way.

"You didn't have to," he said quietly, turning the small wrapped box over in his hands.

"I know, but I did. Don't worry, I'm not presenting you with a designer watch or a brand new sports car. I didn't go overboard."

"You didn't?"

"'Course not," I said breezily. "It's a second-hand sports car."

He laughed then, genuinely, and its sound echoed in my ears long after it had vanished from the air. I couldn't help but smile, too, uplifted by the knowledge that in that one moment, that brief snapshot of time, Luke was truly happy. Whatever he had to return to, whatever was forced upon us in the future, this moment couldn't be taken away. I wasn't sure why that felt like such a reassurance.

It took forever for him to unwrap the gift. His fingers worked meticulously against the sticky tape, each movement careful, nothing like the headlong excitement I would've ripped into it with. The box slid out and landed in his lap, and he lifted the lid.

He stared intently at what was inside, but I couldn't tear my eyes away from his face.

"Oh my God, Corey."

A smile broke out across my face, made up of more relief than I would've liked to admit. When I'd first seen the gift online, I was convinced it was perfect for Luke—but the time it had spent in a bag under my bed had allowed doubt to creep in. Was it too much? Not enough? Overly personal for how long we'd known each other? At one point, I'd been seriously considering not giving it to him at all, but now I was confident I'd made the right decision.

Inside the box was a small, silver key ring with three charms: a pi symbol, an infinity sign, and the letter *L*.

"This is adorable. I love it," he said as his smile stretched so wide it threatened to split his face in half. Then he turned to look at me, and a slight shift in atmosphere made things suddenly more serious. "Thank you, Corey. For doing all of this. You didn't have to."

"I know I didn't have to. I wanted to."

"I have to put this on my keys right now." I watched as he slipped the key ring out of the box, fumbling with it for a few seconds until he managed to hook it onto his car keys. It jangled lightly against the metal, and the silver glinted as it caught the moonlight. "There. You know, every time I see these, I'm going to think of you."

I caught his eye. "Consider that a bonus."

He laughed again, then edged a little closer, narrowing the space between us. Colored lights danced across his features, brightening his smile, until it became so infectious I wondered if we'd ever be able to stop.

Except we did, sooner than expected, when silence wriggled its way in and the air became laden with a heavy atmosphere.

He didn't say anything, but it wasn't like he needed to. His face was already moving closer, the pale slope of his features advancing on mine, eyes shining with wordless language. All at once everything blurred around us; the commotion of the fair became one mess of unfocused light, colors smudged in every direction; the darkness became a distant backdrop. My heart was thumping now, so ferociously I was sure Luke could hear it. I knew what was happening, and no part of me was about to stop it.

When his lips made contact with my own, I felt myself melt, leaning into the kiss I'd wanted to happen since the day we met.

He was gentle at first, his soft lips brushing over mine so lightly I could barely feel it happening. It lasted only a couple of seconds— then I could sense he was about to draw back, to gauge my reaction and determine what to do next. It was in that split second, the moment in which I felt space slip between us once more, that I knew I didn't want to let that happen.

And before I could even process what I was doing, my hand reached for the back of his head, pulling him closer and kissing him back with an urgency I couldn't quite make sense of.

Before, I'd been reluctant to let myself think of Luke in this way, kept in line by the assumption he would never like me as more than a friend. He was the most popular guy in school, with his pick of almost any girl—even Claire. Against that, I couldn't compare. Thinking of him in that way was only setting myself up for disappointment.

Or so I thought.

We broke away when the need to breathe became too much to ignore. My stomach had erupted in a round of butterflies, and I wondered if Luke felt the same underneath his composed exterior. As we leaned back, there came a beat of silence in which we were unable to do anything but stare at each other, struggling to find words to fill the gap.

It was Luke who eventually took the lead. "Whoa."

Coherent thoughts had started to return to my brain, and my

breathing was slowing to a rate that could pass as seminormal. "Took the words right out of my mouth," I murmured.

He smiled coyly, his hand reaching up to scratch the back of his neck. "I was beginning to think I'd never work up the courage to do that."

"Well," I said, "I'm glad you did."

"I really like you, Corey," he admitted. "I don't know what it is about you, but it's crazy. And it's felt like this since I met you that first time. The day you showed up at Franklin, I thought I must've been the luckiest guy on Earth."

I could feel warmth rising to my cheeks. "You *are* lucky," I said, "because it turns out I really like you too."

We stayed on the grass for a while, not talking much, if only because words felt insignificant in the aftermath of what had just happened. Both of us seemed content to just sit beside each other, soaking up the company, letting the atmosphere speak for itself. When the night truly began to wear on, taking the last scraps of warmth from the day, Luke draped his jacket over my shoulders before I could protest.

"You ready to head back?" I asked. "We should probably get home before your dad starts wondering where we are."

A jolt of alarm coursed through him; it was like this was the first time he'd thought about his dad since we'd left the house. I understood how he felt. Spending a few hours on this impromptu trip had been enough to push everything else to the back of my mind, even if just for a short while.

"Oh yeah," he said eventually. "I guess we should."

Pushing himself to his feet, he offered a hand to help me up, and I linked my arm through his as we made our way back across the field. It suddenly felt like a natural movement, and I wasn't going to question it. With the onset of darkness, the wind had picked up, and I huddled closer in an attempt to share some of our body heat.

"Chilly, huh?" I said, as I felt him shiver against me.

"Just a little," he answered, before pulling me closer.

When we reached the car, I didn't argue when Luke went for the driver's seat; I was perfectly content to stretch out on the passenger side and let him take the wheel. After this whirlwind of an evening, I wasn't sure I trusted my sense of direction to get us home without incident.

I made the right decision. With Luke at the wheel, we sped down the highway with ease, smoothly overtaking the few vehicles on the road with us and making it home in forty-five minutes. For the whole journey, I'd allowed myself to relax into the passenger seat—but as soon as we got back into Sherwood and started passing through more familiar streets, an unknown urge forced me to sit up a little straighter.

He was going to take me back to my mom's place, but the journey there involved going past Luke's house. From the moment we pulled onto his street, it was obvious the open house was over. Most of the windows of the house were dark and the parked cars that had gridlocked the street hours before were gone—except one.

"Hey, slow down," I told him urgently. "Is that my—"

He brought the car to a crawl as we went past the house, and by then, I was close enough to catch sight of the license plate of the other car in Luke's driveway.

"Can you pull over?" I said. "What is my mom doing here?"

He did as I asked, and with a pounding heart I threw open the car door and stepped onto the sidewalk. Once Luke had shut off the engine, he wasn't far behind me.

What was my mom *doing*? It wasn't a secret that I was going to the open house, and I had already told her I'd likely be back some time in the evening. I wasn't home late enough for it to be cause for concern—and certainly not late enough for her to come looking for me.

But our arrival seemed to be long awaited. Luke and I only made it halfway up the driveway before the front door of the house swung open.

"Ah." The booming voice of Luke's father was hardly a welcoming sound. "There they are."

Then the second figure came into view. The car had already given her away, but the sight of her perfect posture and impeccable ponytail still made my heart sink. As her eyes swept over me with uncomfortable scrutiny, I wished more than anything I could tell what she was thinking.

"Mom," I said. "What's going on?"

We had reached the porch now, putting Luke and me level with our respective parents, though Mr. Everett still towered over all of us. As his menacing gaze swept from Luke to me and back again, I realized it probably wasn't just the nighttime breeze that was making me shiver.

"I'm sure you'll understand I took the liberty of calling your mother after you disappeared from my house several hours ago," he said in a tone that implied I had no choice *but* to understand. "Since nobody had a clue where you two were, I think she had a right to be concerned."

"Come on, Dad, it's not even that late," Luke pointed out. "You didn't need to go all FBI on us. We're fine."

"That may be, but how do you expect us to know that when you just disappear? Without even a phone call? I thought you would've at least had the decency to stay in the house. You know how important this event is for the business."

"We were there for most of it!"

"Most of it isn't *all* of it, Luke," Mr. Everett said, and it was clear from his voice he was not to be argued with. "What do you think I'm going to do when I have potential investors telling me how much they'd love to meet my son? Do you think it's acceptable for me to have to say that, in fact, I have no idea where you are? You only think about yourself, don't you?"

I could see Luke struggling to come to his own defense. "Look, it's my fault," I cut in, though even I could hear the quiver of fear in my voice. I may not have been Mr. Everett's daughter, but that didn't come with the guarantee I wouldn't be punished. "I was the one who persuaded Luke to sneak out. Don't pin this all on him. It was me."

Mr. Everett's eyes narrowed into slits, looking at me with an expression of pure loathing. "That may be, Corey," he snarled, as if my name left a bad taste on his tongue, "but it doesn't change the fact that Luke agreed. He's just as much in the wrong as you are."

"I think it's time to go home now," my mother cut in, finally breaking out of her frozen stance. I'd never been so relieved to hear her voice. "The main thing is that they're home and safe."

"Of course," said Luke's father, but he hardly sounded convinced.

The good-byes were painfully forced; I knew I'd soiled my reputation in Mr. Everett's eyes, if that hadn't already been the case. Had we been alone, no doubt Luke and I would've moved in for a second round of what we'd started earlier, but I obviously wasn't going to risk being permanently banned from their home by kissing Luke in front of his angry father. Instead, I nodded in a way that I hoped conveyed something more, before bidding the politest good-bye I could muster to Luke's dad.

As I turned my back and started across their front yard, my

mother's steps falling into place beside my own, the atmosphere felt as if it could be shattered with the slightest movement.

The front door closed behind Luke and his father before we got into the car; I heard the resounding slam as I approached the passenger side. As I yanked open the door, in that brief second before I clambered into the seat, I could hear raised voices from inside the house. Their sheer force was remarkable even from a distance.

I tried to block it out; it felt like something not to be intruded upon. What happened behind the closed doors of the Everetts' house was their business, and certainly not mine. But even as the voices remained muffled, actual words indistinguishable from the angry tone, there was something else.

The noise of the crash, dulled through a layer of brick and wood, stood out against the rest. However, the silence that followed was perhaps worst of it all.

CHAPTER TWENTY

Unsurprisingly, my mother's response to the situation was much less harsh than Mr. Everett's.

"You should probably call next time you two sneak off somewhere," she told me in the car on the way home, her voice calm against the quiet hum of the radio. "Luke's dad's kind of weird about that type of thing. His work's important to him."

"You know him?" I asked, slightly taken aback.

"We've met," she said simply, as if unwilling to commit to anything stronger. "He sold me my house, actually. Handled everything. I knew he had a son who went to Franklin, but we don't know each other well."

"Oh," was all I could manage.

The conversation went no further than that; we both seemed content to lose ourselves in our own thoughts about what had happened, the peppy tune on the radio filling the silence between us.

I'd resigned myself to the fact my mother and I would never mend our relationship completely, but at times like these I couldn't help wishing for something more. It would've been easier to stop feeling so detached from Sherwood had she been there to confide in, but our interactions remained as sterile as ever. This relationship was strictly practical, not to be complicated by matters as trivial as emotions.

My mother seemed happy to let the night of Luke's birthday go, but the same didn't go for me. Even when I managed—for the most part—to convince myself I must've imagined the noise behind Luke's door, the doubt still lingered, and there was a part of my brain that just wouldn't let go.

When I got to school on Monday morning, I was bouncing off the walls with anticipation. I just wanted to see Luke, to make sure he was okay, to maybe also work out where to go after that kiss on Saturday night. Something had changed—that much was obvious. The difficult part was working out where we now stood.

We didn't see each other the entire morning, although that wasn't unusual. We shared none of our morning classes, but I thought I would at least see him in the cafeteria at lunch.

As I slipped into my usual seat at Kim's table, opening the lunch box my mother had packed as normal, I couldn't resist glancing toward his usual table.

Claire was nearby, smiling as one of her friends recounted a story, but I couldn't help noticing it didn't seem to reach her eyes. The surrounding tables were filled with their usual occupants, as lively as ever, but Luke's absence put a blank spot in the middle of it all, the empty seat speaking louder than any of his classmates.

Kim noticed my distraction; after zoning out, I was brought back to reality by her hand waving in front of my face. She and George were both interested in how Luke's birthday had panned out, but I didn't want to reveal too much until I was clear on where we stood. All I let myself say was that things had gone to plan, trying to keep a smile from my face as my mind replayed the kiss once again.

That afternoon, I was first in the classroom for precalculus, seated at my desk and watching the door as the rest of the class filed in. Luke was one of the last, hurrying toward his seat at the exact moment the bell rang. I caught his eye as he moved past my seat, hoping for a chance to talk sometime during class, but a stroke of bad luck came in the form of a surprise quiz Mr. Bronowski sprang on us at the last minute.

We remained silent for most of the hour, and focusing on math problems was even harder than usual when all I could think about was the fact that Luke was sitting two desks away. However, I did find some comfort in that I felt slightly less confused than I would've been several weeks ago. My grades still bordered on atrocious, but my tutoring sessions were working a little bit of magic.

After what felt like an eternity, the bell rang. I wasted no time in jumping from my seat and depositing the test on Mr. Bronowski's desk. Outside the classroom, I finally caught up with the guy I'd been waiting to see all day.

"Hey," I said breezily. "I didn't see you at lunch."

"Oh, yeah." He shook his head. "Sorry. I had some homework to catch up on."

"That's okay. I was just wondering."

It was then that I caught the trace of uneasiness across his face. The day was unusually warm, with the temperature inside crowded hallways and classrooms even higher, yet he was wearing a plaid shirt with long sleeves, and another shirt underneath. My own T-shirt had been sticking to my skin all day; I could only imagine how Luke was feeling beneath several layers of fabric.

"God, aren't you hot in that?"

He looked down, as if only just remembering what he was wearing. "I'm okay," he said dismissively, though I could see the little beads of sweat on his forehead. "I thought it was going to be cold this morning. Guess I was wrong, huh?"

He laughed, but the sound came out oddly, nothing like what I'd heard on the night of the fair, with that note of carefree happiness I'd come to adore. My gaze dropped to his arm, where he'd rolled up his sleeve, and I felt my heart jolt in alarm.

"Is that a—"

My question was cut off in perhaps the most unexpected way. Before I could even get the last word out, I felt myself being pressed backward, my back meeting the lockers just as Luke's lips landed on mine. For a moment I kissed him back, more by instinct than anything else, and then I broke away. "What was that for?"

He smiled sheepishly and took a step back. "I don't know. I just really wanted to kiss you again."

And yet the look in his eyes told me it was more than that, as they glimmered with something beyond what his lips were telling me. I remembered then what I'd been saying before I was interrupted, and looked down at his forearms. However, he had tugged his sleeves down, concealing what was once on display.

"What's wrong?" I asked.

The commotion of the hallway had already set in, the noise of hundreds of other passing students making for a louder echo than expected. We were enclosed on all sides by conversations, other lines thrown back and forth, matters that didn't concern us in the slightest, and yet my question rang out louder than all of them put together.

He laughed, but I believed the sound no more than he did. "Nothing's wrong," he said. "Why do you ask?"

"Come on, Luke, don't lie to me. What happened to your arm?"

"Nothing."

But I wasn't about to give up that easily. I lunged forward, making a grab for his sleeve and yanking it upward. My stomach lurched at the sight I was faced with; all the way up his arm were bruises, ugly patches of discolor trailing right up to his elbow; there was even a graze that looked much too fresh.

He snatched his arm away but it was too late. I'd already seen all there was. "Oh my God, what happened?"

"Oh, it was just me being clumsy as usual," he said, though I'd never witnessed a moment of clumsiness in all the time we'd known each other. "I tripped and caught my arm on the side of the dining table. Hurt like a bitch."

There was no way that such a minor accident would cause so many bruises. This was in an entirely different league, something recurrent, lashing multiple inflictions across his skin. I couldn't bear to think about what had caused them.

"Luke," I said, almost pleadingly.

I knew he could see that I didn't believe a word of it; he understood my soft tone, begging for the truth. He swallowed, and for a second I believed he was considering telling me the truth, but then he forced a laugh that sounded even more out of place than the last one had.

"Corey," he mimicked, in a similar tone of voice. "You know I'm clumsy. You don't have to worry about me. I only covered it up because I didn't want the whole school asking me how I'd done it. Honestly, I'm fine. Don't worry."

He said it like that was going to stop me, but we both knew the words were empty. How could I not worry after being faced with something like that? I wanted there to be another explanation, a reason that would convince me that Luke was fine, but there wasn't.

"You know you can talk to me," I pressed, "don't you?"

"Of course," he insisted, "but there's nothing to talk about."

"Was it . . . ?" I could barely bring myself to voice the prospect aloud; the moment I did, I'd be crossing a barrier, and one I certainly couldn't go back on. "Was it your dad?"

He recoiled immediately, my words having the effect I'd been afraid of. "What?" he said, but the pitch of his voice was too high to be convincing. "My dad? Why on earth would you think that?"

"Look, I don't know, it was just something I thought . . ."

"I hit my arm on the dining table, okay?" he snapped. "I told you. There's nothing else to it. Can you quit coming up with crazy suggestions like that?"

"Okay," I said, though it was far from it. "I'm sorry. Just forget I said anything."

The smile returned to his face, strained and unnatural. I tried to smile, too, forcing the expression as best I could. My question about Luke's dad was something that could never be unsaid. Part of me wondered whether I should've remained quiet, gone along with his halfhearted story—even though nobody in their right mind would've believed it.

Maybe it was wrong of me to pry. If he didn't want to tell me absolutely everything about his private life, he wasn't obliged to. Just because we'd now crossed the territory into something more than friends didn't mean I'd been granted the right to know everything about him.

"I'm sorry too," he said. "I didn't mean to snap."

"It's fine."

"Probably not the best start after everything you did for me on Saturday. Can we start over?"

"Sure," I said, feeling myself relax a little more, though I wasn't sure if I was right to. "Nothing happened."

"Do you want to come over to my place?" he asked.

"You want to study there?"

"Actually, I don't know about you, but I'm not in much of a mood for studying. I was thinking maybe we could just hang out instead. How does that sound?"

"Fine by me," I told him, as his hand found its way into mine. I clasped my fingers around his, grateful for the contact that seemed to lessen the rift I'd just created between us. "I don't think we spend enough time together not talking about integrating trigonometric functions."

"Are you kidding? That's my best pickup line." He grinned.

I tried to forget about the exchange as we clambered into his car, heading out of the school parking lot with a sense of relief that things seemed to be slipping back into normality. I forced myself to focus on other matters, pushing the sight of those bruises out of my mind.

The ride to Luke's house was more comfortable than I expected; we didn't venture too close to any touchy topics of discussion, which was the secret to an easy chat. When we pulled into his driveway, though, I found myself looking up at the house with bated breath, my heart lurching at the thought of what I'd overheard behind those doors two days ago.

It was almost like he'd read my mind. "My dad won't be home until later," he said, climbing out of the car. "So we'll have the house to ourselves for a couple of hours."

The relief was so overwhelming I was sure it must've shown on my face. It couldn't have been plainer that Mr. Everett disliked me, and dealing with him had become an unpleasant chore. The prospect of hanging out with Luke, uninterrupted by his father's disapproving glares, was undeniably appealing.

I tailed him up the steps of the porch, waiting as he dug around for his key to unlock the door. The hallway was familiar, even in the absence of middle-aged party guests, painted a deep red that contrasted sharply with the pale carpet. Instinctively, I began taking off my shoes, before noticing Luke had walked right inside without bothering. My mother probably would've passed out at the thought.

"You want something to drink?" he asked, gesturing toward the kitchen door.

"A glass of water would be great, actually."

"Got it," he said, already disappearing across the threshold. "Make yourself at home."

Left alone, I kicked my shoes back onto the mat and headed through the door I recognized as the living room. It seemed smaller than it had on Saturday; the couches had been moved back to the center, angled around an expensive-looking rug, their image reflected in the mirror over the fireplace. I could hear Luke clattering around in the kitchen as I moved farther into the room.

Ornaments were dotted all over the place: intricately detailed vases on either side of the mantelpiece, a globe-shaped sculpture in the corner, sets of figurines shelved inside a glass display cabinet. However, these weren't what caught my eye. Photographs were mounted on each wall, different snapshots from throughout Luke's childhood, none of them out of place in a family house. There must've been at least a dozen, but one in particular made me pause—a small frame perched on the side table, having no reason to stand out from any others, but doing so all the same.

I stepped closer and picked it up for a closer look. It was a slightly grainy photograph, looking like it dated back at least ten years, one edge curling where it had been jammed into the frame. In it were three people, only two of which I recognized. Luke's father looked similar, though his younger face had fewer wrinkles. Luke himself was no older than six, his expression barely visible beneath an oversized sun hat, clutching an ice cream with pure glee. Kneeling beside him, bearing a wad of napkins to stop the melting treat from dripping all over his arm, was a woman I didn't recognize.

Of course, it was his mother. That much became obvious the longer I looked at her face; her features were remarkably similar to her son's, though she had a mop of dark curls in the place of his blond. She was a pretty woman, despite her smile being less than focused in the photo.

Luke had never mentioned his mom before, and I hadn't thought to ask. Only then did it occur to me that I'd never seen her around the house. What had happened to her? And was it even appropriate to ask? Given Luke's track record of sharing details about his personal life, I wasn't sure.

"Look, Corey—I hit the jackpot! Leftover meatballs."

I jumped at the sound of his voice; it had slipped my mind that he was only in the next room. Carrying two glasses and a plate of the canapés I'd devoured on Saturday, he was already halfway across the space.

"Hey, what are you looking at?"

"Oh!" I wondered if my voice sounded as guilty as I was hearing it. "Just this photo."

Setting the glasses down on the table, I felt him come up behind me and peer over my shoulder. "That old thing?" he asked. "God, that was a long time ago."

He didn't seem mad, at least, so I deemed it okay to continue. "Is this your mom?"

My finger hovered over the woman in the picture, smiling back at us, caught in a moment from over a decade ago. Her eyes were slightly squinted, the sun blazing bright in the sky behind her, but there was an essence of happiness about her whole being.

He paused slightly before answering, looking intently at the photo himself. "Yeah," he said eventually, "that's her."

"Is she . . . ?"

"She's still around," he finished for me. "Yeah. She and my dad aren't together anymore. They separated . . . what? Must be four years ago now."

"Oh," I said, my voice small in both volume and significance. "I'm sorry."

"It's okay. Not like you had anything to do with it. It was probably for the best, anyway."

"What do you mean?"

"Well, by that point, they hadn't been getting on for months. When two people are arguing that much, you don't really expect them to stay together for long."

"Do you still see her?"

He flinched slightly. "I haven't seen her since she walked out," he said. "She moved to Washington as soon as the divorce papers were signed. Now she's married again with a baby on the way. What reason has she got to come back, really?"

"Oh."

"Still, I can't exactly blame her. I don't think I'd want to come back either."

The following silence was heavy; I felt bad for bringing the topic up, since it had to be even more of a downer than poring over textbooks for several hours. When Luke had suggested hanging out, talking about the mother who had walked out on him probably hadn't been what he'd had in mind.

"But," he said, seeming to sense it was time to break the settling quiet, "that's old news. Four years is enough time to get used to only having one parent around. And I'm certain my mom's better off where she is now. You can't force things to work out if they're not supposed to, you know?"

My mind drifted back to my own mother, and the painfully sterile relationship that had failed to develop into anything further, even after the weeks it had been given. "Yeah," I said. "I guess that's true."

"It means I don't have to sit upstairs trying to block out the noise of their arguing, at any rate. Which is basically what I had to put up with all through middle school."

I finally brought myself to set the picture back down on the table. "That sucks."

"Yeah. I mean, it was hard to deal with in the beginning. Things were pretty tough when she first walked out. I was so angry at her for leaving me. For giving up, just like that."

"I don't blame you."

"I even walked in on her the night before she left. She was up in their bedroom, packing as much stuff as she could into a suitcase. I knew she was planning to leave. I begged for her to take me with her, but she was trying to get out quickly, so there wasn't time. She promised she'd come back for me later, once she had things straightened out . . . but, well, she never did."

I didn't know what to say. "I'm sorry," was what I settled for eventually, despite knowing full well it sounded weak. "That must've been really tough to deal with."

He shrugged, averting his gaze downward. "Only really at first. Things were pretty bad straight after she left. I was only in eighth grade, but I failed every class. I stopped showing up to school most of the time. Went off the rails a bit. I ended up being held back a year so I could get my shit together."

He trailed off, the ensuing quiet deep enough I could hear the muffled sound of a radio Luke had turned on in the kitchen.

"So what about you?" he asked gently. "I mean, I don't want to pry, or anything, but I know it's just you and your mom at home . . ."

"Oh," I said. "My dad ran off before I was born. Made a stupid mistake and got out of there as fast as he could, apparently. I don't even know his name."

"Man." Luke let out a drawn-out sigh. "Have we got some dysfunctional families, or what?"

"It's never really bothered me," I told him truthfully. "As long as I can remember, I've always had one huge family. The circus was good for things like that. One missing dad didn't feel like a big deal at all."

"I suppose that's true." He looked over at me, as if trying to gauge what I was thinking. It was a while before he worked up the courage to voice the question playing on his mind. "Do you miss it?"

I glanced up. "The circus?"

"Well, that's probably a stupid question," he continued. "Of course you miss it. That goes without saying. I just mean . . . do you really hate it here? Do you still want to give it all up and go back?"

I thought back to a previous conversation, an exchange over one of many dinners at Joe's. We'd talked about it before, though back then, I'd been in Sherwood barely any time at all. Now that I'd had more time to adjust, I'd realized life without constant motion had brought some pleasant surprises. My relationship with my mother was difficult to deal with, sure, but that didn't overshadow everything else. Without the sharp new turn, I'd never have met people like Kim and George, nor would I have experienced high school life as millions of other teenagers did. And, of course, I wouldn't have got to know Luke in this way.

"No," I said, sounding much more sure than I'd been expecting. I was still afraid to disturb the quiet, a fragile state that could be easily broken, but my answer had enough impact. "Of course I don't hate it."

"Well, that's good to hear." The corner of Luke's lips had quirked into a smile. "Of course, I'd never wish what happened on anybody, but I have to say . . ." He paused, like he was going over the words in his head. "I'm really glad we got the chance to get to know each other, Corey."

His words had me breaking out into a smile, whether I liked it or not. "Me too."

Because although my worries about Luke's home life were still lingering beneath the surface, clamoring for attention, that didn't change the truth.

I really meant it.

And that was what scared me the most.

CHAPTER TWENTY-ONE

"I can't believe you didn't tell me!"

Holding the phone away from me, I winced as Kim's loud voice assaulted my eardrum. We'd been talking for no longer than a minute, and already it felt like she'd damaged my hearing. She clearly wasn't going to hold back.

"Calm down," I told her, daring to press the phone against my ear again. "I was planning on telling you."

"What, when you guys announce your engagement? *This* is what you neglected to tell George and me at lunch. You didn't think maybe it was important to mention that you're now dating Luke Everett, a.k.a. the most popular guy in school?"

"We're not dating."

She scoffed, obviously not willing to believe a word of it. "You're not dating, huh? Care to explain why I saw you guys making out against a locker?"

I was suddenly thankful we were having this discussion over the phone, because my face took on a definite pink tinge. "You saw that?"

"It was pretty difficult not to. I think most of the school saw you two sucking face."

"Why are you so worked up about it, anyway?" I asked, keen to move the conversation past my impromptu PDA with Luke. "You're not going to tell me you have a crush on Luke or something, are you?"

"Of course not." Her dismissal was instantaneous, as if the very idea of having a crush was beneath her. "I just thought we were friends. And this is exactly the kind of thing friends tell each other before the rest of the school finds out."

"Is this about your presidential privileges again?"

"It's about my *friend* privileges," she corrected. "In future, I'd like to be informed of gossip like this. Plus, I would be a terrible student body president if I didn't have up-to-date information on whom Luke Everett's dating."

"Not dating, Kim," I told her again.

"Enlighten me, then. What *is* going on?"

I leaned back against the headboard, picking at a thread on the hem of my shirt. "I'm not entirely sure," I confessed. "It was just something that happened on his birthday."

She didn't even have to say anything else; I could feel her insistent curiosity through the phone line, wordlessly pressing me to continue.

"We ended up going to this traveling fair," I said, scooting around the details. Half of me felt bad that I still hadn't told Kim about where I came from. It wasn't that I didn't trust her; I just wanted as few people as possible to know about my past. With that kind of knowledge came a lot of power, and I'd always been weird about depending on others. "It wasn't anything crazy. We had a good time. And at the end of the night . . . well, I don't really know how it happened. But he kissed me."

"And?"

"Well," I said, "I didn't *not* kiss him back."

"So, you snuck off from his dad's open house to go make out somewhere?"

"No! It wasn't like that. It was just something that happened, you know? The right moment, I guess."

"See, I don't know why you'd keep this quiet. Any other girl in school would be dying to tell anybody who'd listen that they'd made out with Luke Everett."

"Stop saying that!"

"Okay, okay," she drawled. "But we both know it's true."

"Do you have to be so sarcastic about this whole thing?"

"'Course I do. You know me—I'm not going to pass up any opportunity to tease you about this. You better prepare yourself."

"Honestly, Kim," I said with a sigh that was only half exaggerated, "I've been preparing from the moment I picked up the phone."

"Proud of you, Corey." I could practically hear the grin in her tone. "Hey, you know what? Speaking of traveling fairs, I just remembered what I've been meaning to tell you."

I froze, my muscles locking as if the slightest movement could give everything away. I should've got over this type of paranoia—especially with somebody like Kim. She wasn't exactly the type of person to take some stupid rumor about vandalism at face value, at least not without looking for the evidence. But I couldn't quite bring myself to take the risk.

"What?" I asked warily.

"I saw the weirdest thing the other day at work," she said, oblivious. "I was around the back of the gym, sorting out the trash, and there was this old poster somebody had pasted on the wall. It must've been there for a while, but I never noticed it. It was for this circus—Mystic, or something? I can't remember the name. But there were all these photos, and I swear to God, one of the girls looked exactly like you."

I could feel my breath quickening, my heart drumming in my chest. "What?"

"Freaked the hell out of me! I swear, this girl could've passed as your twin or something. As much as she could while hanging upside down from a trapeze, I mean. I really thought it was you at first, but what would you be doing on a circus poster, right? Makes no sense."

I forced myself to laugh, though I was sure it sounded much too shaky. "Yeah. That's weird."

"You want to watch yourself," Kim continued. "Apparently, you've got a weird circus doppelganger." Thankfully, she seemed to have overlooked the silence on my end of the line; her voice was as breezy as ever.

"Apparently so," I said, exhaling in relief that the moment had passed. "Thanks for the heads-up, I guess."

"She looked pretty good on that trapeze, you know. You should get up there and see if you've got the same talent." She laughed. "After seeing you climb that rope in gym, I don't think I'd even be surprised."

"Well," I said quietly, "that'd be something."

She had to be onto me. There was no other explanation.

But she didn't say anything else.

I was pulling it off. Somehow.

~

Not much changed over the next couple of weeks—or at least, that was what I would tell anybody if they asked. In reality, there was one big thing that *had* changed, and so drastically everything else seemed to bend along with it—the suddenly ignited spark between Luke and me. Without ever really saying it aloud, the two of us became an item, and it no longer mattered who knew. We didn't think twice about people seeing us arriving at school together, holding hands in the hallway, or sneaking a kiss wherever we could.

It just felt . . . *right*, in a way that I'd expected to take much longer to develop.

And I wasn't going to question it.

Of course, Mr. Everett's disapproval didn't magically disappear. In his eyes, his son deserved someone much better. Unfortunately, the *someone* he had in mind wasn't a figment of his imagination, but a real person—one I had to face every day at school.

I couldn't really blame him. Claire Delaney was a textbook match for his son: beautiful, smart, and with ready-made family connections to the real estate business, she ticked all the boxes. Against her, I fell short in every category. My looks were plain, I was flunking almost all of my classes—and the thought of Luke's father discovering I was fresh out of a traveling circus made me feel sick.

At first, I was worried his father's opposition would take its toll on our relationship, but Luke and I soon devised a system that took out most of the stress. Most weeknights, his dad would stay late at the office, and it was safe to linger at Luke's place until seven or eight in the evening without crossing paths.

I wondered if the amount of time Luke and I were spending in each other's company was excessive, but our alternatives—both of which were empty houses—hardly compared. So, evening after evening, we found ourselves together—sometimes poring over math notes, other times a lot more distracted.

Being with him was unlike anything I'd experienced before. Comparing how I felt with him to afternoons with Dave was like trying to bring two separate universes together. With Dave, things were easy, and my thoughts went no deeper than deciding on pizza toppings or what TV show we should watch next. When I was around Luke, he pulled my world to a standstill, and our moments stretched wide with endless possibility.

It wasn't that the choice was easy. Instead, there didn't seem to be one in the first place.

That particular Friday evening started off the same as any other. We had a test in precalc the next week, but the books I'd lugged over remained unopened in my backpack. I knew we should've been studying, but as soon as Luke had suggested putting on a movie and curling up on the couch, the temptation had been overpowering.

"We've been working hard all week," he assured me, scrolling through the choices onscreen. Then he joined me on the couch, not quite snuggled up together but close enough so our legs were touching.

"I guess we've got all weekend to study," I said.

"That's the spirit."

When I looked over to catch his eye, I became suddenly aware of how little space there was between our faces. The last of the black eye had long since faded from his skin, but it had taken a strangely long time. It still felt like new relief every time I saw the large expanse of pale skin, unscarred by any physical impact.

I wasn't sure either of us was paying much attention to the movie. Characters appeared and disappeared, delivering lines that barely registered; I was more focused on determining whether Luke really was watching me from the corner of his eye, or if I was just imagining it.

By the time the two love interests, soaked in pouring rain, began delivering passionate declarations of love in between gulps of breath, I realized he had turned his head completely. He wasn't watching the screen. He was looking at me instead.

I glanced over. "What?"

All he did was grin, shaking his head slightly.

"Aren't you watching the movie?"

"Not really," he admitted, not sounding sheepish at all. "I much prefer looking at you."

My heart may have fluttered a little, an involuntary reaction, but I still moved over to nudge him in the side. "You try way too hard to be a charmer."

"What are you talking about? I don't have to try. I am a charmer."

I laughed. "Of course. Your moves are *so* smooth."

And then suddenly he pulled me closer, my whole body shifting so that we were turned toward each other. "You say that," he said, his voice low and breathy, "but you're not watching the movie either."

There was no time to draw breath, let alone think of a comeback, before we were drawn together, our lips colliding in a messier version of what we'd shared over and over the past few weeks. It wasn't the first time we'd ended up like this. Countless other times we'd found ourselves pressed into the couch, locked in make-out sessions that lasted way longer than they should. It was strange, I'd come to realize, how much time could pass when your lips were pressed against someone else's.

Something was different about this, though. Our mouths

moved sloppily against each other, in a way I would definitely have been embarrassed to see anybody do in public. Before long I was struggling for breath, gulping air in the seconds we were apart. My hands trailed up Luke's back, fingers finding their way up to tangle themselves in his hair, wondering if this exploration would be what finally disheveled its ever-perfect style.

The movie had become suddenly irrelevant. Faint music played in the background, the flickering light of the TV set casting shadows across the dimly lit room, but neither of us was paying attention. In that moment, I doubted whether I could even recall the name of it.

I realized then what I wanted, and pulled my lips back to reposition them a few inches from his ear. "You want to go upstairs?" I asked softly.

He knew what I meant of course. The underlying question was obvious, asking how far we were going to take this. It wasn't completely new to me—during the last six months of the circus, I'd had a couple of flings. But those guys had been outsiders, and from the start I knew nothing would come of it. If they'd wanted something more than a good-night kiss after the show ended, or a stolen moment at a party I'd wrangled an invite to, I'd certainly not been about to give it to them.

This was different. This was Luke.

And I knew he was exactly what I wanted.

He nodded. "Yeah, okay."

He took my hand to lead me up the stairs, and I felt dizzy when he pushed open the door to the room I'd since become familiar with. It was comfortably messy: the bed was only half made, piles of textbooks teetered on the edge of the desk, several crumpled T-shirts were strewn on the floor. As I stepped backward, my foot collided with something on the carpet and I stumbled, staggering toward the bed and pulling Luke with me.

His face hovered above mine, sweeping over my expression, and my heart thudded with anticipation.

"Are you okay with this?" I asked, because I was sure I could see an underlying nervousness beneath his expression.

But then his lips found my neck, their movement spelling out the answer. "I am."

After that, we were kissing again, more slowly than we had been downstairs, as if suddenly aware this wasn't something to be rushed. Luke's hands began wandering; I could feel them trailing up my back, having edged their way under the fabric of my shirt. The sensation was strange, more unfamiliar than anything else, my skin hot beneath the movement of his fingers.

He broke away for a moment when he brushed the clasp of my bra, wordlessly asking for permission to keep going. I nodded, watching his face, before leaning up to capture his lips in a gentle kiss. There was more fiddling than expected, and he drew back a little, his brows creasing into a concentrated frown. I couldn't help but smile.

"Need help?" I asked.

"I'm getting there," he assured me, but his cheeks were growing redder. "Sorry. If I'm being honest, I-I've actually not done any of this before."

"That's okay." All at once, he got it, and I felt the clasp come undone. "Neither have I."

I was beginning to relax a little more now, my fingers brushing the hem of his shirt. I went to pull it upward, but only made it a few inches before I felt his hand enclose mine.

I looked at him questioningly.

"Sorry, I . . ." He took a deep breath, slowly removing his hand. Then he shook his head. "It's fine."

I wanted to ask him what he'd been about to say, but it didn't seem like the right time. Instead, I carried on with what I'd originally been trying to do, tugging his shirt up until his head emerged again in a tangle of disheveled blond. I could tell he felt exposed, with his whole torso on show, but it was only when my eyes trailed downward that I realized why.

I wish I could've stopped myself from drawing in such a sharp breath, which sounded far too loud in the quiet space. But the sight was overwhelming: not the expanse of Luke's pale skin, but what had been inflicted across it.

The bruises I'd got an earlier glimpse of, all those weeks ago, didn't stop at his arms. His whole chest was dotted with similar injuries: purple-red patches on his shoulder, back, and stomach. A particularly sore-looking slash stretched across his shoulder, the surrounding skin angry and inflamed.

"Luke," I breathed, unable to muster anything else.

My realization was obvious to both of us. There was no question about it now, regardless of how much Luke tried to deny it. We both knew what was going on, and this was something serious.

"Don't say it," he whispered. I was taken aback by the pleading note in his tone. "Please."

"But . . ."

"Can we just have this moment?" he asked quietly, cutting me off. We were looking right at each other, no avoiding gazes, his striking blue eyes piercing my own. "Even if it's just for a little while . . . can we pretend it doesn't exist?"

I didn't know what to say. He'd as good as told me what was really going on, about the abusive home life he worked all hours of the day to cover up. We'd have to discuss it at some point; there was no way we could brush this under the carpet. I couldn't forget it. And yet there was something swimming in his eyes, a desperate look that broke my heart, a silent longing for our moment to continue untainted.

After everything, didn't he deserve that? Just one moment?

I wasn't heartless enough to deny him.

We tried our best to resume what we'd started. However, the sudden awareness that had swept over me was hard to ignore, my eyes wandering down any time they were given the chance. I only let my fingers skim his skin, terrified of causing more pain, though I could tell some of the injuries were weeks old. Everywhere I looked I saw damaged flesh, red and inflamed like the anger that had caused it in the first place.

Luke wanted to forget about its existence, pretend we were still wrapped up in the moment. But it was proving impossible to return to that desperate desire, when all I now wanted to do was hug him.

"Does it hurt?" The words escaped me on impulse, hardly louder than a whisper, causing Luke to freeze.

A second's pause had his gaze flickering over my face. "Not anymore," he said quietly. "I'm fine. I promise."

There was no chance to question further, though I wasn't sure whether I'd been about to. At that moment, an unmistakable sound from downstairs rang out loud enough to shock us to our senses, both at the same time. The jangling of keys. The slam of a front door. Footsteps, loud and angry, pounding against floorboards.

I'd never seen an expression of fear as intense as the one that appeared across Luke's face. He jumped away from me instantly, stumbling in a desperate attempt to get off the bed. I didn't need to ask what was going on; a jolt of equally intense panic was pulsing through my blood. Luke reached for his shirt just as I yanked mine back down, pulling it over his head as the footsteps grew louder, closer, more intimidating.

"*Luke*! I thought I asked you to send those spreadsheets to Mr. Delaney!"

The voice was everything I'd been afraid of, booming, every word erupting with anger. Seconds later, the door was thrust open with such force it bounced off the wall. All I could do was sit there, half-tangled in the bedsheets, fully dressed but more exposed than I'd ever felt in my life.

"Dad," Luke breathed, though it was clear that the word would do nothing to calm the figure in the doorway, who'd frozen on the spot. "I was just—"

"Oh, you've got a little friend over, have you?" Mr. Everett said, his eyes darting toward me with a look of pure disgust. "Now *this* is an arrangement you didn't tell me about. I suppose this is something you two have been doing every afternoon I'm at the office?"

"Corey and I were just studying," he said, but he'd picked the weakest of all excuses. His disheveled hair, now sticking up in all directions, not to mention my spot on the bed were clues enough. It didn't even matter that there were no textbooks in sight. "We have a math test next week and I—"

"Don't lie to me, Luke. I'm not an idiot."

"I'm not—"

"Not only have you been breaking rules when I'm not here, it's also your fault that I've been forced home early. Those financial spreadsheets for Clearview were meant to get to Mr. Delaney today, no later. I told you to send the file. But apparently you've been too busy jumping in bed with random girls to even—"

"*She's not a random girl!*" Luke yelled, in a tone so sharp it

237

seemed to slice the air in half. I'd never heard him speak to his father like that before; it was slightly unnerving to witness. Maybe I should've been flattered, in some weird way, but it was difficult to think of anything other than Luke's bruised torso and what the consequences might be. "Jesus, do you have to be so rude? Corey's my *girlfriend*, how many times do I have to tell you? For crying out loud, have some manners!"

The deathly silence that followed was even worse than the shouting. All that could be heard was the sound of our ragged breathing. The atmosphere had become a pane of glass, threatening to shatter under its own weight. One movement could set everything off.

"I think you should leave now, Corey," said Mr. Everett.

I didn't need to be told twice. My limbs were trembling as I stumbled off the bed, struggling to get to my feet. I ran a hand through my hair in an attempt to tame it.

I wasn't sure what to do. Luke was already ushering me out of the room, moving to herd me into the hallway and down the stairs. Every step felt like a mistake, a warning against leaving them alone—because if I did, who knew where Mr. Everett's anger would take him? Would Luke be sporting another black eye the next time I saw him?

"I'll see you at school, yeah?" Luke said to me when we reached the bottom of the stairs, his voice remarkably level.

"Yeah," I breathed in response.

The fear pressed in on me from all sides, squeezing the air right out of my lungs. But I'd already lingered much too long. There was nothing left to do but take a shaky step out the front door and try not to look back when I heard it close behind me.

I made it to the end of the driveway, my pace agonizingly slow, before stopping. I finally realized why my shoulder felt so much lighter; the school bag I'd lugged over was laying forgotten in the living room, textbooks untouched. For a moment I considered just leaving it there, before remembering I'd be without my math notes all weekend if I did. With a test on Monday I really had to study for, there was no alternative but to go back for it.

My hands, at least, had stopped shaking by the time I got up to the house. The front door was unlocked and I slipped inside with ease. For the briefest of seconds, there was quiet, and I felt a swell of relief that Mr. Everett's anger may not have been as intense as first thought. But the feeling was short lived; seconds later, the sound of yelling started up from somewhere downstairs.

The noise was muffled; I couldn't make out the words, only that the shouting seemed to be coming from both sides. They were each holding their own pretty firmly, though I wasn't sure whether to be glad about this.

I opened the living-room door slowly, hoping the noise was coming from the kitchen. It sounded some distance away—not right on the other side of the door, at least. I figured I could dash in, grab my bag, and make a break for it without being noticed.

But I'd got the door only a quarter open when I froze.

"You worthless piece of *shit*!"

The words barreled out of Mr. Everett's mouth with more force than I'd heard before; it was almost like the loathing had a sound of its own. Suddenly, they both moved backward, slipping into view of the crack in the door.

"Oh yeah? Isn't that what Mom said about you before she left?"

This, it seemed, was the final straw. Before I even had time to react, Mr. Everett launched forward, shoving Luke back with all the strength he could muster. His son, unprepared for the force, lost his footing completely. He stumbled backward into the wooden bookcase with a loud crash before falling to the floor.

Silence fell across the room, but all I wanted to do was scream.

CHAPTER TWENTY-TWO

I couldn't bear to watch.

Blood pulsed in my ears, drumming with a roar that drowned out all other noise. Not that there was any—Luke wasn't making much sound as he lay motionless on the floor. Above him, his father was heaving huge breaths, towering over his son's crumpled form.

Maybe I should've rushed in, thrown myself into the middle of it—whatever it took to make sure Luke was okay—but my muscles had locked into place, leaving me hovering in the open door and feeling far too exposed.

As I stood there, frozen, I couldn't take my eyes off Luke—and that was when I saw his eyes flutter open. A rush of relief came over me, but it didn't last long; there soon came a lurch through my chest instead when his eyes locked onto mine.

He'd seen me. There was no question about it, and the few seconds of charged eye contact seemed to convey more than any words we'd ever spoken.

I didn't need his lips to move to know what he was telling me.

Go.

Leaving him was unthinkable, but what other options did I have? I couldn't run in there and save the day; the least I could do for him was what he wanted. So, with great effort, my muscles managed to unstick themselves, and I fled the house with a speed I would later be ashamed of.

All the way home, I considered going back. It was a wonder I even managed to find my way. My feet moved of their own accord, one step after another. As I walked, I felt like I was breaking into fragments, and by the time I reached my mom's house, I felt sure there should have been nothing left of me.

The place was quiet, eerie, leaving too much open space to be comfortable. I wanted to scream just to fill it. All I wanted was warmth, sound, a sign of life—if only to distract myself from the bleakness inside my own head.

"Corey?"

The voice stopped me dead in my tracks as the door clicked shut behind me. Any hope of slipping in unnoticed had been well and truly crushed, but I stayed still anyway, like that would make a difference.

When I didn't respond, my mother's voice called out again. "Is that you?"

"Yeah." My voice came out so feebly that I was surprised she could even hear me from the living room. "It's me."

Until this point, I'd held it together so well. The hard part was over; all that remained was a tiny stretch, the simple matter of making it upstairs and closing my bedroom door. After that, I would be free to fall apart in private—to cry, crumple, come apart at the seams.

She appeared suddenly in the doorway, her hands curled around the frame, shiny acrylic nails on view. Her eyes were wide and questioning, but I wasn't sure why. It was near enough the time I'd told her I would be back, but it was like she sensed something, a feeling that things were a little off, a shift in atmosphere even as I walked through the door.

Something about the sight of her made me pause. Maybe it was her expression, tinged with concern despite the iciness that had plagued us since being forced together. Regardless of the circumstances and our history, she was there—and she was my mother.

I couldn't help it. I burst into tears.

Even through the broken lines of my vision, I could see she was startled. I turned away, ashamed of my moment of weakness, especially in front of my mom. It wasn't her problem. This was on me, and me only.

"I'm sorry," I said, already heading for the stairs.

But the hand on my arm came even before I'd made it to the first step. She hadn't grabbed me, or anything close, but her touch was like a vice grip in itself; I couldn't move a muscle.

"Corey," she coaxed. "What's going on?"

I heard the concern in her voice, and for the first time there was no sense of the detachment that kept us at arm's length. She genuinely wanted to be let in.

I was beyond being able to stop crying, the tears already brimming over, streaking down my cheeks one after another. I couldn't say anything. The words were caught in my throat, fusing with each other to form a lump I couldn't swallow. Somehow, though, my mother knew exactly what to do.

Moving closer, she put an arm around me.

It could've felt weird. It could've felt unnatural as she pulled me against her, my head fitting into the space above her shoulder. For weeks we'd been separated by an intangible barrier, with no idea how to go about breaking it, but I could feel it all shattering. The previous awkwardness didn't matter. The past fifteen years didn't matter. In that moment, even if that was all it turned out to be, I felt like her daughter again.

She led me to the living room, ushering me onto the couch before fetching a box of tissues. These remained balanced in her lap while I curled up as small as I could, the tears showing no signs of letting up.

"Corey," she said from beside me. Her voice was gentle, edging its way closer. "What's the matter?"

What could I say? My head was hopelessly scattered. It felt like hours had passed since I'd staggered away from Luke's house, and yet the scene kept flashing across my mind like it was still playing out right in front of me. I couldn't escape it, no matter where I turned.

My façade of independence was crumbling; the tireless effort I'd devoted to maintaining a composed exterior suddenly felt wasted. I was supposed to be able to hold it together, but here I was, falling apart in the messiest and most vulnerable way.

From this, there was no going back.

Maybe that was what made it easier to start talking.

At first, I could barely get the words past the lump in my throat. I wondered whether I was betraying Luke just by speaking of it. But I soon realized there was no way I could keep it all to myself. Once I got started, off-loading felt like a colossal relief, and I wasn't sure I could stop.

My mom was patient. She sat still through the whole thing, occasionally reaching over to hand me another tissue, a dozen of which were now balled up on her spotless couch. I thought this would make her restless, but it didn't seem to bother her at all. Instead, she kept nodding, listening intently to my every word.

"I just don't know what to do," I choked out, finally drawing to the end. "I can't pretend I don't know what's going on, but . . . I'm afraid he'll hate me if I do anything about it."

"This isn't something you can keep to yourself," she said, her voice calm enough to steer me back into reality. "Whether or not he was trying to keep it a secret, it can't stay that way. It's not fair on you or him."

"What if he never speaks to me again?" I whispered. "I don't know if I can live with that."

"You don't really have a choice."

"Did you suspect anything?" I wasn't sure what made me ask, but the words were out before I had a chance to think twice. "His dad, you said you'd met before. Did you know . . . ?"

She shook her head. "Of course not. But then I wouldn't think it possible for anyone to do something like that to their own child . . ."

She hadn't meant it that way, but the words seemed to linger in the air anyway, ringing out louder than the rest. I realized then that I was holding my breath in what had become a charged atmosphere.

"Corey," she breathed eventually, after a silence that felt like it had stretched fifteen years. "Everything that happened . . . you know I didn't mean for it to turn out that way."

I wasn't sure of the right response—and since risking a wrong one seemed dangerous, I stayed quiet.

"I was a stupid teenager, thinking it made me cool to make all the wrong decisions, whatever it took to get my parents riled up. I didn't mean to get pregnant so young, and after that, everything seemed to fall apart. I made some stupid, stupid decisions. If only

I'd been older, and in a better state of mind, things could've been so different . . ."

She ducked her head, low enough that her hair would've hidden her face had it not been scraped back into its tight ponytail. "I just wish it all could've happened another way. From the day you were taken from me, I've been labeled a bad mother. And I was. I'm not stupid enough to deny that. I thought maybe this could be my chance to turn it around, but it's been fifteen years and it's like I haven't changed at all . . ."

"You have," I said, but my quiet voice was hardly convincing.

"I'm sorry." The two words were definitive, startling. "I talk about Mr. Everett like that, but the reality is my selfish decisions could've completely ruined my own daughter's life."

"It's not like that," I told her. "You know it's not like that."

"I'm sorry, Corey. You deserve better. You always have."

"Don't say that."

"It's true."

"No, it's not!" I only realized I was shouting once the words had escaped me. But I couldn't help it. After witnessing what happened behind closed doors at the Everetts', the situation with my mom seemed like a dream in comparison. We may not have been close, but at least I could trust her not to throw a punch.

"You did everything you could," I told her.

She looked at me then, eyes wide and focused, glinting with something I couldn't work out but appreciated all the same. We didn't say anything, but there was no need to. And when she reached over, a tissue in hand to dab away the last of the tears still shining on my face, I felt the unmistakable sensation of something falling together, a loose end being tied up, jigsaw pieces finally slotting into place.

I only wished it hadn't taken such an awful situation for it to happen.

~

Later that evening, I returned to my room. For the first time ever, dinner had been something other than an awkward affair, although my stomach was far too unsettled for me to eat much. It was our opportunity to have a real conversation, once I'd ridden out the worst of the emotional aftermath and was better able to think things through. And we talked about a lot. It was a relief to listen to somebody else's perspective, to bounce my concerns off something other than the inside of my skull. Things seemed so much clearer.

I'd reached a decision. A solution may have been out of my own hands, but I had the power to enlist the help of somebody else. If only it hadn't taken me so long to realize that.

In a way, it felt like treachery, but I knew it was the right thing to do. Even if he didn't agree at first, he would surely come around.

I was counting on it.

My hands trembled as I picked up the phone and dialed the number copied onto a scrap of paper in my mother's impeccable print. I hesitated after the tenth digit, stalling in those few seconds before pressing Call.

After that, there would be no going back.

I held my hand still enough to bring the phone to my ear, waiting with bated breath as the call rang through. A few seconds later, I heard the voice that would change everything.

"Sherwood Police Department, how can I help you?"

CHAPTER TWENTY-THREE

Over the following week, things were unnervingly quiet.

I may have been imagining it, but there seemed to be a heightened sense of anticipation in the air. Everything was hanging in the balance, set to go up in flames at the first spark. I was on constant edge, teetering on the brink of—well, *something*. If only I knew what.

Luke had been absent from school the entire week. Every morning I scanned for his car in the parking lot, and the first two minutes of each lunch period were spent searching the cafeteria for a head of carefully tousled blond hair. By Wednesday, my hope was beginning to waver. I was itching to speak to him, to finally tackle it all head on; at least then the words would be out in the open. But even his phone kept up the wall of silence, remaining switched off at all times of the day, no matter how much I cluttered his message inbox.

Naturally, I expected the worst. Visions of him lying in a hospital bed—or even worse, at home—haunted my mind, growing so unbearable I almost went over there. But each time I began slipping my arms into a jacket, half-ready to walk out the front door, I remembered the call I'd made and what it would change.

It wasn't intentional, but I withdrew into myself. In class, I did nothing more than stare out the window, the teachers' voices reduced to background noise. At lunch, I took my usual seat at Kim and George's table but shied away from most conversation, picking at my food instead.

They noticed, of course. At first, they assumed I was having a bad couple of days and didn't ask many questions. By Friday, however, I could sense Kim's irritation even through my haze of disinterest.

"Corey?"

I looked up from the sandwich I was picking apart. "Hmm?"

"Are you even listening?"

My eyes met hers, detecting the challenge within them. Beside her, George ducked his head, as if sensing the confrontation that was coming.

"What's up with you?" she asked outright, her tone caught somewhere between concern and exasperation. I couldn't work out how I felt about it. "You've been acting strange all week. Is there something wrong?"

The truth was obvious, especially to somebody like Kim. And yet with so much still in limbo, it felt wrong to talk about it. How could I even begin to explain what I couldn't grasp myself?

So I did what was second nature to me. I shut her out.

"Nothing," I said. "I'm fine."

"Well, you're obviously not fine," she continued, setting down her fork. Her eyes peeked out from beneath her impeccably straight bangs, scrutinizing, as if I were a puzzle she was trying to figure out. "You've barely said two words to us all week, and all I see you do is pick at your food. Did something happen with Luke?"

"I told you," I said, "I'm fine."

"Jesus, Corey." The exasperation written across her face was kind of scary, enough to warn me against ever getting on her bad side. While Kim was honest, rational, and straight talking, those same qualities only intensified when she was pissed. "What do you expect us to do here? This is me and George we're talking about. Not some kids in the hallway looking for gossip to spread. We're concerned."

"You don't need to be."

This, apparently, was the wrong answer. "You know, this is exactly your problem. We're your best friends. You're meant to tell us stuff. How on earth are we supposed to help you if we don't have a clue what's going on?"

I had to admit that her guilt-tripping was working. My gaze flickered over the pair: Kim, leaning forward on the table and radiating fiery determination; George, pushing his glasses up his nose, only just daring to raise his head. She was right, they were my best friends—two of the handful of people I'd really got to know during my time at Franklin.

I'd never really had anything of the sort before. There'd always been Dave, of course, but even that was different, in a way I couldn't quite explain. The circus had a strange knack for skewing things that would've otherwise been normal, as if a whole other world altogether existed within the walls of the tent.

I owed it to them to say something, even if it was just one corner of the huge picture. And yet when I opened my mouth to speak, I couldn't find the words.

"This is exactly what you always do," Kim continued, having

sensed I had nothing with which to defend myself. "You bottle everything up, keeping secrets left and right. As if we can't be trusted. Is that what you think about us? That we're about to go publishing your personal life in the school newspaper or something?"

"That's not it," I protested, but my voice was weak, especially against Kim's.

"Well, what is it then?" she demanded. She'd stiffened in her seat, her back straight, and suddenly looked several inches taller. As if I wasn't already intimidated enough.

"Kim . . ." George's interjection was tentative, as if worried she might turn on him too.

"You can't keep people out forever, you know," she said. "I don't know what's going on with you and Luke, but if it's that much of a secret, maybe I don't want to know."

She stood up then, pushing her tray away, even though her lunch was only half eaten. "I've got a student council meeting to go to," she declared, still looking straight at me. "If you decide to stop freezing me out anytime soon, you know where to find me."

The cafeteria felt painfully quiet as George and I watched her stalk off, though the noise level hadn't dipped at all. We were surrounded on all sides by other conversations, lines of chatter being thrown back and forth, even if we had nothing to say.

There was something hopeless about the sight of Kim's retreating figure, already halfway across the room. When she—the girl who was more likely to stay up all night figuring out a tricky math problem than throw in the towel—had given up on me, it felt like confirmation that I was beyond fixing.

As it turned out, however, the face-off with Kim was a mere warm-up compared to what I was to deal with that evening.

In the absence of an alternative, I resorted to my usual pastime—

the gym. Even running the risk of bumping into Kim wasn't enough to keep me away from the temptation of exercise machines and physical exertion. I killed a couple of hours there, returning to my mother's about seven thirty, my gym bag slung over one shoulder. I intended to take a shower before dinner, but once in my room, I hadn't even started peeling off my clothes before there was a knock at the door.

My mother would be out late; she'd already told me that morning. She was staying behind at the office, then heading out for dinner with a few colleagues. A serving of lasagna was waiting in the fridge for me, cooking instructions printed on a sticky note. For the time being, at least, I was home alone.

I considered ignoring the knock, figuring it was a door-to-door salesman. All I wanted to do was strip off my sweaty sportswear and hop into the shower. But then the knocking sounded again, this time louder and more insistent.

I padded down the stairs, irritated, hoping it would be something that could be dealt with quickly. But as soon as I pulled open the front door, I realized that wouldn't be the case.

"Luke," I breathed. Words suddenly failed me, strangled by the sight of him right in front of me. "What are you doing here?"

"Sorry, did I show up uninvited?"

It was an odd thing to say, let alone in such a clipped tone. I frowned.

"Do you want to come in?"

He didn't bother answering, instead stepping across the threshold and into the hallway. As I closed the door behind him, a strange quiet fell across the room, broken only by the sound of a ticking clock from the living room. With every passing second, the more Luke's gaze weighed on me, and the clearer it became that something was very wrong.

"Are you okay?" I asked, partly because I was genuinely concerned, but also because there didn't seem to be any other suitable words to fill the space.

Clearly, it was the wrong question. He laughed, but the sound was almost mocking. When he cast his gaze upon me once more, I could feel myself shrinking. "Are you *really* asking me that?"

I swallowed. "What are you talking about?"

"You know exactly what I'm talking about, Corey. I know it was you."

"Luke, I—"

"You called the *police*? What the hell were you thinking?"

Half of me expected it, but the other half flipped straight into defensive mode. I wasn't about to stand there and be lectured about what was, inarguably, the right thing to do. I thought better of myself than that.

"What was I thinking?" I echoed disbelievingly. "Oh, I don't know, Luke. Maybe I was thinking about how I saw your dad almost knock you out. Or maybe about all those bruises I've seen. Or the past three black eyes you've had, which you've been lying to me about this whole time . . ."

"I told you I was fine!"

"You don't exactly have a solid record of telling the truth, though, do you?"

Something in his eyes sparked, a flame of anger I'd never seen in him, let alone seen directed at me. "That isn't the point. You shouldn't have gone behind my back."

"You're being ridiculous."

"I suppose it was your idea of doing the right thing, huh?" he said, the words backed by a sense of real distaste, as if it was something to be ashamed of. "Reporting my dad for assault. Anything to get it off your own conscience."

His words were unfair, every comeback twisting the situation into something that could be pinned on me. In a situation where neither of us was the culprit, it certainly didn't feel that way. And for that, I was suddenly livid.

"What did you expect me to do?" I shot back.

"I expected you to come to me first!"

"What, and have you talk me into keeping the whole thing quiet? Because *that* would've been the right thing to do?"

"That's just the thing, Corey. You *don't* know the right thing to do. You don't understand any of this."

"I know I don't. And you know why? Because you don't give anybody a chance to, Luke! You sit in silence for God knows how long, trying desperately to cover everything up. Anything to make it look like things are fine. But they're not fine. They're anything *but* fine. And nobody's got a clue, because you've made damn sure of it . . ."

"Because look what ends up happening!" He threw his hands up in the air, frustrated. "I had the cops show up at my door. My dad thought it was me who'd called them, so of course he lost his temper. Next thing I know, he's in handcuffs. What the hell am I supposed to do then?"

"That's *his* fault, Luke," I said, "not yours."

"It wouldn't have even come to this if you hadn't started interfering!" he shot back. "You think it's easy for me to watch my own dad being arrested? Do you know what an assault case is going to do for his criminal record?"

"Then say you don't want to press charges," I told him. "Go back to living in that house and wait for him to put you in the hospital."

"You think I didn't try that already?" he asked, his voice rapidly shooting up in volume, like he couldn't believe I was being so stupid. "Of course I did. I was taken in for questioning, and it was the first thing out of my mouth."

"Then what's the problem?"

"They didn't believe me," he spat. "They thought he was pressuring me into it, making me do things against my will. Kept muttering to themselves about the psychological damage domestic violence can do. As if any of that bullshit actually applies to me. The case is still ongoing. I'm not even allowed in my own house right now. So what do you think I've been forced to do?"

My voice had retreated somewhere inside me, but I had a feeling that silence wasn't going to sit well with Luke. Or at least not this angry version of him. "What?"

"I've had to call my mom."

It was hardly the unthinkable resort I had anticipated. "Well, that's a good thing, isn't it?"

"You've got to be kidding me." If anything, he looked disappointed now, as if he couldn't quite believe that I wasn't grasping it. His eyes locked onto mine once again, with an intensity that sent a chill down my spine. "I might be old enough, but I don't have the money to make it on my own. And do you think I'm welcome in her new life? She left me behind for a reason. How do you think it's going to go when I waltz in there and screw everything up?"

"Look, I'm sorry, okay?" I said, wishing I didn't sound so close to pleading. "But I had to do something. I can't just forget it all."

"Oh, don't worry," Luke shot back, his tone caught somewhere between sarcasm and spite. "You did something, all right. No doubt about that one."

"I did what I had to do," I said, but my voice had grown quieter, no longer fueled by the same fire. I was overcome by a new sense of fear, as if I'd only just realized I couldn't handle it. This was *Luke*. The same Luke who'd consumed my thoughts, in one way or another, for weeks on end. The one who'd held it together for so long in a way I could only dream of. The one whose absence was almost impossible to imagine. "I couldn't sit by and bear the thought of you trapped in that house with him."

"Well, it's done now, isn't it?" A humorless smile appeared on his face, but it was perhaps even more difficult to face than a glare. "There's no taking it back now. If anything, you've single-handedly sent my dad to jail. I hope you're happy."

"Luke, I—"

"See, *this* is why I keep things to myself. You make it out to be such a bad thing. You make out like you're the noble one, sweeping in with one phone call that'll magically make everything better. That's the trouble. You think you understand what I want. You might think you've fixed it all, but you've just made it worse."

It hit me all at once, the full force of his words and the bracing dose of truth that came along with them. Until now, I'd been convinced Luke was being irrational. How could he have expected me to accept the fact he was suffering serious abuse at home?

And yet suddenly, in that one moment, I saw what he was saying. The last threads of hope were always the strongest. When one person was his last option, he'd do anything to hold on.

"Luke," I began, but I didn't get any further.

"Don't," he warned, his voice stern enough to cut me short. "I don't want to hear anything else. You've done enough."

"I just wanted to help you get out." All my anger had melted away, until it felt like it should've been in a puddle at my feet. Every action, even the simple matter of moving my lips, seemed to take of the last dregs of my energy.

"Well, that's where you got it wrong." The beat of silence that passed between us felt years long. "I didn't want to get out."

"He was hurting you."

"He's *family*. And in case you hadn't noticed, I don't have a whole lot of that. It's all right for you, with your traveling circus and *we're-all-in-this-together* bullshit. Well, you're here now. Welcome to the real world."

"Luke—"

"I don't want to hear it."

"But I—"

"Jesus, Corey!" His voice rang out louder than expected, and I found myself flinching. Instinctively, I stepped backward, my back brushing against the wall. "You really don't know when to quit, do you?"

I wanted to say something more, to at least try to defend myself, but words failed me. My mouth opened and closed, until I finally resigned myself to silence. Maybe it was better that way.

"Thanks for your concern," he said, painfully sarcastic. He stepped forward, already moving toward the front door. "But as it turns out, I'll be a lot better off without it."

I couldn't say anything as he yanked open the front door, already making for the porch steps and the street outside. Even if I had been able to find my voice, I doubted any words would've been enough to stop him, let alone make him turn back. The sight of his retreating form—the second one I'd had to deal with that day—caused a lump to form in my throat, and soon I could barely piece together the broken fragments of my vision.

When I finally gathered the strength to close the door, there was nothing to do but sink down against it, put my head in my hands, and slowly fall to pieces.

CHAPTER TWENTY-FOUR

When Kim turned up outside my house on Monday morning, I knew things were about to get worse.

We hadn't spoken all weekend; she'd kept up her wall of silence for three days, and I hadn't tried to reach out. This, of course, left George caught in the middle, flitting between the two of us, trying as best he could to diffuse the situation.

I did feel bad. Kim's words continued to ring in my head, and it was perhaps the truth of what she said that echoed loudest. I *had* been keeping things from her—and in more ways than she knew about. Telling her the real story would make it even worse.

So, like always, I kept my distance.

Until now.

My mom and I were halfway through breakfast when Kim's car pulled up outside. My seat at the dining table had a clear view of the front window, and at first, I couldn't believe what I was seeing. But once the petite figure climbed out of the driver's seat, there was no mistaking Kim.

My mother noticed her too. "Oh," she said, surprised. "Is Kim giving you a ride to school?"

She was closing in on the front door, with a speed that had me rising from my seat. "Something like that," I replied, pushing my plate away. The last thing I needed was a confrontation in my mother's presence, and the only way to avoid it was to get out quickly. "I'll, uh, see you later."

"Sure," she answered. "Have a nice day."

I was out of the room in seconds, pulling on my shoes and opening the door before Kim had a chance to knock. When it swung open, she froze on the spot, her arm lifted.

I didn't know what to say, and I figured she'd have something up her sleeve—she always did. So I stayed quiet, just waiting.

"Corey," she said slowly. Both syllables were well balanced and equally calculated, and I wondered if she'd been practicing. "What do you say to a ride to school?"

It was bizarre; she didn't seem mad, miles away from her outburst in the cafeteria just three days ago. In fact, there was an air about her that I couldn't quite put my finger on. Managing a smile, her eyes remained unreadable beneath the heavy bangs.

"You're talking to me now?"

It hadn't meant to come out as a challenge, but it did anyway.

She leaned in, lowering her voice slightly. "Look, there's something we need to talk about. I really think it's a good idea for me to give you a ride."

Now, of course, I was wary. There was something about the look on her face, one that was completely out of place on Kim, that had my heart pounding. "What do you mean?"

"It's hard to explain."

Her smile was pleading. It was unnerving to see Kim like that; she was someone who was usually so confident in everything she did, words always flowing at the speed of light, intimidating even at five foot two. Only now did I register her height, like she'd taken off a pair of heels I had never noticed.

"Okay," I said, stepping forward and shutting the door behind me. "Let's go."

We walked in silence toward her car. Whatever Kim had to say—however bad it turned out to be—I was going to find out in a matter of minutes. My heart thumped in time to the pace of my steps.

I slipped into the passenger seat and sat tight as Kim fumbled with her keys, taking longer than usual to find the ignition. When the car roared to life, I jumped unnecessarily, already on edge.

The car's interior was too warm to be pleasant; beads of sweat were forming on the back of my neck. We moved off, heading down the street, Kim's careful driving taking a while to pick up real speed. The farther we went, the more ominous the silence became.

When she hit the blinker to take the next left, I couldn't take it any longer.

"What's going on?"

I immediately regretted blurting it out, as the resulting tension fell across the car like a smothering blanket.

After what felt like a lifetime, Kim took a deep breath. "There's something I have to tell you," she said again, as if this wasn't clear enough. "Before we get to school, I mean. I have to let you know."

I glanced to my left, but she was staring straight ahead, eyes fixated on the road. "Kim, come on. You've got me worried now. Tell me."

I watched her swallow. There was a beat of silence, and then the words were out. "I know everything."

It could've meant anything, but my heart was pounding already:

the steady *thump-thump-thump* beneath my shirt was the only thing I was certain of. Everything else—her nervous tone, the slightly jerky movements of the steering wheel, the radio on the lowest volume—I found myself doubting. She couldn't mean what I thought. She couldn't.

"What are you talking about?"

"I couldn't help it, okay?" she said, all in a rush. "I was curious. I've always been that way. The slightest bit of suspicion, any inconsistency, I'll go after it. It's just in my nature." She shook her head. "What I'm trying to say is . . . I did my own research."

I could guess what she was getting at, but that didn't make it any easier to hear. It was really happening—what I'd been trying desperately for months to avoid. When I found my voice once more, it was surprisingly quiet. "On what?"

She looked over at me, guilt written all over her face. "The circus, Corey. I know all about it."

I'd been right, but hearing the words aloud ignited my panic at once. *She knew.* Her eyes flitted between me and the road with more urgency than was probably safe, like she was trying to gauge my reaction. All of a sudden, the temperature inside the car felt unbearable.

"I—I don't . . ."

"I wasn't trying to invade your privacy, or anything. I swear. I was just interested."

Finally, the word tumbled out. "How?"

She managed a smile, but it was humorless; she was well aware I was not in the right frame of mind for jokes. "You leave more of a trace than you'd like to think, Corey," she said. "It wasn't that difficult. You can find almost anything on the internet. Your name isn't an exception."

"So you Googled me?"

"You'd be surprised at how many times your name pops up. Articles, mostly. Reviews of the show. *Budding trapeze star, new on the scene . . .* you should hear it. They're raving about you."

I was being tugged from every direction, each reaction holding a different corner of me, like a blanket about to rip. On the one hand, I was panicked, overwhelmed by how much Kim really knew about me. I usually called the shots on how much people were allowed to know, but that was clearly no longer the case. On another, I was angry. What gave her the right to research me like I was some kind of school project? Just because there was information available didn't mean she was entitled to go looking for it.

"How long have you known?"

I wanted specific answers: dates, times, right down to the exact moment she'd broken through my guard. What she had to offer hardly compared. "A while."

When I didn't say anything, she took her cue to go on. "Look, I'm sorry, okay? I kept waiting for you to tell us, dropping hints to see how you'd react. We're friends, you know? I thought it would happen eventually. And then suddenly all these weeks have gone by, you're still as secretive as ever, and we're as clueless as the rest of the school. It was like you didn't trust us."

"It wasn't that."

"Then what?"

"Kim, please don't pretend you don't know what people in this town think of the circus," I said. "You know what happened last year. The vandalism at Clearview, how it was all blamed on us . . . how there's at least one person in this town who hates us enough to try to burn us alive."

She opened her mouth to say something, but I kept going.

"We're not criminals. We had nothing to do with what happened at Clearview. And it doesn't matter if you tell me you don't believe the newspapers, because practically every other person in this town does."

"There was no evidence," she said. "They never had anything that pinned it to you guys."

"That's not enough to change people's opinions," I told her. "And you know that."

Her silence served as confirmation.

"This is what I mean," I continued. "This is why I didn't want to tell anyone. I only get one shot in Sherwood. If I blow it, I don't get to pack everything up and start over. I'm stuck here, whether things are good or bad."

She looked uncomfortable, and chewed on her lip. "There's something else."

"What?"

I watched her teeth graze her lip, again and again, rubbing the flesh raw. "God, I don't know how to tell you this."

Though I didn't say anything, my silent insistence could be felt in the air, urging her to continue. She'd said it now; there was no going back.

"I was mad the other day, okay? It all got the better of me. I was mad that you still didn't trust me—at least not enough to tell me on your own. I snapped at you, and I was in a bad mood all through the council meeting . . ."

She inhaled deeply and shook her head. We were approaching a line of traffic, a red light somewhere up ahead, and the car rolled to a stop. "Claire caught up with me afterward. We were talking for a while, and she asked me if everything was okay. I didn't mean to tell her, but you know what she's like. Too nice for her own good.

That girl could talk anyone into telling her their secrets. Even me."

"You . . . you told Claire?"

"I know. I'm sorry. It wasn't my place to go spreading it around, but I was mad, and Claire wanted to listen . . ." She trailed off. "I guess I didn't emphasize the *secret* part strongly enough. She went back to a couple of her teammates—I guess she wanted to tell them she'd cracked your secret to doing so well in gym. I didn't know she would gossip."

My mouth had gone dry, my tongue suddenly feeling like sandpaper. There were so many things I could've said, but at that moment, none sprang to mind. The realization was too big to swallow, like a pill that wouldn't quite go down.

I didn't want to believe it. I *couldn't* believe it.

"I'm sorry, Corey. I shouldn't have told anyone. It's my fault."

"What are you saying?" I managed to choke out. "Are you saying that everybody . . . ?"

"I don't know how many people know," she said, in the matter-of-fact tone I'd come to associate her with. Even now, Kim was as consistent as ever. "I don't know how far it's spread. I just think you've got the right to know what you're walking into."

She glanced over, as somewhere up ahead the light turned green and the first cars started to move off. "I really am sorry," she said, and something in her voice told me she was sincere. "You've got every right to be mad."

I knew she was right. Surely that was the typical reaction for a situation like this one. My best friend had jeopardized the secret I'd been trying to keep for months. I didn't deserve it, and yet it had happened anyway.

But, strangely, I didn't feel angry. The rising unease overpowered everything else, causing me to focus instead on what would happen when I stepped into the school hallway. Who knew what would be waiting for me? The thought alone was nauseating, but there was also something else.

A note of finality. Deep down, I knew something like this had to happen eventually. I couldn't coast through the rest of high school—if I was stuck here for that long—with something so big still hidden. As Luke's situation had proved, the weight on my shoulders would crush me eventually—and the secret would have to come out, one way or another.

Really, it was as if Kim had done me a favor.

I had to face up to things eventually. Living in fear was no way to get by, even in high school. The time had come to tackle the consequences head on.

"Well, I know what I'm walking into," I began quietly, as Kim eased her foot onto the gas and the car moved forward again, putting everything into motion, "so I guess I need someone to walk into it with."

I'd never seen a smile so full of relief as the one that appeared across her face. "And that," she said, "is where I can help."

~

As it turned out, our optimism—and what I now couldn't help thinking of as *we're-all-in-this-together* bullshit—didn't last long. We were confident as we pulled into the school parking lot, but once Kim shut off the engine, and I realized we actually had to get out of the car, things started to go downhill.

We headed toward the main doors, where Kim shot me an encouraging smile. But once we made it through them, emerging in the hallway that was already buzzing with activity, it was clear I was going to need a lot more than gentle reassurance.

Perhaps I imagined it. Perhaps it was my overactive mind coming into play. But I was pretty sure a wave of quiet *did* fall over the hall as I set foot inside. Several dozen heads turned in my direction, and I was suddenly under the scrutiny of everybody in the vicinity. Kim sensed it too. She stepped forward with unnatural purpose, each foot carefully placed in front of the other, as if one wrong move could thrust everything into chaos.

I walked with her, slowly, feeling like the pair of us were edging our way into a lion's den. Once we'd moved several yards forward, the whispers broke out. Everywhere I turned, someone would lean toward their friend, murmuring something just out of earshot; I didn't have to be a genius of Kim's caliber to work out they weren't compliments.

Others weren't so careful. As I strode past a huddle of sophomore girls, with as much confidence as I could fake, the words *trailer trash* crossed the space between us, with no effort to lower the tone.

"Come on," Kim muttered, tugging on my arm. "Let's get away from here."

Wherever we went, however, there was no improvement. The junior hallway was just as bad as any other. Kids I recognized from various classes—most of who would have politely acknowledged me before—were now making no effort to conceal looks of distaste, and some even stepped back as I moved past.

It felt like I was carrying a contagious disease.

Farther down the hall, I spotted Landon, who, to acknowledge my arrival, put down the freshman he had pinned against the wall. As I brushed past, praying for him to keep quiet, his voice rang out more viciously than any other.

"God, can you believe I almost hooked up with that?" he said loudly, pulling a face. "Now there's a lucky escape—who knows what I would've caught from her?"

Just like that, something in me snapped. I spun on my heel, putting Landon and me face to face, despite the inches he had over me. A slight pressure on my arm told me Kim had grabbed it, but the words were already out of my mouth.

"The only person who would've caught anything, Landon," I spat with confidence fueled by anger, "is *me*. God knows how many STIs you're carrying."

Landon stepped forward threateningly. "What did you just say, you little shit?"

"You heard me," I said, forcing myself to keep our eyes locked. His own beady pair were narrowed, while a twisted look of loathing soured his face, but I was determined not to give him the satisfaction of making me run.

"You've got some nerve," he growled. "As if I'd ever want to go near you again now I know what you are. Fucking circus freak."

I wanted to hit back with something, but I didn't get the chance. Kim's grip on my arm tightened, and she pulled me away. Landon called something after me, but I didn't catch what. It was probably better that way.

"He's not worth it," Kim said, as we pushed through the small crowd that had gathered. "None of these bullies are worth it. They're all idiots."

"Easy enough for you to say," I replied quietly. "You're not the circus kid fresh off the back of a trailer."

Though most people weren't bold enough to start anything like Landon, the whispering was just as bad. The news had traveled like wildfire, spreading through the entire student body, with no freshman or senior left in ignorance. Things like this didn't happen often, and novelty had its attraction.

Every whisper and muttered remark sapped my strength. Where

I'd once been confident, ready to deflect Landon's comments with a sharp retort, I could feel myself shrinking. What I'd been afraid of all this time was now reality. I was stuck in a nightmare, with no option but to face it head on.

"Corey?"

It was the first time I'd heard my name instead of an insult, but when I turned my head, the reality hit me harder. Because there was Claire, standing in the middle of the hallway, her face washed out by a noticeable lack of makeup, and her eyes glazed with a guilty sheen. She was reaching out as if to touch my arm, but instinct pulled me away before she could get there.

"I need to talk to you," she said, almost pleadingly. "Please give me a chance to explain."

I could see no trace of maliciousness in her expression; upon first glance, it really did seem like she regretted what she'd done. But the damage couldn't be undone now, and the last thing I wanted was to stand there and listen to her excuses. Not here, not now.

"Don't bother," I snapped, and with that, I was already walking away.

When I finally reached my locker—the area surrounding which was strangely deserted—it only got worse.

Last week it had been plain blue metal. Now, splattered across the locker in thick white paint, were two words. Two single words that sent my heart plummeting.

Circus freak.

I couldn't help it. At any other point in my life, the words would've been water off a duck's back, and yet they suddenly felt like the final straw. Everything hit me at once: the embarrassment, the stinging sensation of everybody's eyes on my back, the realization that this time, there was no running away.

It was all too much. Tears pooled in my eyes, though I was doing all I could to hold them back. I could feel myself crumbling, whole chunks breaking right off, forming a pile of dust at my feet. I had spent so long building myself up, and it was all coming down. Just like that.

Kim sensed it; she was looking at me, her eyes full of concern. "Corey."

But I wasn't going to stick around to hear it. I couldn't stand another minute in the hallway, where so many eyes were trained on me, judging, like they knew me at all. Nausea rose from the pit of my stomach, my head spinning. I had to get out of there.

There was no need to shove as I dashed down the hall; everyone seemed to clear a path anyway, maintaining the safe distance of a quarantine. The colors of the hallway blurred into masses of blue and white, but I managed to stumble my way to the nearest bathroom.

Thankfully, it was empty. I didn't have any strength left for myself, let alone enough to hold it together for anyone else.

Once safely inside a stall, the door forming a much-needed barrier between me and the rest of the world, I collapsed onto the toilet and sobbed.

After everything, I had nothing left.

~

I expected the worst—and I was right.

The kids at school already had their opinions, and they weren't about to change them. Sherwood's local media—and no doubt the anger of wealthy parents who'd had stakes in Clearview—had burrowed deeper under their skin than the redeeming personality of a new classmate ever could. One stupid newspaper editorial had taught them all they wanted to know about circus life, and drawn the boundary that stopped them taking about anything else. Their bottom line was clear: we were criminals, lying and stealing to make a living, and leaving damage in our wake.

Only a few assholes piled on the real abuse, but nobody else made an attempt to step in. No longer could I walk down the hallway or into a classroom without being followed by a trail of whispers. Most kids took to ignoring me, out of fear of being picked on by Landon or the other main perpetrators if they did anything else.

And that was all it came down to, really. The fear of what other people would say—it had taken over all of our lives.

Even mine. Especially mine.

A day was all I had strength for. I was close to tears by the time I returned home again, making an excruciating attempt to hold myself together in Kim's car as she drove me home. Luke had been absent from school again, though I'd expected nothing less. I didn't know what was going on with him, and it didn't seem likely I ever would.

I put on a brave face for my mom, unable to get up to my room fast enough. Once inside, with the door safely shut behind me, I fell onto the bed and buried my face in the pillow. Only here, the one spot of isolation in an entire town, could I get away from it all.

Maybe I'd made up my mind already, in some subconscious way. Or maybe it was just the thought of returning to Franklin to repeat the whole thing tomorrow, and countless times after, that did it for me. Either way, when my eyes wandered over to the cell phone on my desk, it had never been clearer. I knew what I had to do.

My hands trembled as I dialed the number, a combination of digits I hadn't pressed in weeks but still remembered perfectly. I struggled to keep my breathing under control as I lifted the phone to my ear, waiting for the voice on the other end.

After this, there'd be no going back.

Which was probably what made it so appealing.

When the ringing was cut off, and the voice on the line sounded in my ear, it was so unexpectedly familiar that I struggled to keep it together.

"Dave," I forced out, just as my voice threatened to crack. "It's me. Listen, I don't care what Aunt Shelby says—I'm coming back."

CHAPTER TWENTY-FIVE

There was a moment of silence on the line, and it seemed to go on forever.

When I did get a reply, it wasn't the one I'd been holding out for. "What?"

At first, I wondered if I hadn't made myself clear enough. "It's Corey."

There was another pause, along with some rustling in the background. "No, no, I got that part. I just . . . what are you talking about?"

"What else would I be talking about?" I asked, frowning. "This place, of course. And the circus. I'm coming back."

He laughed then, though I couldn't see the humor in the situation. "Good luck with that. I mean, you can try, but you're dreaming if you think Aunt Shelby won't march you right back where you came from."

"I don't care. She can't force me. Tell me where you guys are."

"Corey."

"*Dave*," I pressed, impatience seeping into my tone. "Seriously, I'm not playing around. I know she's not going to be happy that I've gone behind her back, but I don't care. I'll deal with that later. Tell me where you guys are staying right now, because I'm coming to find you."

With that, I could sense a shift in atmosphere between us, and every trace of joking evaporated from Dave's end of the line. "Whoa, whoa, whoa. Slow down. What's going on?"

"I can't do this anymore," I told him, pulling myself into a sitting position on my bed so my knees were against my chest. "The kids at school found out about everything."

All at once, Landon's stinging words came back to me with as much impact as the first time around. *Fucking circus freak.* Just like that, the label was scrawled on my forehead, with all the permanence of a tattoo. The damage was done; no amount of scrubbing would get rid of it.

The other end of the line stayed quiet, so I took this as my cue to continue.

"This town . . . it's something else," I told him. "It's got history I didn't know about. They think Mystique vandalized a luxury housing development last year, and rumors have been flying around since we left. People are looking at me like I'm a criminal."

"What are you talking about? We didn't vandalize anything."

"I know we didn't," I said, unsure why I felt so defensive when it was Dave I was talking to. "But try telling that to anybody here. There were no other leads, and we were in the wrong place at the wrong time. We were the easiest people to blame."

"Corey, I think you might be overreacting. We didn't have anything to do with it, so they can't have any evidence—"

"Evidence doesn't *matter*, Dave," I interjected, unable to soften the cutting edge of my voice. "It's the way people look at me, how they treat me, like they can't even stand to be *near* me—"

"Corey." There was something in Dave's voice I couldn't put my finger on, something that was completely foreign to our dynamic. Our opinions overlapped more often than not, whether by coincidence or a choice on his end, and disagreements were few and far between. I'd grown so accustomed to reassurance from him that a clash of opinion was a shock to the system. "You can't be telling me that *everybody* at school hates you."

"Well, maybe not," I said, "but they're all too scared of those who do to say otherwise."

There was another pause on his end, and I was beginning to take each one as a bad sign. The conversation definitely wasn't swinging the way I thought it would; part of me was wondering if Dave had been the right person to turn to after all. I'd been seeking reassurance, a source of comfort. The one person I'd thought guaranteed to give it was proving me wrong.

"How long has it been?"

I stopped, confused. "What do you mean?"

"How long have you given it? Since they found out, I mean."

I started chewing on my lip, already guessing what was coming. "Well, I mean, it only happened today, but . . ."

"*Today?*" His disbelief crackled through the line. I probably should've expected this reaction, but everything felt so hopeless already—surely I didn't need to face another day to confirm what I already knew. "Come on, Corey. Are you honestly telling me you're ready to give all this up after one day?"

"Well, yeah." I could imagine him shaking his head somewhere, cooped up within the boxed walls of his trailer. "But it's not going to get any better. I know that much. You should've seen them today. They were acting like I had some kind of disease they were afraid of catching. I can't go back and face that."

"Why not?"

The sudden urge to raise my voice came over me, but I managed to restrain myself. One thing was clear—the phone call was helping to curb my tears, even if it did make me want to scream in frustration. "What do you mean, *why not*? Isn't it obvious?"

"Come on, Corey."

I took a deep breath, listening to the sound of his voice, now slow and soothing. Something familiar, at least, to latch onto. "You're just like the rest of us. We've been dealing with this kind of shit all our lives. You know how to handle it."

"This is different," I said, quietly. "You know it is. I can't move on from all this. I'm stuck."

"Okay, so you can't physically move on," he admitted, "but that doesn't mean you have to run away. It's been *one day*. You don't know what's going to happen tomorrow or the next day or the next. I don't know how long it'll take, but it *will* get better. Eventually."

Fresh tears were already brimming in my eyes, though I wasn't exactly sure why. Maybe it was having the truth laid out so plainly in front of me—and from the person I had least expected it from. One day wasn't an indication of forever, and I knew that, as much as it was hard to admit.

There was no way to gauge the long-term situation at Franklin from one day. The news was so fresh, everybody's heads still reeling with the discovery. Gossip would move elsewhere as the weeks melted into each other. But that didn't make today any easier.

It appeared that I had vastly underestimated Dave. Though it could have been the separation, which had dragged us further apart than ever before, it felt like something more. Maybe I'd never really known him that well at all. It had seemed a safe bet that he'd sneak me back into the circus the moment I reached out. I thought that was what we both wanted.

And yet, in the space of a phone call, that view had been shattered.

"Everything's going to be okay," he said, in a voice so calm and level it almost had me believing him. "I can feel it. Things are going to work themselves out."

"How long?" I asked.

"What do you mean?"

"How long do I have to give it?" I repeated, closing my eyes and clutching the phone a little tighter to my ear.

I wanted specifics, but that didn't seem to be on offer. "Long enough," he replied simply. "Look, Corey. You don't need to worry about that. Things will straighten themselves out more quickly than you think, and then you'll wonder why you even called me in the first place."

"I miss it," I whispered. "I miss the circus."

I wasn't quite sure what made me say it. Something inside, powerful and heady, had taken over, a wave of nostalgia for everything I'd been without for the last three months.

I wanted to go back. Of course I did. That fact would always remain, hidden in the back of my mind, no matter how much things in Sherwood improved. For as long as I was away from it all, I'd miss the five a.m. wake-ups, mornings spent wrapped around that flimsy trapeze. I'd miss the glint of pride in Silver's eyes each time she watched me nail a new routine, and the way she clapped me on the back the moment my feet hit the ground. I'd miss the buzz of anticipation, the excitement that came with arriving in a new town, the roar of the crowd on opening night. I'd miss the people who had been my true family.

It seemed like such a simple case of wanting, but Dave's next words forced me to reconsider.

"I know," he said, in a quiet voice not unlike my own. "So do I."

And in that moment, I understood. What had happened that first night in Sherwood had not taken me away from the circus; it had taken the circus away from all of us. It didn't matter that I'd been forced out for my own well being by Aunt Shelby, separated from everybody else. Even for those still moving from one temporary pitch to another—wherever those happened to be—things had shifted beyond recognition.

Going back wouldn't solve anything. It wouldn't erase the fire, the turning point at which our world had changed around us. I may have moved on, but that didn't mean I'd left it all behind. Whatever I'd been left with—no less than the others—I'd taken with me.

I didn't know what awaited me at school the following day, nor if it would be better or worse than what had been thrown at me that morning. Only one thing was certain: I was going to have to walk straight into it.

~

I didn't tell anyone about my conversation with Dave. Not Kim, not George, and especially not my mother. In a strange way, it felt like a dark secret; I was ashamed of the fact that I'd considered giving up, even if I hadn't gone all the way.

The next day at school was pretty much the same, but as the week wore on, things got a little easier. Dave's advice had given me a new sense of realism, and I'd come to accept the fact that change wouldn't be instantaneous. Idiots like Landon would still be there each morning I showed up to school, as would the comments he threw loudly across the hall whenever we crossed paths. Still, I felt like I was building up some kind of immunity to it. The more insults he threw my way, the easier it became to ignore them, and most of the time I would laugh about their stupidity afterward with Kim and George, and his increasing desperation to get a reaction actually made for some hilarious conversation.

Landon and his cronies' opinions ruled the school; most people either agreed with them or were too scared to say otherwise. Still, as the days wore on and gossip turned to fresh scandals, it seemed the contagious plague I carried began to dissipate. People no longer went out of their way to ignore me, and several acquaintances even struck up a conversation.

It was stupid that this was any kind of milestone, but the progress was reassuring nonetheless.

Luke, however, had turned into a mystery of gigantic proportions. Contact had dried up since our argument, and all attempts to call him only got me as far as his voice mail. The silence between us swelled with each day, and I was starting to wonder if we would ever speak again. He hadn't shown his face in school since it had all happened, and judging by the snatches of gossip I overheard in the hall, nobody had heard from him.

I soon resigned myself to the fact that I had ruined it completely. I had no idea where Luke was even living; for all I knew, he could already have left for Washington, two states away. After the argument, I wasn't expecting a good-bye.

My chance was gone. I had to focus on something else.

And as it turned out, about a week after my phone call with Dave, that *something else* came right to me.

It was the end of the school day, and I was at my locker retrieving the books I needed for that night's homework when someone appeared behind me. Their lingering presence was impossible to ignore; at first, I just assumed it was somebody waiting for me to move so they could get to their own locker. But once I slipped my books into my bag and turned around, I realized it was much more than that.

"Claire," I said, surprised.

She looked slightly more put together than the last time I'd seen her, her face bronzed by a light layer of makeup and her hair pulled back into a slick ponytail—but that couldn't mask the uncertainty in her eyes, or the way she'd left a safe distance between us.

"Corey," she began. "I completely get it if you don't ever want to see my face again, but . . . is there a chance we could talk?"

I thought it would be easy to walk away. Claire was the reason I'd had to endure this nightmare of a week, and that hardly made me want to reach out for a catch-up. But there was something about the sight of her that stopped me.

"Please," she said, when the silence between us stretched slightly too long. "I'm not going to try and justify what I did. I just . . . I really want to talk."

There was no obligation for me to give in. If I wanted, I could walk away right then, and never have to speak to her properly again. I *thought* that was what I wanted. But with the choice right in front of me, I couldn't bring myself to shake my head.

"Okay," I said, closing the locker behind me. "I'm willing to listen."

The smile that spread across her face was full of relief, and I could almost see the weight being lifted from her shoulders.

"Thank you," she breathed, like the air was rushing out of her all at once. "Shall we go somewhere quieter?"

The bustle of the hallway had blurred into one continuous backdrop, one I'd got so used to in my time at Franklin that I barely noticed it anymore, but I knew she was right. If we were going to do this, we should do it properly.

So I nodded. "Okay," I told her. "Lead the way."

CHAPTER TWENTY-SIX

School was letting out, with streams of people making for the exit and parking lot, so Claire and I headed for the football field. It wasn't completely empty; there was a practice going on at the far end, where I could see the football players running through drills in the distance, balls sailing through the air as the players passed them to one another. The late afternoon sunshine warmed our backs as we climbed to the top of the bleachers and sat down.

There were a few people watching the practice, but they were at the other end of the field. We were in no danger of being overheard.

For a long while, we didn't say anything, both of our gazes fixed on the football practice.

Eventually, she looked over. "I know you probably don't even want to be having this conversation," she said, her voice low and quiet. "You probably hate me . . . and I don't blame you. I kind of hate myself too."

"I don't hate you." I was surprised to hear myself say it, but it was true.

Claire just looked at me. "Well, you *should*. It was obvious there was a reason why you hadn't told anyone in all the time you'd been at Franklin—just like it was obvious what that reason was. I knew it was going to hurt you. And believe me . . . I've felt nothing but guilt since."

She sounded sincere, but it was nowhere near enough. All I could bring myself to do was look blankly at her. "Why did you do it, then?"

Her eyes dropped to her lap, where she'd laced her fingers together, rubbing her thumb over one patch of skin again and again. "I'm about to tell you something I haven't told anyone at school," she said. "Not on my own terms, at least. And this isn't supposed to be an excuse, or a justification . . . I just want to explain myself."

I stayed silent, waiting for her to continue.

She took a deep breath. "I've always known . . . I wasn't exactly straight," she said, and paused. "I've struggled with it for a while now—not being able to figure out what I want, pinning my whole identity on the slightest hint of attraction to anyone, boy or girl. It's only in the last couple of years that I've started to come to grips with how I feel. To stop feeling like I have to put a label on it. I've been scared of that label for a long time, but what I do know is . . . I like girls."

It seemed like she was squeezing her hands even tighter, gripping them with all her might. "It shouldn't even be a big deal," she said, "but you know what Sherwood's like. Everybody knows everybody's business, and once they know it, you can be sure they're going to judge you for it. Maybe they wouldn't say anything to my face, but they'd definitely be whispering behind my back. And I don't know, the thought of it . . . I can't handle it. I just want to be me, you know? I don't want there to be this dramatic reveal, all this gossip. Why can't I stay the person I've always been?"

Her words resonated deeply, and she must've known that. But I still couldn't resist chipping in. "Yeah," I said. "I know the feeling."

"It hasn't really made a difference until this point, to be honest," she continued. "I've never had a girlfriend, or even anything close, so there's been no reason for a big announcement. The first time something changed was when you walked into the gym, actually."

My eyes met hers, questioning; I wasn't convinced I'd heard her correctly. "What?"

"I thought you were cute, okay?" she said, with an embarrassed smile. "It feels weird to admit it now, but I did. And for the first time in my life, I thought *what the hell*—I'm going to strike up a conversation. If it didn't go anywhere, it didn't go anywhere, but it was worth a try."

I couldn't deny that I was taken aback. For all the suspicions I'd had about Claire's intentions, none of them had been even remotely close. "Wait, really?"

She nodded. "Yeah. Don't worry, I wasn't too heartbroken when I realized you were straight. Even just working up the courage to talk to you felt like a milestone to me."

There was a lingering smile on her face, a thoughtful expression that seemed to take her right back to that moment, but as the silence wore on it faded. "I guess it was that kind of confidence that got me into trouble."

"What do you mean?"

There was so much behind her eyes I couldn't decipher, a whole other world inside her head I was just beginning to see. But then she looked away, her gaze drifting toward the football field. "There was this girl at my party," she said eventually. "We got talking, and somewhere along the line we wound up kissing. It was such a breakthrough moment, you know? The first time I'd felt anything so *real* . . . but then it all came crashing down. Landon caught us. Of course, he thought he'd hit the jackpot. Couldn't wipe that sleazy smile off his face. I knew he'd be a dick about it, but . . . I really didn't expect him to hold it over my head and threaten to tell the entire school."

"No . . ."

"I *know* I've got nothing to be ashamed of. I *know* it shouldn't bother me. If I had any kind of integrity, I would've let him tell anybody he wanted and walk through it all with my head held high. But I just couldn't. I wasn't ready, and he had me trapped. I knew it would change everything . . . and I was willing to do whatever it took to stop that from happening."

Only then did I realize I was holding my breath, bracing myself for what was to come—because I felt like I had an idea already.

"When Kim told me about you, I thought it was the perfect distraction. I knew Landon had told a few of his idiot friends about me, because they all kept sniggering and making stupid gestures at me in the hallway. It was only a matter of time before it spread further. I thought . . . if I told everyone about you being in the circus, it would be big enough news that I could stay under the radar."

My fingers had curled themselves into my palms, leaving half-moon marks where the nail dug into the skin. There was anger . . . but there was also something else. Claire's explanation wasn't a bandage that would magically make this all better. Really, it couldn't change anything. But I also couldn't overlook the rawness of her expression, the way shame was carved into the lines of her face. She wasn't looking for a justification, a get-out-of-jail-free card. This entire conversation was drawing something out of her, from deep within, and she was giving herself over to the pain that came with that.

"I'm so sorry," she said. "And I know you probably won't believe me, but I regretted it as soon as I realized what I'd done. Realized I'd just deflected all the shit onto you because I was too weak to take it myself. And when you walked into the hallway that day . . . God, I've never hated myself more."

I looked at her. "As much as everyone else hates me?"

Whatever she'd been about to say seemed to get lost, because her mouth closed without her saying anything. It was only after a couple of seconds of tense silence that she spoke. "If they hate you, they're idiots," she said. "Total and utter idiots. Which is why it makes me even more pathetic that I'm scared of them seeing the real me. You've been nothing but nice to everybody, but because of some stupid rumor, you're suddenly the worst person to walk the Earth? Maybe I'd have believed it before, but not now. Not now I know you."

"Well," I said. "That makes one person."

"It's not just me," she insisted. "Not everyone thinks that way. And if they *do* decide to believe the shit that comes out of Landon's mouth, then are they really worth associating with? That's what I'm trying to tell myself. That I know who my true friends are, and . . . well, fuck everyone else."

I couldn't manage even the smallest smile. "That's brave of you," I told her. "I wish I could think the same way."

She stared at me strangely. "Are you saying you *don't*?"

I shook my head. "Not really," I said. "Maybe it's supposed to feel liberating, now I no longer have the weight of this huge secret on my shoulders. But it doesn't. Instead, I've spent the whole week wishing I could go back to how things were."

"Well, you definitely don't show it."

I raised my eyebrows.

"No, really," she went on. "I'm not just saying that. I don't know anybody else who would've walked down that hallway with their head held so high. And what you said to Landon—I certainly wouldn't have the nerve. Give yourself some credit."

It was, of course, entirely possible that this was just a sweetener, a neat coating of sugar so her apology would go down easier. The more skeptical side of me could argue that all day. But she couldn't fake the glint in her eye that told me it *was* something resembling admiration. And once I'd seen it, I knew she was sincere.

"I really am sorry, Corey," she said. "And I don't expect you to forgive me. I know what you've been through must make my issues seem pathetic, but I'm still here saying it. It's just something I need to get out there."

She was right. She'd had her chance to explain herself, and I'd already been generous by giving her that. Despite the fact it had been a heavier conversation than I'd been expecting, and all the clues in her mannerisms that confirmed this wasn't one big sympathy act, I still didn't owe her anything.

"Honestly," I began, "I'm not mad at you anymore. I know I should be, and I can't deny that I was for the first few days, but I just don't have it in me anymore. Yeah, it was a shitty thing to do, and people reacted just as shitty as I expected. But . . . I couldn't stay hidden forever. Sooner or later, the truth was going to come out."

There was something more to my wistful gaze, which got lost as I stared into the distance, focusing so far beyond the pitch that the football players became a single blurred haze. The truth *had* had to come out, and though it had been far from painless, it did feel like something had aligned in the process. I'd been convinced I had to force down one side of me, but there was only so long I could do so before it jumped back up like a coiled spring. I wasn't plain old Corey anymore. All of me was on show, and I had no choice but to deal with it.

I knew the people who were worth anything were still by my side. Kim and George hadn't gone anywhere, and the people in the circus were only a phone call away at any time of day. But there was one person in particular I kept thinking of, one I desperately wished was here to see it through with me.

Claire and I had slipped into companionable silence, her apology having settled between us, but I knew I had to ask.

"Claire," I said.

She looked over. "Yeah?"

The question was out before I could stop it. "Have you heard anything from Luke?"

Her eyes gave away the answer before she could say anything, and I got a good enough glimpse before she ducked her head. A stab of hope—or was it dread?—shot through my chest, forcing an intake of breath that stayed there until my lungs felt like they were going to burst.

"Yeah," she said eventually. There was so much balanced on the single word that it threatened to crack under the weight, and the pause that followed was even more precarious. Just when I thought I couldn't bear it any longer, Claire looked up. "Look, I don't think I should say too much. It's not fair to him. He's had a rough week, but . . . he's okay. I promise."

There was much more to it—that was obvious—but I could understand her apprehension, and her reasons for being so vague. It wouldn't feel right coming from her, anyway. If Luke had something to say, he would have to say it himself.

Perhaps Claire could sense my resignation, twisted with disappointment, because she leaned in a little closer. "I know how it feels," she said, "but sooner or later he's going to realize he needs you."

~

It was this line that echoed in my mind long after Claire and I finished talking. I was still hearing it as I made my way through the near-empty school, and, as the buses were already gone, began the walk home.

I so badly wanted to believe it, to cling to the hope that Luke would show up again and stay long enough for us to straighten things out. I needed him to know I only wanted the best for him—then and now. But there was only so much reassurance a fleeting comment from Claire could give. And what did she know, really? She hadn't seen the vicious edge to our last conversation, and the way it had created a bottomless rift between us. Perhaps there was no coming back from that.

I'd all but convinced myself that was true when the message came through just a day later.

I was coming out of precalculus when my phone buzzed in my pocket. I assumed it was Kim, asking if I wanted a ride to the gym, like she'd been giving me a couple of times a week. Instead, when the name *Luke* flashed onscreen, I almost tripped over my own feet.

I'm sorry. Can we talk?

And then, a second message, almost like a nervous afterthought.

Can we meet at Joe's at 5? If not, I'll understand.

My heart pounded as I wove through the busy hallway, staring down at my phone and narrowly avoiding the oncoming stream of students. A million questions ran through my mind, but I wasn't going to get the answers to any of them from two short lines of text.

This was what I'd been waiting for, but suddenly I was doubting myself again. Was this even the right thing to do? Would going to meet him interfere with my attempt to get back on track, if all he had to break was bad news?

However, the thought of ignoring the message—of leaving him sitting at Joe's alone—was too much to bear. I couldn't walk away without getting answers. Whatever lay ahead, I knew I had to face it.

I got home, threw my stuff down quickly, and paused just long enough to leave my mother a note. She was more than used to my after-school arrangements, and probably wouldn't worry upon coming home to an empty house, but it was a habit that seemed wrong to break. The words came much more easily now, without the worry that she would scrutinize each one. I was out of the door by four forty-five.

For the entire journey my heart was in overdrive. I couldn't work out anything from Luke's cryptic text, and there was no way to know what I was heading into. But I kept going. Because when it came to Luke—the guy I could never get out of my head, however hard I tried—there was no other option.

I approached Joe's with a sense of weighty anticipation. It had been a while since I'd visited; it had felt wrong to go back without Luke, like I would've been betraying tradition by going alone. The diner, however, looked the same as ever—the flashing sign was still missing several bulbs, and the parking lot was almost empty, the entire place looking like it could do with a little love. It wouldn't have felt right any other way.

I took a deep breath before I stepped inside, the bell tinkling as the door opened. I could see him at the counter, a head of blond, caught dead center between neat and messy, turned away from the door. He must've heard someone come in, but I wondered if he was afraid to turn around.

I forced myself to take a step closer, and then another, each one shaky and uncertain. There was no time to have second thoughts, because before I realized it, the space had dwindled into nothing. I was there.

Ready for whatever was coming next.

CHAPTER TWENTY-SEVEN

I was at home on the trapeze.

To most people, it probably seemed strange that I felt most comfortable suspended way above the ground, where all that existed was me and a simple rope setup. Up there, it was nothing but muscle: a careful balance of strength and flexibility. No complications. Practice made perfect. I always ran the risk of falling, of course, but for the most part I was in control.

Here, right now, things couldn't have felt more different.

Luke, sensing my presence behind him, eventually turned around. And that was it. We were face to face, with no opportunity to run away.

He didn't look how I expected. His face was brighter than usual, slightly nervous but containing more life than ever. Out of habit, I found myself searching for signs of infliction—receding bruises, tiny scratches, inflamed skin—but came up short. Even the skin around his left eye was clear.

He spoke first. "Hi."

My own greeting got lost somewhere in my throat. Just as Luke started looking at me strangely, it managed to break through. "Hey."

I wondered if the awkwardness was spreading beyond our own little space; surely the whole diner could feel it. And yet all around, life was ongoing: quiet chatter formed a continuous backdrop, coffee mugs clattered on metal tabletops, the jukebox shuffled a quiet selection. This was a matter that concerned only us, and everybody else went about their own business, blissfully ignorant.

His eyes flickered to the stool beside him, and I took that as my cue to lower myself onto it. My jacket had barely been shrugged from my shoulders when the waitress appeared at the counter.

"You two again?" she asked, with a smile that suggested she was completely unaware of the underlying tension. "Our real regulars. We've missed you these past few weeks."

She put me on the spot, but Luke's charm was effortless, unfaltering. "I've been missing this place too," he told her, with a smile. "Couldn't keep myself away for too long."

"Tell you what," she said. "I'll fix you two those favorite milk shakes of yours—on the house. Since you haven't been around in so long."

"Thank you," I said, smiling gratefully, as she scurried off to the kitchen.

There was nothing left to do then but turn to face Luke, whose presence beside me was having a disconcerting effect on my ability to speak. Trying to maintain a level tone, I said, "So. What's going on?"

He brought his hands onto the countertop, already beginning to twiddle his thumbs. We were both visibly nervous, almost like we were drawing it out of each other. I watched him swallow. "I think we, uh . . . have a few things to talk about."

"Yeah," I said. "No kidding."

"Well, first things first, I guess." He took a deep breath. "I just . . . I really have to apologize for everything. There's no use jumping into this conversation before we establish that."

"Right." My voice came out louder than I expected; my confidence was slowly returning. Thank God. "Apologies."

"I know I was out of order. Me coming over to your house that night . . . Jesus, I can't believe I acted like such a dick. I guess it all came as a shock, you know? Everything seemed to kick off all at once, and I was just mad about it all. You seemed like the easiest person to blame at the time."

"Well," I said, "you did have a point."

"No, I didn't." The words were definitive. "And I shouldn't have made you think that I did. It was completely uncalled for, showing up like that, causing an argument. Anger got the better of me. I wasn't thinking straight.

"Of course you were worried about me. You watched my dad almost knock me out, for crying out loud. I guess . . ." His voice trailed off, slipping into a small pocket of silence among the hubbub of the diner. "I guess I forgot that wasn't a normal thing to see. It's just, when you're living in the middle of something like that, you kind of get used to it . . ."

He shook his head, as if trying to think better of it. "Of course, it's not normal. It took me a little while to remember. It was unreasonable to expect you'd keep quiet after seeing something like that. And then for me blow up at you for doing the right thing—"

"It wasn't that simple," I pointed out. "There wasn't a right and a wrong—"

"No, Corey." The interjection cut me off, but his tone remained soft. "There was. I knew it, really. It was going to happen eventually.

It *had* to. I guess I'd just got so used to everything being a secret, realizing that somebody actually knew was kind of overwhelming."

"I understand."

"But now I owe you one huge apology. None of this was your fault. I have to stop blaming everything on other people and focus on who's really at fault: my dad.

"I've spent so long covering up for him. God knows how many times I've had to lie through my teeth trying to protect him. Like he even deserved protecting in the first place."

Luke yet to take his eyes off me, that striking shade of blue piercing my own. With anybody else, it probably would've been unsettling, but Luke seemed to have retained his knack for making everything between us feel natural.

"It's just crazy that it's taken me so long to see it, you know? Some of the stuff I did, I just . . ." He ducked his head, like the shame was truly starting to seep in. "Like that fight with Landon on your first day. You remember that, right?"

"Yeah," I said. "Pretty hard to forget."

He grimaced, like it hurt to recall. "It wasn't really a fight at all. My dad . . . well, he lost his temper the night before. Threw something and it hit me clean across the face. In the morning I woke up with this horrific bruise. I knew everybody would be asking me what happened."

I knew what was coming; the realization echoed with every pulse of my heart, even before the words were spoken aloud.

"I picked a fight with Landon on purpose. Said whatever I could to get him riled up. And when he took a swing at me . . . well, there was my explanation."

The waitress had dropped off our drinks without a word, appearing to sense we were in the middle of something, vanishing to leave us to it. When the word escaped my mouth, it was barely louder than a whisper. "Luke . . ."

"I know. Sounds crazy when you put it like that, right?" He sighed. "And yet at the time, it seemed so *normal* . . ."

My heart was pounding now, an unrelenting drumbeat in my chest. I'd assumed I knew the worst of what had been going on with Luke, and yet somehow I was in for a second round of shock. All I could think about was how much he'd been dealing with all the time we'd known each other. Though he wouldn't want me feeling guilty, that was hardly enough to stop me.

"Still. Things are changing, and I feel like it's finally time to start moving on, you know?"

"So what happens now?"

It was the question I'd been terrified to ask, but it had to happen sometime. The truth was already on its way out, ripping through the fabric of our relationship, and we couldn't hold it back any longer.

The look on Luke's face was impossible to decipher. "Well, that's kind of one of the things I wanted to talk to you about."

"Oh," I said. "Okay."

"You don't need to look so worried," he said with a small smile. "It's not that bad. Well, I mean . . . depends how you take it, I guess."

"And you tell me not to be worried."

He started fidgeting again, rubbing one thumb against the other in a repetitive motion, unable to meet my gaze.

"The police case got pretty intense. Somewhere in the middle of it, they realized how serious things were. I told too much of the truth to go back on my word. My dad was arrested, and they detained him right away. But that wasn't all. They started searching the house for evidence to build a case, and . . ."

As his words trailed off, our eyes locked in a way that held more significance than it should have. "I swear, I didn't know, Corey. You've got to believe me on that one. What they found . . . I had no idea until the cops told me."

My heart was in my throat, and I tried desperately to swallow over it. "What?" I pressed. The suspense was suffocating. "What are you talking about?"

"I want to tell you this myself. I have to. Before it comes out everywhere else."

"Come on, Luke." I forced myself to laugh, but the sound was painfully unnatural, and we both knew it. "Don't keep me waiting here."

"The fire at the circus . . ." His voice trailed off, dwindling into silence before he willed himself to continue. "He was involved. I mean, maybe he didn't do the real dirty work, but he was definitely involved."

"What?"

I could barely hear my own voice. The ringing in my ears had overtaken everything, leaving no room for anything else. The words coming out of Luke's mouth seemed to have an impact of their own, threatening to shove me backward. My head was reeling, unable to focus, and though Luke was talking, I could barely distinguish each word from the next.

"He's always been damn good at keeping secrets, but *this* . . ."

"What?" I whispered, too quietly for anybody to hear.

"He didn't know I was there that night. He didn't know he could've killed his own son—"

Suddenly, the words broke through the barrier, and my confusion was replaced with something else: white-hot, stinging anger. "It was *him*?"

"I swear, Corey, I didn't know until now. I never thought he'd do anything like that."

"Why?" I blurted out, way past the stage of being able to think about what I was saying. "Why the hell would he do something like that? Why would *anyone*?"

Luke ducked his head, and I could see his hands fidgeting in his lap. "They found evidence," he said, in a small voice. "Emails and messages on his computer. Correspondences with whoever else was in on it."

"Why?" I repeated.

"Do you remember I told you before that my dad's company was responsible for marketing the properties in Clearview Heights?" he asked, and I nodded. There was a pause. "Well, I may have played that down a little . . ."

"What?"

"You'd just found out about all the rumors, and I didn't want you to think I was part of spreading them, okay?" he said. "He *was* doing the marketing . . . but what I didn't mention is that he's also one of the investors in the development. When the sale prices went down . . . he lost a lot of money."

"And that makes it okay, does it?"

"No!" His voice was loud enough to cause several other diners in the vicinity to turn around. "Of course it doesn't. It's sick, and twisted, and I can't believe I'm related to somebody who would even *think* about doing that. You have to trust me when I say I had *no idea* . . ."

"What's going to happen to him?" I asked. "Surely after all that, he won't be able to just walk free?"

"As it's looking right now," Luke said, "he hasn't got a chance. If he's charged with arson, not to mention assault, he'll be locked up for years. Even if he gets the best lawyer in the business, the amount of evidence the cops have got on him is crazy. He'll never get off."

That, at least, came as some relief. I wasn't sure I could physically handle anything stronger than what was already rushing through me, let alone the knowledge that Mr. Everett would walk away unscathed. The thought of him in a jail cell was a mild comfort, although it did nothing to diminish my newly unearthed anger. It had been there, dormant, for a while now—three months with no progress in the investigation had buried it, but it wasn't gone. As it stood now, however, I realized I'd probably never get over it. How could I? Why one person would decide to destroy the livelihoods of over a hundred, risk the lives of hundreds more, for one pathetic bit of revenge, I'd never understand. Even from someone as ruthless and evil as Luke's father.

"There's something else," Luke said slightly nervously.

I looked up warily, which he noticed. "Don't worry, it's . . . an improvement. On what I just told you, anyway. Kind of.

"Mine and Claire's dad have pretty much equal shares in the real estate business. With my dad on trial, Mr. Delaney's taken over. Temporarily. Nothing's down on paper yet, but he's as good as told me he's looking to sell."

"Right," I said, not quite seeing the relevance.

"Claire's dad's always been a decent guy," he continued. "Got a bigger conscience than my dad, at least. He's putting the whole business on the market for someone else to take over, and there are a couple of buyers interested already. The deal's practically signed and sealed. And, well, here's the thing. The biggie, I guess."

"What?"

"He wants to set up a fund. A percentage of the profits from the sale will go into it, which will be . . . well, it'll be a shitload of money, put it that way. And he wants to donate it to the circus. To Mystique."

I heard the words, but in that moment I was convinced I'd got it wrong. "What?" I said, even though the echo of his voice was ringing in my head, amplified a million times over.

He wants to donate it all to the circus. To Mystique.

"He wants to help them set back up, Corey," Luke said. "The circus will finally be able to get back on its feet."

It was all a joke. It *had* to be a joke. He couldn't be telling me this, right here in the middle of Joe's, as an afterthought to everything that had already been uncovered. I felt ready to burst into tears, cry with laughter, or scream at the top of my lungs. Maybe even all three at once.

"What are you saying?" I murmured between the deep breaths I was now taking.

"I'm saying sorry," he said simply, as if that was all there was to it. "I'm saying sorry for everything, for all the ways me and my family screwed you over. And I'm saying you have a chance to start again. The chance you deserve."

"I can't . . . I don't . . ." I was stammering now, the words tangling themselves somewhere on the journey from my head to the open air. "You think I should leave Sherwood?"

I thought I saw a trace of confusion cross his face, but then again, maybe it wasn't wise to trust my brain in a moment like this one. Thoughts raced at the speed of light, ricocheting off the inside of my skull. If I didn't come out of this with a headache, I would consider it a miracle.

"Isn't that what you want?" he asked.

Suddenly, I found myself being transported back, an intense feeling of déjà vu, to our first moment in this very same spot. In front of me was a very different Luke, and yet so many things about him remained the same. Like the way he looked at me, as if I was a puzzle he wanted to figure out.

Before, it had been about trapeze. Now, though, it was all me.

"To go back to the circus," he continued. "That's where you belong, right?"

He was right, of course. Mystique was my home, and a couple of months spent in any town would never be enough to change that. Residence with my mother had always been a temporary arrangement, and while I had finally started to feel comfortable there, the circus was where I belonged.

But it also wasn't that simple.

"I don't . . ." I was struggling to get a grip on the words I wanted. "I mean . . . what about you?"

Luke's expression made it obvious we weren't done; there was still more to come. "Well," he said, suddenly shifty. "About that."

Part of me was afraid to hear what would follow, but the other part couldn't stop listening. It was like watching a horror movie, feeling so terrified that you found yourself hiding behind your hands and yet unable to resist peeking through your fingers anyway.

"This past week, I've been crashing at Claire's," he said, "but, uh . . . well, I can't stick around forever. Obviously."

"Yeah." I smiled weakly. "Right."

"I don't really have any other option. There's no way I can stay in that house, even if my dad never comes back to it. It's just too much. So, like I told you . . . I've been talking to my mom."

"What did she say about all this?"

"Well . . . the whole thing actually went better than I expected," he said, daring to let our eyes lock. "We started off emailing, but then we got to talking on the phone. I told her all about what went

300

on with my dad. I thought she would see it as a nuisance if I had to move to Washington, but . . . she's really on board with the idea."

Once again, my heart had started thumping. "She is?"

"Yeah."

I stayed still as his eyes searched my expression, but I was trying my hardest not to give anything away.

"I wouldn't have to move in with her new family if I didn't want to. She said she was willing to lend me what I needed to put a deposit on a place of my own, at least until I can get to the money my dad put away. I could start making plans for college. And then . . . we'd take it from there. If I wanted."

The question hung in the air between us, swelling with each moment, with so much presence it felt like I could reach out and grab it.

"Do you?" I asked eventually, fighting to keep the words even.

For a moment he didn't say anything, and for a second time I could feel the quiet seeping back between us. Behind us, the rest of the diner continued unconcerned, but I could only concentrate on Luke. Against a blurred backdrop, he'd never been more in focus.

He was looking right at me, and somehow that told me everything, before the words had even left his mouth.

"Yeah," he breathed eventually, and all at once the silence shattered. "I think I do."

The sensation that washed over me was an odd one; I couldn't work out whether things were being pieced back together or falling apart. Usually the two were polar opposites, boundaries cleanly cut and separated by miles, but this was different.

"When do you leave?" I managed to get out.

"Next week," he told me in a low voice. "I'm sorry."

"Why are you apologizing?" I asked, but my vision was already cracking, fragmented behind the sheen of my brimming tears. "This is a good thing. You're moving on."

"I know," he said quietly, "but it's not that simple. There are some things I don't want to move on from."

"You have to." I stopped then, correcting myself. "*We* have to. Both of us."

The words sounded so definitive, so sudden, that it felt as if I should take them back. But the fact stood that I couldn't; no matter how hard this was, both Luke and I had to face up to the truth. Our loose ends may have been tying themselves up, but that came with no guarantee that our ends would be knotted together.

"I'm sorry." Luke looked up at me then, and as soon as our eyes met, I felt the connection through every inch of my body. "I'm sorry that things couldn't work out between us."

"It's not your fault," I breathed. My eyes, still full of tears, reached their limit then, and I felt a single drop roll down my cheek. There was no going back.

I swallowed, remembering one of the things he'd said on that first afternoon in his house, a photograph of his mother between us. A moment that was both worlds away and as vivid as the day it happened. "You can't force things to work out if they're not supposed to, you know?"

He smiled then, a watery one, and it was as if I could really feel my heart aching. "Just promise me one thing, Corey."

I looked over. "What?"

"When I move, and you go back . . . promise that Mystique won't forget to set up in Rennerdale, Washington, sometime soon."

I laughed then, the sound contrasting sharply with the fresh tears now spilling over my cheeks, and let myself be pulled into the hug Luke was offering. As his arms locked in place around me and I rested my head in the space above his shoulder, I tried not to think about the fact that this was soon to be over. In a week he'd be gone, but right now there was nothing to do but immerse myself in the moment; we'd deal with everything that came after later.

"We won't," I said into the fabric of his shirt. "I'll make sure of it."

"I'll see you around, Corey Ryder," I heard him say from above me.

"You will," I told him. At that point, I lifted my head, meeting his gaze with a firm smile. "But I can't promise I'll hang around for long. Remember, we supercool trapeze artists are on a tight schedule."

We both laughed then, loudly and genuinely, until the only thing left to worry about was what would happen after we stopped.

SIX MONTHS LATER

This was it.

The glare of the spotlight danced across my face—not just the light, but blazing heat, too, a hot wash over my skin. Every muscle in my body ached in protest. Sweat pooled at the back of my neck, a sticky patch right at the base of my ponytail, but I kept going.

As if my heart didn't feel ready to burst right out of my chest. As if my arms weren't trembling under the strain of my entire body's weight.

I wouldn't stop. I couldn't stop. Because, in that moment, I'd never felt more alive.

I swung myself under the trapeze, hands gripping the wooden bar, with enough strength for the momentum to leave me vertical. Two seconds of perfect balance, toes pointed in the air. And then it was time to move on. A moment to right myself again, before my legs were curling themselves in the rope, my torso bending with them. I could hear nothing but the raw beat of the music, with none of its instrumental embellishments: just the pulsing rhythm to which I had to match my exact movements.

The track was swelling, my pace increasing with the knowledge that the end of the routine was approaching. Silver had changed some elements over the past few months, but our big finish remained the same. I uncoiled my legs from the rope, my feet landing on the bar. Then, I rolled forward, until I was beneath it all again.

A kick of the legs, perfect timing, and I was launched into the air. For a brief moment I was soaring, before the time came to tuck myself into the tight somersault I now had down to a T.

As I landed on my feet, arms stretched above my head, the applause was deafening. It was almost like I could feel it working its way into my body, fighting off the fatigue already seeping into my muscles, filling my head with a euphoric sensation nothing else could induce.

It continued long after the lights were shut off, plunging the ring into darkness. As I made my exit, I felt as if I were riding on it: a tangible mass that carried me all the way backstage.

~

"You were incredible out there!"

I heard the voice before I could determine where it was coming from. Seconds later, emerging from behind a crowd of people congregated backstage, I saw Silver rushing toward me. Although it was a show night, she wasn't in costume; instead, the first hints of a baby bump were visible beneath her plain T-shirt. Although it hadn't erased the pain of her previous loss, she'd been overjoyed to find out she was pregnant again, and the rest of us were just as happy for her.

I barely got to my feet before she threw herself at me, pulling me into a bone-crushing hug that rendered us both motionless.

When I was finally released, I let out a breathy laugh. "Thanks, Silv."

"God, you two make me wish I was still up there with you," she said, sighing a little wistfully.

Silver may have had a hard time stepping down from trapeze, but I knew she was excited for new challenges ahead. Initially, we'd considered finding a replacement to preserve the act that had always been a trio, but she soon made other plans. We didn't even need her, Silver decided before sitting down to rechoreograph the entire piece for two. Kendra and I had been skeptical at first, but a few shows in we came to realize it actually worked.

Tonight was no exception. Ever since I'd heard where we were set to pitch, I'd been a little nervous. There was definitely a stigma about performing here, and I'd been worried that lingering memories could throw off our perfect routine. We weren't quite in Sherwood, but being in this area of Northern California was the closest I'd come in six months.

"Maybe after the little one arrives," I said, gesturing toward her stomach. "So what's it going to be? A baby trapeze artist?"

"You know, I was actually considering rooting for aerial silk."

I turned my head, following her gaze, which had landed upon Rhona's crew a few yards away. Even having the circus torn apart and stitched back together hadn't changed the rift between our groups; any hopes I'd once had that the ordeal would be a bonding experience had been well and truly crushed. Rhona still glared jealous daggers at us whenever we crossed paths, and the arts of trapeze and aerial silk remained worlds apart.

"Kidding!" Silver assured me, placing a hand on my arm. "Of

course it's going to be trapeze. Even if it's a boy, he's going to be Mystique's first male trapeze artist."

"A real prodigy, huh?"

"Well, duh. It's got half my genes, hasn't it? There's got to be a kickass trapeze artist in there somewhere."

I shook my head, but I was grinning. "Always so modest."

"You know me, babe." Her gaze drifted away from me, focusing on something past my head. "Looks like you've got a visitor. I'll see you later."

At that, I spun around, ending up face to face with someone very much unexpected. There, right in front of me, stood my mother, looking happier and more at ease than she had nine months ago. Perhaps the most striking thing about her was that she'd finally lost that tight ponytail, long brown waves now framing her face. It took years off her.

We hadn't seen each other since I'd left. I expected awkwardness, but ended up being pleasantly surprised.

Telling my mother of my plans to return to the circus, all those months ago, had been one of the most difficult parts of the transition. Sitting down on the couch to break the news was a moment that would likely never leave me; I wouldn't soon forget her expression, that misty look in her eyes as I told her of my plans to leave.

There had been tears. Still, we felt better for it afterward, and I kind of liked the proof that a couple of months spent together had actually meant something. After so long spent living among what felt like Arctic ice, such warmth came as a huge relief.

But the biggest weight off my mind was that my mother understood. It was what I'd been dreading the most—a misunderstanding between us, the mistaken notion that my departure had anything to do with what had happened fifteen years ago, when her life had spiraled out of control.

This time was different. We'd parted as equals, a mother and daughter with the mended halves of a relationship between them. The stitching may have been slightly wonky, patchy in some parts, but all that mattered was that it did the job.

Now, with her standing in front of me, I managed to breathe one word: "Hi."

"Corey." She leaned in a little closer, requesting silent permission for a hug, which at last felt natural to accept. As her arms closed around me, I realized I could feel no trace of Arctic chill.

"I didn't know you were coming to the show."

We broke apart then, and a smile crept across her face. "After I heard you guys were close by, I couldn't resist. I thought I at least owed it to my daughter to see what she was so good at. And you really are, Corey. What you did out there tonight was amazing."

"Thank you," I said, and really meant it.

"I was thinking maybe if you weren't doing anything tomorrow, I could take you out for dinner or something. To catch up?"

The hopefulness in her expression warmed my heart; there was no way I could possibly say no. "Sure," I said quietly, my breath escaping in a cloud of relief. "I'd like that."

Suddenly, I heard a noise from across the room, something carried above the background buzz of the performers, all still talking excitedly about the night just past. It wasn't just a noise, but voices—more specifically, two of them.

"Corey!"

The Australian inflection on my name had my heart leaping.

Then there was an almighty crash; my head jerked around instantly, just in time to catch sight of Rhona tumbling to the floor. Above her, two figures stood—one tall, the other very much the opposite—looking sheepish, unsteady after the impact but at least managing to remain on two feet.

"Shit, sorry!" Kim's voice rang out loudly across the backstage area, which had got a lot quieter in the commotion. She looked down at Rhona, who was now sprawled unflatteringly on her stomach. "Didn't see you there!"

"Yeah, sorry!" George echoed, pushing his glasses up his nose.

They didn't wait for Rhona to right herself; once our eyes locked, they dashed over, coming to an abrupt halt just inches short of my mother and me. As I was pulled into a hug by an overly enthusiastic Kim, I saw Rhona drawing herself to her feet, though not before shooting a lethal glare in our general direction. There was sure to be hell to pay later, but it would be worth it.

My mother shot me a smile, excused herself with a wave and the promise of seeing me tomorrow. I returned it as best as I could when Kim finally let me go, watching her retreating back, which soon slipped into the surrounding crowd.

Turning my attention back to my friends, I didn't have time to get any words out before I was pulled into a second hug by Kim's taller counterpart.

"You came to the show!" I said eventually, once I'd been released.

"Are you kidding? We wouldn't have missed it for anything," Kim told me as I looked over at her. "When we heard you were here, we booked tickets right away. Still, I can't believe we had to wait six whole months to see you in action."

"Which, by the way, was out of this world," George chipped in. "Sorry about knocking over your friend, though. We were just excited to congratulate you."

"Don't worry about it," I said, lowering my voice as I noticed

309

Rhona muttering something scathing to her friend. Her perfect blond ponytail had been messed up in the collision, and the sight was more satisfying than I liked to admit. "She's not my friend. Feel free to knock her over again, actually."

"Noted," he said, with a surreptitious wink.

"Seriously, though, Corey," Kim continued, "no wonder you were such a pro at that rope in gym. God, if only Coach could see you now. I think you'd probably send him into cardiac arrest with pride."

I laughed.

"So how are things back here? Sure seems like you're enjoying yourself."

I paused, taking a moment to consider. There were so many thoughts swirling around in my head, but I wanted to choose my words carefully. Returning to the circus, and everything that had come with it, had made for a whirlwind of a six months, a torrent that had moved by so quickly it was difficult to sum everything up in a sentence. Still, I had to try.

"I am," I told her honestly. "I just . . . it's crazy, you know? How so much has changed. And yet it feels right. Like I'm finally back where I belong."

"Glad to hear it," Kim said, smiling warmly. I could tell she really meant it, but that didn't stop the mischievous glint from appearing in her eyes. "So have you and Luke jumped into a long-distance relationship yet?"

My first instinct was to roll my eyes, but I wasn't able to stop the flush rising to my cheeks. "Stop it."

"Oh come on." She gave me a pointed look. "Don't try and tell me you two haven't kept in contact."

I couldn't deny that much. Just because Luke had moved away, cutting all contact just wouldn't have felt right, and more emails had gone back and forth between us than I would ever admit to Kim. Now that we were no longer in the same place, the dynamic between us had changed, but there was an undeniable spark of *something* still there. There would be the occasional line in his emails that would make my heart flutter, but the feeling was only ever temporary. The verging-on-flirty edge to our conversations didn't *mean* anything, but it kept me on my toes all the same.

Kim could see there was something I wasn't telling her. "Corey . . ."

"It's nothing serious, okay?" I said. "We just email each other occasionally . . ."

"*Email?*" Kim looked as if I'd just told her we kept in contact via carrier pigeon. "Wow. Retro. Then again, I guess Luke doesn't seem like the type of guy to slide into your DMs."

"We're just friends," I told her, though I knew I didn't exactly have her convinced. "Although . . . Mystique is due in Washington next month, and he won't be far away."

Kim looked like Christmas had come early, clapping her hands together as a huge grin spread across her face. "Well, that's settled. Something's *definitely* going to happen then, and there's no way you can tell me otherwise."

I shook my head, resigning myself to the fact I couldn't take the idea out of her head now that it was there. Still, the mention of it had tightened the knot of nerves in my stomach. As much as I wanted to see Luke again, and as much I'd thought about him since we'd both left Sherwood, I couldn't help feeling apprehensive about our reunion. So much had changed for us both, and things between us could never be quite the same.

As far as I knew, he was doing well. The situation with his mom was better than he could've hoped for. They'd had a long, much-needed conversation, in which she'd broken down in guilt about the past four years. It seemed it was another situation in which Mr. Everett had been interfering; each time she tried to make contact, stories were spun to go with vicious messages telling her that Luke didn't want to speak to her, and they were better left alone. One apology wasn't going to fix everything, but it was a good place to start.

She'd helped him find an apartment just a short drive from her own place, and the gradual introduction to her new family was going well. That summer they were going to tour colleges together. Everything was working out for him.

It had taken six months, but I'd realized the truth. Luke and I couldn't be together. But us both being happy, separately, was the next best thing.

"Anyway, enough about me," I said, keen to change the subject. "How are things with you guys? Anything big happening in little old Sherwood?"

Kim looked over at George, like she was seeking inspiration, but all he had to offer was a shrug. "Not really," he filled in for her. "Same old, you know?"

"Sounds riveting." Something occurred to me then, a random thought that reminded me of Claire's party, when one thing George had said had stuck in my mind. "Hey, how are things going with your mystery girl? Married yet?"

I wasn't sure of the reaction I'd expected, but it certainly wasn't the sudden silence that fell over them both, the awkwardness threatening to smother us all. I looked from George to Kim and back again—and that was the moment I noticed they were both blushing the same shade of bright red.

"No way . . ." I said slowly, as realization dawned.

They didn't say anything, but Kim's reluctance to make eye contact spoke for itself.

"Oh my God, really?" I asked, my jaw hanging open. "Are you serious? When did this happen?"

Unusually, it was George who met my gaze first, though the evidence of his embarrassment was still splashed all over his cheeks. I decided it was kinder not to mention it. "Uh . . . a few weeks after you left," he said, reaching up to scratch the back of his neck. "I guess you inspired me to finally work up the courage to tell my 'mystery girl' how I felt."

"Nice one, buddy," I said, unable to contain my own grin. It only got wider when I turned to look at Kim. "Kept that one quiet when you were teasing me about Luke, didn't you?"

"Oh shut up," she said, but she was smiling, too, and it didn't escape my notice when her hand found its way to George's. "My point still stands."

"If you say so."

"So," she continued, clearing her throat. "Word on the street is that Claire Delaney's throwing a party in Sherwood tonight. The kids at school seem to think it's the place to be. I don't suppose you two are up for it—you know, for old time's sake?"

I thought back to my first experience: being hit on by the world's most repulsive football player, stumbling my way through a crowd of drunk people in the hope of spotting somebody familiar, spending the whole time wishing for it to be over. Six months may have passed, and a lot had changed in that time, but I wasn't exactly inspired to try again.

"Actually," I said, "I was kind of thinking more along the lines of late-night pizza. How does that sound?"

"Sure," she said. "That works too."

Something caught in my line of vision then, a familiar figure skirting the periphery, making his way through the dense throng of people backstage. I would've recognized the plaid shirt and scruffy hair miles off. Though I wasn't quite sure what made me do it, I found myself calling over to him.

"Dave!"

He looked over in surprise. When our eyes locked, he smiled warmly, before heading over to close the distance between us. "What's up?"

"We were just about to head out for pizza," I told him, gesturing toward Kim and George. "You want to come?"

He looked slightly taken aback, as if the invitation hadn't been expected, not in the presence of my Sherwood friends. I noticed the flicker in his eye—the mild spark that most others would've overlooked—that told me he was more flattered than he would let on.

"Sure," he said. "Sounds great."

"Okay." I twisted the eye mask I was holding around my wrist, reaching up to pull my hair from its tight ponytail. "Just let me get changed first. I'll definitely turn a few heads if I show up at the pizza place looking like this. Meet me outside in ten minutes?"

I was met by collective assent, which I took as my cue to turn away and head for the changing room.

Once there, I stepped out of the glittering black leotard, reaching out for my usual jeans and T-shirt. I could feel the transformation even as I pulled them on. It happened this way every night—with the costume that I peeled off and each layer of makeup I scrubbed away, I was separating myself from the trapeze. For so long I'd assumed that without all that, I was no longer the same girl from the stage. I thought we were two separate beings, the union of which could never be achieved.

And yet something had changed. As I took a makeup wipe to my face and began scrubbing, the real features of my face coming back into view, I realized that the boundaries were not so cleanly cut. I didn't have to pick and choose between Corey and the trapeze: plain or striking, closed or bold. There didn't have to be the barrier that I'd drawn up between them.

I could be both at once.

And, really, that had been the case all along.

*

05/14/19 03:12pm

To: Luke Everett (luke_everett@gmail.com)

From: Corey Ryder (cryder@gmail.com)

**Subject: Your invitation to the most spectacular show
you'll ever see**

Attachments: <tickets.pdf>

Luke,

The big day's almost here! I can't believe it's come around
so quickly, but we're all packed up, ready to hit the road—
and it's next stop: Rennerdale, WA.

After all the strings I've pulled, I'd better see you in the
crowd on opening night. I've even managed to get you free
tickets (they're attached—just print them off to show at the
door) so you've got no excuse. Not that you'd pass up the
opportunity to see me anyway . . . ;)

It feels really weird to be able to say this, but I'll see you
soon (!!!)

Corey x

05/17/19 09:03am

To: Corey Ryder (cryder@gmail.com)

From: Luke Everett (luke_everett@gmail.com)

Subject: Re: Your invitation to the most spectacular show you'll ever see

Corey,

Thank you so much for last night. I don't know about you, but I'm still playing it over and over in my mind. The show was incredible—and so were you.

I know you probably won't be around for a while, but please let me know when you next rock up around here. I wouldn't miss it for the world.

Luke x

ACKNOWLEDGMENTS

Firstly, to everyone at Wattpad—and particularly I-Yana—for the incredible opportunities and unwavering support you have given me over the years. I wouldn't be the writer I am today without the amazing community you have built, and this story would not have come so far had you not believed in it as much as I do.

To Jane Warren, the most wonderful editor: it has been a joy to work with you on this project. Countless times you have been able to express exactly what I was thinking, and you have helped shape this story into something I am truly proud of. I have also learned so much about my writing in the process—things that I will remember for all my future works.

To Emma Szalai and Lydia Carr, for being there in the group chat to provide writing advice at pretty much every hour of the day. I always know I can ask you the questions I wouldn't dare ask anyone else.

But most of all, to the thousands of people who have supported me on Wattpad in any shape or form over the last eight years. It feels like a long time since I wrote this story for fun at age eighteen, back when I would post a chapter at a time and wait for your comments to come pouring in. I appreciate each and every one of you (whether you reacted well—or not so well—to the ending in the comments section), and I'm so grateful that we get to continue this journey together. With any luck, this will only be the beginning.

ABOUT THE AUTHOR

Leigh Ansell is the author of *Trapeze*, *Human Error*, and a number of other titles on Wattpad. Since she began posting her works online at the age of fifteen, she has accumulated over 130,000 followers and her stories have been read over thirty million times. Leigh is the winner of two Watty Awards and the Wattpad Prize for Best Love Story. She lives in Berkshire, England, and has a day job in marketing.

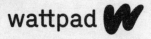